T0031209

Praise for Kirsty Manning and

THE PARIS MYSTERY

"There are few things as glamorous (or decadent) as 1930s Paris, and Kirsty Manning's new book brings it to life with a twist." —*New Idea* (Sydney)

"In the tradition of Agatha Christie . . . [*The Paris Mystery* is] a suspenseful ride, filled with twists and turns." —Lisa Ireland, author of *The Shape of Us*

"Meticulous research, stories with social importance, pioneering characters, and effortless flitting from one epoch and city to another underpin Kirsty Manning's cut-above historical fiction novels." —*The Australian Women's Weekly* (Sydney)

"One of Australia's best historical fiction writers." —*The Daily Telegraph* (Sydney)

Kirsty Manning

THE PARIS MYSTERY

Kirsty Manning grew up in northern New South Wales, Australia. She has degrees in literature and communications and worked as an editor and publishing manager in book publishing for more than a decade. A country girl with wanderlust, her travels and studies have taken her through most of Europe and the east and west coasts of the United States, as well as pockets of Asia. Kirsty's journalism and photography specializing in lifestyle and travel regularly appear in magazines and newspapers and online. She lives in Australia.

Also by Kirsty Manning

The Jade Lily

The Lost Jewels

The French Gift

THE PARIS MYSTERY

THE
PARIS
MYSTERY

A Charlie James Mystery

Kirsty Manning

VINTAGE BOOKS

A DIVISION OF PENGUIN RANDOM HOUSE LLC

NEW YORK

A VINTAGE BOOKS ORIGINAL 2023

Copyright © 2022 by Osetra Pty Ltd.

All rights reserved. Published in the United States
by Vintage Books, a division of Penguin Random House LLC,
New York, and distributed in Canada by Penguin Random House
Canada Limited, Toronto. Originally published in paperback,
in slightly different form, in Australia by Allen & Unwin,
NSW, in 2022.

Vintage and colophon are registered trademarks
of Penguin Random House LLC.

This is a work of fiction. Names, characters, places,
and incidents either are the product of the author's imagination
or are used fictitiously. Any resemblance to actual persons,
living or dead, events, or locales is entirely coincidental.

Cataloging-in-Publication Data
is available at the Library of Congress.

Vintage Books Trade Paperback ISBN: 978-0-593-68554-9
eBook ISBN: 978-0-593-68555-6

vintagebooks.com

Printed in the United States of America
10 9 8 7 6 5 4 3 2 1

For Sara James,
fearless reporter, inspirational friend.
Thank you x

Also,
for my very own Charlie,
who brings a smile to every setting.

'I'm going to make everything around me beautiful.
That will be my life.'

—Elsie de Wolfe

THE PARIS MYSTERY

Prologue

The tightrope walker staggered along the highwire as if he were drunk. One slip and he would plummet to certain death.

Drums rolled. The orchestra struck opening chords as the elegant hostess, Lady Eleanor Ashworth, stepped into the spotlight dressed in a black tulle Chanel gown draped with a cobalt cape. Behind her, the outline of Château de Versailles shimmered in the distance. The hostess raised her hands in the air and dangled a whip from her right fingers.

A collective gasp.

She teased the audience, circling the whip above her head as the music started to crescendo and the spotlight glowed. Fireworks exploded and screamed into the inky sky. Thousands of coloured stars hissed and fell.

With a flick of her arm, Lady Ashworth lashed the whip down onto the sawdust, and a dozen miniature ponies wearing sequined headpieces entered the ring, fanning out behind her. On their backs rode burlesque dancers in matching burgundy masks and under-bust corsets, their muscular legs braced for balance, bare breasts bouncing.

The women in the audience laughed and rolled their eyes at one another while their menfolk loosened bow ties and leaned forward on the cushions to catch a better view.

With the next beat of the drum, the hostess cracked her whip again, and the ponies broke off into pairs and cantered in a pretty circle.

Four storeys above, the acrobat leaned forward and dropped onto the highwire, doing the splits. The wire swayed slightly with the gathering wind.

The audience cheered.

When the acrobat bounced up onto his toes, he spread his arms wide to balance. The wind kicked up and howled, and he disappeared from view as the arena lights blinked out. The orchestra paused, the drum faded.

An outraged black swan waddled across from the lake, spread its wings and hissed at the crowd.

The mood had shifted with the wind. Chatter faded to nervous whispers. The rhythmic thud of hooves became a panicked patter as the skittish ponies tucked their ears back and whinnied.

Guests leaned towards one another in the dark and murmured.

'I bet *that* wasn't part of the party plan.'

'*Mon dieu!* Those poor ponies.'

'Be a dear and hold my Krug.'

The seasoned hostess needed to soothe her guests. Behind her, trainers could be heard shushing the ponies.

The late-night breeze continued its mischief through the gardens of the Villa Trianon, making the red-striped marquees billow and flex, ropes straining against anchor posts. Some of the crystal coupes were blown from their neat rows on tabletops and shattered on the ground. The candles flickered out, and the only light was the bobbing flames on the ends of the tightrope walker's pole as he rushed to the safety of his platform.

Someone found the generator, and the spotlight in the main arena flashed back into action. Guests stood clutching cushions and blankets to their chests with one hand, masks and feathered fascinators with the other. Men draped their white tuxedo jackets over the bare shoulders of women. On the main arena, a trainer haplessly tugged at a white pony that reared up on its hind legs, whinnying and tossing its head about.

'Music!' Lady Ashworth snapped, clicking her fingers at the conductor. Her neck muscles were as strained as the guy ropes tying down the marquees.

The orchestra started up again. As the clarinet and saxophone trilled, a higher note could be heard above the wind.

Off pitch.

The conductor waved his baton, cutting the music. The other note continued.

Nobody spoke.

Instead, hands covered mouths as the guests huddled closer together. For it was not music they were listening to: it was a terrifying scream.

Chapter 1

Charlie James smoothed her jacket, righted her cloche hat and slipped on her gloves. Not even the painful squeal of brakes on steel tracks could dim her excitement as the Night Ferry train pulled into Paris.

Gare du Nord spanned as far as the eye could see, and the air was thick with hissing and clacking as trains pulled in and out of platforms. Porters in neat caps struggled to push trolleys loaded with luggage; families huddled in tearful reunions or farewells. Men with booming voices ambled along each platform, carrying trays of newspaper cones filled with warm chestnuts, while a young woman with a white chef's hat, a hot plate and nimble hands produced paper-thin crêpes drizzled with lemon and sugar at breakneck speed.

Paris. Charlie thought of her former husband's surprise when she'd told him she was leaving Sydney. *That's quite a stretch.*

Perhaps. But when she'd heard six months ago that *The Times* needed a new correspondent for their Paris desk, she had sent off her clippings along with a cover letter and resumé in flawless French. Four months later she was boarding a vessel for Britain, directly followed by the Night Ferry train to Paris.

A conductor in a neat blue hat opened the carriage door, and Charlie stepped onto the platform and made her way towards a handwritten sign.

CHARLIE JAMES, *THE TIMES*

She sucked in her breath and allowed a ripple of excitement to run down her spine at the sight of her name next to her new masthead. She had a longed-for by-line on one of the most famous newspapers in the world, but to achieve this she had moved to the other side of the world. Her chest fluttering with homesickness, she wished her parents were here to witness her achievement.

Resolved to make the best of her new life, Charlie took a deep breath and allowed her eyes to linger on the sign for a second time. Holding it was a beautiful young woman who looked as though she'd stepped from the pages of *Vogue*; she was dressed in a blush Chanel bouclé suit, kitten heels and a matching pillbox hat. A cream Hermès handbag dangled nonchalantly on her wrist. Beside her stood a greying, balding, portly gentleman in a crumpled dark suit. Charlie presumed this was her new boss: the head of the Paris bureau, George Roberts.

'Charlie?' He scratched the back of his head, face pumice. His voice was deep and very British.

'Short for Charlotte,' she replied as wine barrels were wheeled up the platform.

'I can see that.' His voice was a little sharp with frustration.

'Charlie James.' She extended her hand, and he shook it. His hand was fleshy, his grip firm and businesslike.

He narrowed his eyes slightly and studied her face—here was a man used to sizing people up quickly. 'But, your by-line . . .'

'I would hate for people to read my work differently.' Charlie jutted her chin out. 'Like Louie Mack.'

'Louie Mack, eh?' Her new boss nodded, but his tawny eyes twinkled with curiosity. 'Then you have big shoes to fill. I'll need a solid feature right away—a Paris story to prove to our man in London you are up to this desk.'

'Understood, sir.' Charlie's stomach lurched: she'd been put on notice even before the porters had unloaded her luggage.

She'd wanted to be a foreign correspondent ever since her mother had taken her to a Red Cross lunch when she was ten. Over lukewarm chops, peas and mashed potatoes, the Australian war correspondent Louise 'Louie' Mack had spoken of her adventures in German-occupied Antwerp, where she'd sheltered from bombs in a hotel cellar. A plain, slim woman clad in a simple white linen dress, her dark hair spun into a knot at the top of her head, she'd held the floor with tales of hiding in cellars to escape bombs and running along deserted streets to catch glimpses of enemy troops. To escape Antwerp she had dressed as a maid, buried her notebooks deep in her luggage, and borrowed a local woman's passport. She'd travelled from Belgium to France and London, then all over Europe after the war—filing features, hunting stories.

Big shoes to fill indeed. Charlie wanted to ask her new bureau chief if he'd ever met Australia's most prolific—and perhaps bravest—reporter, but thought better of it. George Roberts was clearly a true newspaperman, focused on the here and now. With each sentence, his expression flickered between curiosity and ruthlessness.

'Right then,' he said. His face was returning to a more normal colour and had the whisper of a smile at the corners. George beckoned for a porter to carry her suitcase, then he ushered her along the platform towards the exit. 'You'll start Monday. The Paris desk is as important as those in Rome and Berlin. Chamberlain is steering blind. All his talk of appeasement . . . well, it's crucial we report what's happening here on the Continent. The French are in his pocket—they want to play it safe too. Understandable after that last car crash of a war. But the Boches are gathering steam. Everyone's bloody worried about their own economies, and our collective balls are going to be squeezed by Italy and Germany if Chamberlain and his cronies don't pull their fingers out.'

'Got it,' said Charlie.

'One of the most prominent Brits here, Lord Rupert Ashworth, keeps to himself. He used to have close contacts in Downing Street, but rumour is he's been pushed aside because he was too close to King Edward—backed the wrong horse.' George scratched his head and hitched up his pants.

The beautiful woman beside him said nothing, but she gave Charlie an encouraging nod and a warm smile.

Charlie took a moment to digest the information being volleyed at her, knowing she'd need to record it in her notebook as soon as she reached her new apartment.

'There's a lot happening in Paris.' George pointed at Charlie. 'You need to make Lord Ashworth your business. The Prime Minister made sure Lord Ashworth was posted to Paris as a diplomat when King Edward abdicated. He's lost face in London with the top brass, but he still has friends in high places right across the Continent—people in governments and industry. And his wife, Lady Eleanor Ashworth, knows everyone who counts in this city. Hook both of them, get access to their network. We need a cracking feature. Make a splash. She has her annual party coming up—a Circus Ball. Cover it. Make contacts. Chamberlain might not listen, but the people will. We'll give them the truth.'

'Understood.' Charlie had been in the copy room and on the news desk in Sydney long enough to ignore the blunt talk of newspapermen. George was no different from her chief of staff back in Sydney.

At first, her male colleagues had been assigned the major homicide, election and police corruption stories, while she had been given lost children, deaths and society marriages. It was only when she took over a murder story from an unfortunate junior beat reporter who'd had his appendix out that her boss had noticed she had some serious writing prowess. He'd raised his bushy eyebrows as he'd read her homicide copy and passed it to the subeditors, barking, 'No changes,' before adding quickly, 'but make the by-line *Charlie* James. We want people to read it—it's not the case of the missing handkerchief.' He'd sauntered out, slamming the door behind him. Standing in the middle of the room, typewriters whirring around her, Charlie had had the strangest sensation of being both hugged and slapped.

She must have earned his respect over the next two years, as he'd insisted she apply for *The Times* Paris correspondent position, and he'd written a letter of introduction recommending that his 'best beat reporter' be given the job.

As they reached the street, George handed her his embossed name card. 'Be at tomorrow's editorial meeting by 10 a.m. sharp.'

Charlie reached out to shake the younger woman's hand. 'Pleased to meet you. Do call me Charlie.'

'Oh, sorry!' barked George. 'Bloody rude of me. This is Violet Carthage—she runs my office. She'll escort you to your apartment and help you settle in. If there's anything you need, Miss Carthage will help you find it. And, James?'

'Yes, sir?'

'You ever pull another stunt like this, and I'll march you back to London myself. I demand integrity.'

'And you'll have it, sir. My word.'

George guided her into the back seat of a black taxi and loaded her leather suitcase into the curved boot, rapping his knuckles on the metal to indicate that the driver should proceed.

Violet, who was sitting beside Charlie, cast her an admiring look and whispered, 'Nicely played, Charlie James.'

'*Arrêtez-vous ici! Merci*,' Violet said to the driver as he pulled into a narrow cobbled alley and parked in front of a stone apartment building with wrought-iron Juliet balconies. 'Welcome to your new neighbourhood, Charlie: Saint-Germain-des-Prés. The Luxembourg Gardens are at the end of your block, and a decent fresh produce market is around the corner, along with every kind of bookshop you could hope for. Perfect for a writer.' Violet's smile dropped. 'This apartment is small, but . . .' She waved her hand out the window as if to say, *But you get to live in this beautiful street*.

Charlie eyed the avenue of manicured plane trees and had to agree.

'I've had a cleaner through since the last correspondent left.'

'I'm sure it's wonderful,' said Charlie.

After the taxi driver pulled her suitcase from the boot, Violet indicated he should carry it to the fifth floor, stuffing a fistful of francs into his suit pocket and patting it with a sweet smile. Charlie traipsed behind him and Violet up all those flights of shiny marble stairs to the top-floor apartment.

'Home,' said Violet encouragingly as she jiggled the key in the latch and threw the door open. The driver deposited her bag and bid the women a cheerful *bonne journée* with a tip of his hat.

The apartment was one large room anchored by an oversized window, which looked out over slate rooftops into the avenue below. A double bed was made up with fresh white linen and someone had placed a small vase of daisies on the rattan nightstand. The parquetry floors were a deep caramel, worn but freshly polished; the room smelt faintly of lemons. Directly beneath the sash window was a walnut desk topped with a shiny new typewriter and piles of paper. Delighted, Charlie ran her fingers over the keys.

'It's a British machine, a beauty. George insisted on a new one. I'm afraid the one at the office is a bit clunky.' Violet pulled a face.

'Don't worry,' said Charlie, 'I'm used to old typewriters, and to working late into the evenings.'

Violet clapped her hands together. 'Doesn't every reporter work around the clock?' She laughed softly. 'George expects a lot from his staff, but he's fair. And because of the time zones, you'll often have to call your stories through to the subeditors—' She pointed at the telephone in the corner. 'If you can't get them, call me, and I'll take your dictation.'

'Thank you, so kind.' It was impossible not to warm to the thoughtful woman. 'This is a beauty indeed.' Charlie playfully tapped the T key before she continued to explore her new home. One wall was built-in wardrobes with striped linen stretched across the doors. The kitchenette comprised a narrow walnut bench with a fridge and a gas burner that Charlie supposed someone had cooked on once, or at least heated up their coffee percolator; she made a mental note to buy a small coffee pot tomorrow.

'Let's get that window open,' said Violet.

'Agreed!'

Charlie now realised how the newspaper had been able to secure such a charming studio in a premiere location at a bargain price: the apartment was too warm because all the day's hot air accumulated just below the attic. Stepping across the parquetry, she kicked off her court shoes then tugged open the sash window.

'Better,' said Violet as a breeze lapped into the room. 'I've stocked the fridge with milk, yoghurt, a pretty chablis and some chèvre. You'll find a baguette and crackers under the sink. The best *boulangerie* for croissants is next door, but get bread three doors down. The *poissonnerie* across the road is the best in the neighbourhood, and the *épicerie fine* beside it will sell almost everything else. I suggest you make your own coffee. The French make *everything* more beautiful'—she gently rubbed the linen duvet cover between her thumb and forefinger—'except coffee. Oh, and there's the view. See!' Violet pointed out the window.

Charlie stood on tiptoe and leaned to one side to catch her promised 'prime view of the Eiffel Tower'. She could just make out the peak.

'Best in Paris,' Charlie said with a grin. 'Thank you again.'

Violet's eyes sparkled, and she pointed to the diamond solitaire brooch Charlie had pinned to her lapel. 'Oh . . . *très jolie.*'

'*Merci*. It was a farewell gift from my *maman*, Sylvie. A family heirloom.' She tried to ignore the lump in her throat. 'She's French, from Normandy. Moved to Australia with her family before the war.'

'Your father, is he French also?'

'No!' Charlie laughed. 'He's a true Sydneysider, with English heritage a few generations back. He's a barrister. Loves tinkering with his little yacht down by the harbour.' She smiled as she pictured her father, Jonathan, at the rudder, then resolved to write to her parents that night.

Violet gazed at the diamond. 'So your pretty brooch has found its way home. You're a native speaker?'

Charlie winced. 'Hardly! This is my first time in France.' She touched her brooch and remembered watching her parents, brother Freddie and two younger sisters Juliette and Madeline on the Sydney wharf as her ship blasted its horn and pulled away. Her sisters had cried and waved like maniacs, running the length of the wharf beside the stern. Their slim mother, dark curls tucked under a subdued, elegant silk scarf, looked too sad to admonish her youngest daughters; instead, she leaned into her tall, sinewy husband and stood still while Charlie waved goodbye. As her family became dots on the wharf, she pulled out the envelope her *maman* had slipped into the pocket of her travelling suit as they'd hugged. In it was a farewell letter, and the brooch.

Dearest Charlotte,

This brooch was my mother's and hers before that. Now it's yours.

It breaks my heart that you would not accept money from your father and I to begin your new life in Paris, but we understand. You have always been so proud and independent. First your job, then keeping your maiden name when you married.

This brooch is a little token of our love and support to take across the sea with you.

Bises, Maman xxx

For Charlie, keeping her maiden name had actually been an easy and pragmatic decision. Her editor hadn't wanted to change the by-line: why would popular Sydney reporter Charlie James (*inferred: Charles*) suddenly switch names? It was a matter of circulation numbers.

Now that Charlie was about to be divorced, she was glad she'd kept that part of herself. As for the money and divorce settlement, who knew when that would be wired to Paris, if ever? But she was a grown woman—a foreign correspondent—and she would take care of herself. She was certain that Louie Mack wouldn't have accepted handouts.

Violet looked up from the brooch and into Charlie's eyes. 'You miss your family?'

'Very much. It's silly . . .' She tried to suppress a yawn.

'Sorry, you must be so tired.' Violet gave her forearm a reassuring squeeze. 'See you tomorrow. Don't be late for the meeting at ten!'

After saying goodbye to Violet, Charlie swung the door closed, walked across to the bed and fell back onto the duvet, closing her eyes as dappled evening light danced across her walls.

The next morning Charlie took a rickety elevator to the top floor of a sober, elegant stone building standing proud on a grand boulevard overlooking a green square. She was greeted at the glass entry doors to *The Times* office at nine forty-five by Violet, who was clad in a figure-hugging navy pencil skirt and magenta silk blouse. If she found Charlie's beige skirt suit wanting, she was too polite to let it show. '*Bonjour*, Charlie James, walk with me,' she said as she strode down the corridor. 'I've booked a car to collect you from your apartment and take you to Versailles at eight-thirty tomorrow morning. Afterwards we'll have lunch, and you can tell me *everything*.'

'Versailles?' Charlie shook her head, confused.

'Yes! Keep up, dear Charlie: an interview with Lady Ashworth. Your first feature.' She bit her lip, hesitating, before she continued. 'You really need your first piece to be brilliant. I know you can do it. The clippings you sent impressed him.' Violet gave her a reassuring smile. 'I've arranged for you to meet Conrad Mackenzie when you are at Versailles. He works for Lady Ashworth as an assistant, but he's fast making a name for himself as a photographer since graduating from the prestigious Rhode Island School of Design. Most of ours are stringers, so we could do with adding a part-time photographer to our books. Mr Mackenzie is surely eager to work for a major newspaper, and *Le Monde* are such snobs—they'd rather chew off their arms than hire an American.'

'Got it: one interview, one photographer,' Charlie said, nodding.

'Here's the run sheet for the editorial meeting.' Violet handed over a typed list, plus half a dozen clippings. 'This is some background reading on Lady Ashworth. She has decorated houses from Minneapolis to London, and the Atlantic is practically her corridor. I've heard she was to redecorate Buckingham Palace, before the . . . trouble with the Duke and Duchess of Windsor. They are part of the same circle; unchanged since the abdication, just more time for bigger parties.' Violet coughed, dropping her eyes.

Charlie shot her a grateful smile. 'Amazing, thanks. So, tell me, how did you come to run this office?' It was clear that the impeccable and clever Violet Carthage was far more than George Roberts's assistant.

She laughed and ushered Charlie past a row of cluttered desks. 'My papa attended school—Westminster—with our chief of staff, then was posted to the East as a young officer. He met my mother in Singapore and stayed. I did the last part of my schooling in Britain.' She shivered. 'And that will be the last of *anything* I do in Britain. Try growing up in Singapore and then being forced to eat British boarding-school food for three years—cardboard smothered in gravy, three different ways, with a side of soggy potatoes or squash. But my parents are in London, running their investments, lunching at their various clubs, and writing me long letters with the details of their friends' eligible sons. My mother even sends me underlined clippings from *Tatler*.' Violet rolled her eyes.

She was from serious wealth, which explained her cut-glass English accent, and her couture.

'I know what you're thinking—that I got this job because of my connections—but I assure you, I speak seven and a half languages.' Violet laughed.

'Half?'

'When I was twelve, my Russian tutor resigned in disgust— a shame, really, because I would have enjoyed the language if I'd stuck to it. All those devilishly attractive, maudlin writers.'

Charlie smiled. Her new friend seemed far too vivacious for Tolstoy and Dostoevsky. 'Apart from French and English, what do you speak?'

Violet counted them on her fingers. 'German, Italian, Spanish, Mandarin, Malay—'

'And a half of Russian.'

'I know enough for the evenings.' She flashed her cheeky smile and gestured Charlie into the meeting room with a flourish. 'Gentlemen, please meet Charlie James, all the way from Sydney.' Violet took the time to walk her around the table, introducing her to a few subeditors in almost identical dark pants, striped shirts and braces.

George Roberts sat at the head of the table, tapping a pen and sipping tea, clearly waiting for his rookie correspondent to be seated and the day's business to begin. Violet walked off to attend to her duties, and Charlie sat down, unbuttoned her satchel and pulled out her notebook, knees knocking with nerves under the table as the men shifted in their seats, cracked their knuckles, and straightened their pens and notepads.

'First item: welcome, Charlie James,' boomed George. 'We need your first feature to be top notch. This bureau runs on the smell of an oily rag!' There were hearty chuckles around the table. 'Bloody Berlin and Rome get all the dough.' He scratched his ear. 'Be smart, James, and don't let us down.'

Charlie opened her notebook. 'I'll do my best, sir.'

Chapter 2

At nine-thirty the next morning, Charlie stood on the front steps of Villa Trianon and watched her taxi swing about on the expansive gravel and disappear down an avenue of oak trees. She took a deep breath and pressed the doorbell. Her usually steady hand was shaky, so she smoothed her jacket, then her hair.

She had spent her second night in Paris at her little desk sipping chablis, snacking on goat cheese smeared over pieces of still-warm baguette, and reading the clippings on Lady Eleanor 'Ellie' Ashworth, who had been the subject of headlines from New York to Paris for more than fifty years: first as an actress, then a home decorator, and now as the artistic director and international hostess of the elite circle known as *le tout-Paris*.

To stay in Paris, Charlie would need to get Lady Ashworth onside, and to gain access to her British husband, Lord Rupert Ashworth, as well as their contacts in high places.

As Charlie waited for someone to answer the door, she peered into the depths of the garden beyond. Villa Trianon sat at the fringe of the Parc de Versailles. Marked on the title deeds was a passageway reserved for the King of France to slip away from the main palace and the prying eyes of the court in order to visit his lover. So very French! Though who would have wanted to run away from Marie Antoinette? Relationships were complicated—even royal ones, Charlie thought sadly. As she looked to the high wall between the villa and the park, she wondered which was the path for someone who wanted to disappear for a clandestine liaison, or even just a quiet moment to oneself?

A butler in a sharp morning suit swung open the oversized door. '*Bonjour.*'

'*Bonjour.* Charlie James from *The Times* for Lady Ashworth,' she said in French.

'*Oui*, of course. Lady Ashworth will meet you in her salon,' he replied in English and directed Charlie inside with a sweep of his hand, closing the mighty door with a click. As he led her through the villa at a brisk pace, she noted its typical French symmetry: sixteen rooms divided by a broad hallway. She pulled out her notebook and quickly sketched a floorplan to annotate later, noting the rooms towards the back had a wall of French doors that looked out to the terrace and garden.

She had never before seen such chintzy luxury. It was as if all the best designs of the Continent had been artfully arranged for an exhibition. Walls were lined with gold and fuchsia silk paper; overstuffed sofas and animal hides stretched across the parquetry. *Every* room was 'the good room'. She couldn't imagine sinking onto a sofa here, a piece of toast between her teeth as she scribbled out her notes.

She furtively swiped a finger on a shelf—no dust.

Villa Trianon's owner was equally well kept. Lady Eleanor Ashworth was dressed in a blue couture blazer and trousers and her neat feet were tucked into ballet flats and crossed just so at the ankles. She had the small, wiry body of a gymnast, and her pale green hair was coiffed into an immaculate chignon. Charlie knew from the clippings that Lady Ashworth was close to sixty, but with her bright skin, bright hair and electric brown eyes, she could have passed for a far younger woman.

Under Lady Ashworth's scrutiny, Charlie adjusted her beige jacket and smoothed her pencil skirt.

'Miss James, welcome to Villa Trianon. Have a seat, won't you. Tea?'

'Thank you. Please, call me Charlie.' She smiled as her host poured tea from an ornate porcelain teapot into a matching yellow Limoges teacup—gilded, of course.

They sat silently for a beat, each sipping tea and studying the other. Charlie opened her notebook and pen, dating the top of a fresh page.

'I must admit when your glamorous colleague Miss Carthage called and asked if I'd meet with you, I'd rather assumed that Charlie James was a man. But you are decidedly *un-masculine*! With your auburn curls and heart-shaped face, you could be on my wall. In fact, I think you are.' Lady Ashworth gestured to a voluptuous nymph in an oil painting behind her.

Charlie's face grew warm with embarrassment. 'The only people who call me Charlotte are my parents. To everyone else, I'm just Charlie.'

'Well, Just Charlie, it's a pleasure sitting with you.' Lady Ashworth beamed graciously. 'Where do you want to start, my dear?'

Charlie gathered her wits. 'This is quite the villa! But you're a long way from home.'

'As are you! Australian, judging by your accent?'

'I am.' Charlie's cheeks burned. Her flat vowels ricocheted between silk-lined walls. Of course, her accent was irrelevant to this story. George's parting words from the night before thrummed in her ears: *If you make a good impression on Lady Ashworth, the rest of Paris will open their salons to you. Don't muck it up.* It was already clear that the woman was no ornament—scratch the gilding off and she was all steel.

As Charlie jotted her initial impressions in shorthand into her notebook, she mused that if Marie Antoinette were still living at the palace that abutted this villa, these formidable, flamboyant women would be firm friends. Or enemies—often there was just the faintest line between the two. Charlie shivered.

In response, the older woman raised her eyebrows and smiled. 'Did someone just walk on your grave?' She passed her guest a cashmere throw from the back of her peacock-blue velvet sofa.

Charlie straightened her back and smoothed the shawl across her lap as she admired it. 'This is lovely. You clearly have an expert eye for décor. How did you come to develop it?'

Lady Ashworth thought for a moment. 'I have a flair for the dramatic, and in my twenties I took to the stage in New York. I brought my own wardrobe—audiences are forgiving of mediocrity when you are dressed in French couture. Some of the high society women in the audience would invite me to their homes. I'd admire their taste and mention I knew someone who could supply exclusive French antiques. My decorating business grew from there. I'd buy furniture from Paris, ship it and charge commission, then charge as well for styling their enormous brownstones. I then began to set up my own homes, starting in New York.'

'So tell me,' said Charlie, 'why did you decide to purchase this villa and devote your energy to it? I'm told it wasn't quite so grand when you bought it, and that you've been restoring and decorating it for almost two years.'

Lady Ashworth sipped her tea. 'My goal has always been to make everything beautiful, and I enjoy a challenging project. My parents were comfortable—back in Minnesota, my father was a surgeon—but they frittered away their money. Lost everything!' She twisted a diamond bracelet about her wrist.

'Lost?' asked Charlie, then she sat back and silently counted to ten. She often found that when she waited for her subjects to fill the gaps, they revealed more about themselves than they intended.

She kept waiting. A clock ticked on a far wall.

'Lost,' Lady Ashworth confirmed as she shook her head with disappointment. 'My father was a gambler. First the horses. Then the stock market. Phoosh!' She moved her hands to mimic an explosion.

Charlie sucked in her breath.

Lady Ashworth's gaze sharpened. 'You too? Who was it? Your parents? A lover . . .'

Charlie turned a page in her notebook and looked her subject directly in the eye.

'Touché! Well, whoever it was, I can see their reckless behaviour hurt you. I was certainly put in a predicament! My parents no longer had the standing for me to make a suitable match. They moved to smaller lodgings on the edge of the city, and the last of the funds shipped me to Scotland where I stayed with relatives for "finishing". I resolved to be nothing like my parents. When my aunt presented me at Queen Victoria's court, I wore my first pair of silk stockings and borrowed a burgundy evening dress, and I knew my future was to be beautiful. Soon I was travelling the Continent, and I promised myself I would build a home in Paris one day.'

'You promised yourself?'

'Yes, and I keep my promises. In this case, that wasn't so difficult. Paris opens her arms to all of us—heiresses, writers, poets, artists . . . reporters. This city shimmers with optimism. It's possible to find magic here in Paris.'

As Charlie transcribed these sentences, she couldn't help wondering if she would find magic in Paris. Her chest tightened as she recalled her husband's face, his muscular arms, the taste of his sweat when she traced the dip of his neck with her tongue. She'd once thought that what they had was magic; now, she wasn't sure if she still believed in it.

She took a breath. 'And what magic have you found?'

Lady Ashworth brushed her left hand over the blue velvet, as though it were a beloved pet. 'Last year, I was showing a group of my husband's visitors through, and one of them was an English aristocrat, bankrupt and bitter. He whispered to his wife something about American industrialists and their *crass* inherited wealth. She scorned me by saying it was *simple* to make a beautiful home with a pile of new money! When I served them tea, I quietly told them that my parents had been buried with holes in their shoes and darned clothes, leaving me with nothing but a pretty child-hood. Well, *then* he apologised. "I beg your pardon, madam, my mistake." He couldn't even look at me! But he'd mistaken more than my heritage—he'd mistaken my motives. It was always my goal to make a beautiful life, not just a beautiful house.' She leaned back and took a long swig of her tea, before exhaling and fixing

Charlie with bright smile. 'The *magic* of Paris, my dear, is that you can let go of whatever dreariness you left behind and be whomever you damn well please.'

Charlie stopped transcribing and met the older woman's eyes, willing her words to be true. She needed this feature to prove to George Roberts that she was up to the job of foreign correspondent. To stay in Paris. Charlie needed to work a little magic of her own to get Lady Ashworth onside, because she needed access to her British husband, Lord Ashworth. But Lady Ashworth was no socialite or ornament—scratch the gilding off and she was all steel.

A framed military cross sat on the mantlepiece tucked between two unlit candles. The award looked small and humble in this grand room.

'You chose to stay in Paris during the war, rather than returning to America?' asked Charlie, trying to keep her head and stick to her list of prepared interview questions.

'Yes. Paris has been very good to me. It seemed hardly fair to abandon her in her hour of need. My father was a doctor, my mother his nurse. I knew enough basic medicine to be helpful so I volunteered as a nurse treating burns patients. A hideous injury. Slow to heal and *so* painful.' She winced and offered a slim cigarette from her case to Charlie before taking one for herself.

'No, thank you.' Charlie continued as Lady Ashworth lit her cigarette and inhaled. 'My colleague Violet told me it was you who showed the Americans, French and Brits how to give the Ambrine treatment to burns victims. Then evacuated the hospital. You were given two bravery awards, including that one, for carrying eighty patients downstairs to avoid a German attack on a hospital?' Charlie pointed at the Croix de Guerre on the mantle.

'What choice did I have? It was *war* . . . no time to sit around. That's not heroism; that's just being helpful.' Lady Ashworth shrugged and brushed a fleck of dust from her woollen pants. 'Besides, my maid helped.' She blew an elegant line of smoke up to the ceiling.

Charlie swallowed, trying to disguise her shock. Lady Ashworth spoke as if having her maid alongside her during four years of war were the most natural thing in the world. Also, how lightly she wore her bravery. War had kept Lady Ashworth strong and humble—even as her own fortunes rose. She continued: 'That may be so, but not many people go on to raise millions of dollars to rehabilitate the people of France and their wounds.'

'Enough do. Most of my acquaintances make *substantial* gifts to my various charities.'

Lady Ashworth watched Charlie closely and smiled. 'The world shifts and you adapt a little,' she said. 'You must understand, Miss James—sorry, Just Charlie—what it's like to be an outsider, as an Australian in France.'

'I suppose I'm getting a taste of it.' Charlie shifted slightly in her seat—*she* was supposed to be asking the questions. 'And actually, it's Mrs, not Miss . . .' She looked down at her notebook and swallowed, unsure why she'd felt the need to clarify that.

'Oh!' gasped Lady Ashworth, as if that was the most interesting thing Charlie had said since they were seated.

Charlie's stomach sank. 'I *was* married. It's . . . complicated.' She had no intention of revealing how difficult—how humiliating—it had been to prove the fault for the dissolution of their marriage lay with her husband. It was the only way divorce would be granted to a woman in Sydney courts. She shook her head and drew a tiny star in the corner of her notepaper, avoiding her subject's eyes.

Lady Ashworth nodded slowly. 'Yes, husbands are certainly complicated. But enough chitchat! Come walk with me.' She stood up smoothly, before Charlie had the chance to answer. 'Don't worry, my dear, there will be plenty of time later for the rest of your questions. I've arranged some coffee and macarons on the terrace for your meeting with my assistant Conrad Mackenzie.' Charlie closed her notebook, got to her feet and followed Lady Ashworth from the room. 'I understand *The Times* is courting him. He is a talent, but we'll have to share. I can change coffee for rosé champagne if you like? After all, it's nearly 10 a.m.' Lady Ashworth talked as fast as she walked, gliding between rooms and topics.

'I'll take coffee, thank you,' Charlie said, thinking of the article she'd need to begin drafting that afternoon.

'Very well, Just Charlie. How very modern you are, with your short hair! I think we shall get along famously.' She looped her arm through Charlie's as they walked; Charlie couldn't imagine anyone not falling in step with Lady Ashworth. 'Do you know,

I *pored* over paintings of the fêtes given by the Sun King—King Louis XIV—at his summer palace Chateau de Marly, and I decided I'd re-create their whimsy with my very own decadent party for the summer solstice. We've hired performers from Cirque d'Hiver—the most famous circus in Paris—and if you look out the window there, you'll see the circus tents.'

Charlie peered out a sash window to see a team of sweaty, shirtless men working in the blazing sun, cursing and banging hooks into the ground to hold the guy ropes for the various tents.

'This ground floor has been set up for two hundred guests. That tent is my big-top circular bar.' Lady Ashworth took off again, and Charlie had to hurry to keep up—for a very little person, Lady Ashworth was exceptionally fast. They stepped onto the terrace shaded by grape vines, where a marble table was laden with the promised silver coffee set and plate of raspberry macarons, which sat beside an open bottle of rosé champagne on ice and three flutes. 'Won't you join me, Charlie? It's too warm for coffee!'

Charlie couldn't resist—and to refuse would be impolite. 'Of course, thank you.'

A strapping young man dressed in a sharp three-piece suit appeared with a black folio under his left arm. 'Conrad Mackenzie,' he said in a Southern accent, thick as treacle, as he offered his free hand to Charlie. His brown fringe swept across his forehead, partially concealing amber eyes. He gave a shy smile as he shook her hand gently, polite yet reserved.

'Conrad, please meet our latest *Times* correspondent, Charlie James.'

'Real pleasure to meet you, ma'am.'

'Please, call me Charlie.'

'Alrighty then, Charlie. Allow me.' He let go of her hand, set his folio carefully on the table, and poured a flute of champagne for each of the women. The bubbles frothed at the lip. Charlie wondered if Lady Ashworth was unimpressed at this crude overpour, but the woman said nothing. Charlie noted he poured himself a modest glass of bubbles.

'Show Charlie your folio, dear.' Lady Ashworth smiled and waved her hand at Conrad, who immediately flipped it open.

'I know I don't take standard photos,' he said. 'I like to capture people's inner world. Show what they least expect.'

Stepping forward, Charlie flipped though black-and-white images of models and movie stars with dark lips, sculpted waves and brooding eyes, then a leopard-print sofa caught in a shaft of light by a long window, and a brownstone façade pattered with the shadows of leaves. Though all the images were staged, they seemed candid, almost intimate.

'These are beautiful!' she exclaimed.

'If you say so, ma'am—Charlie!' Conrad shifted his weight and stared at his feet as his cheeks turned pink. Although he was in his late twenties, with a sweet face and corn-fed glow, his slightly hunched gait and strained eye contact suggested he was not always at ease with his body, or certain company. Yet although Charlie had worked with plenty of photographers in Sydney, none had the emotional range of this young man. Underneath his mousy fringe and shyness was great depth. It took strength and maturity to produce images like this. What had drawn a fresh-faced man from the American South to the glitz and shadows of Europe?

'I'll take this folio back to the office with me,' said Charlie, 'but that's just a formality. Mr Roberts and I will put together some terms, and we'll send you a contract soon. You'll still be able to freelance for other publications.'

Lady Ashworth nodded and sipped her champagne. 'Lovely! George Roberts can be stubborn as a goat. Likes the battle-hardened lads, if I recall. Not fooled by Chamberlain, and I suspect he keeps counsel with Churchill.' The older woman was fishing a little.

Charlie said nothing. Discretion was best in her line of work.

'Thanks, Charlie,' Conrad said, dipping his head respectfully. 'I'll leave you ladies to enjoy your champagne and conversation.' He gave a slight bow to Lady Ashworth, one that would have been almost mocking if she wasn't his employer, and held Charlie's gaze for a beat—as if trying to gauge whether he could trust her. Then he took a few backwards steps, turned and rushed inside.

'Has Mr Mackenzie worked in Paris long?' asked Charlie.

'I met him in New York a couple of years ago. He attended the Rhode Island School of Design, then took leave from his full-time assistant position at *Vogue* to travel to India with me last year, and now to stay here in Paris to help me organise my Circus Ball.'

Charlie wondered where Lord Ashworth figured in all this. 'Is Lord Ashworth involved in the planning too?'

'Oh, he's not interested in that sort of thing,' Lady Ashworth replied airily. 'Just in hosting,' she quipped. 'We play to our strengths.

'I actually have *two* themed summer parties planned for this year. The second will be strictly private, for eighty or so of my inner circle. It will be a gala at the Louvre, which I'll co-host with a fellow patron, the prominent banker Maxime Marchand to launch the season's exhibition. But that's not for another week or so. I'm not sure who decides whose party is the *best*—that's something you people in the press like to put a label on.' Her eyes twinkled. 'On the night of the Circus Ball, arrange for your driver to drop you off at 10 p.m. sharp. Wear something fabulous. Don't be late, Just Charlie. Trust me, you won't want to miss a thing!'

Charlie gulped down the rest of her champagne, thrilled and nervous at the prospect of her first Parisian soiree.

Chapter 3

Charlie's lunchtime martini at Café de Flore numbed her throat. The soft summer sun had coaxed Parisians outside. Women promenaded in slim-fitting suits and demure hats, and carried small fluffy pooches in matching cream and caramel tones. Men draped their suit jackets over one shoulder, rolled up their sleeves and tilted their faces back like sunflowers. The heat flowed through the city like a gentle ocean swell. Ties were loosened; legs lolled about under tables. Red pelargoniums spilled from the cafe's window boxes, and hedges clipped into neat cones sprouted from shiny pots.

Under a striped umbrella, Charlie sat with Violet in rattan chairs on the footpath, snapping off chunks of complimentary breadsticks. The owner of Café de Flore was sympathetic to his loyal following of correspondents, writers, painters and musicians, who flocked to his establishment for the top-shelf liquor, bitter coffee, and free bread and green olives.

Charlie adjusted her hat to stop the sun hitting her face. Parisian sunshine was softer than in her homeland, but with fair skin, auburn hair, and ribbons of freckles across her nose and along her arms, thirty years of experience had taught Charlie it was better to cover up than risk a nasty case of sunburn that would see her skin blister and peel.

Violet had brown skin, twinkling dark eyes and jet-black hair courtesy of her Malay mother, and she wore a spectacular zebra-print pencil skirt and matching jacket that would have swallowed anyone else. She sashayed around with a Hermès bag slung on her wrist, dressed head to toe in couture, chin held high as if she were about to lunch with the president rather than run errands for her curt bureau chief.

Paris was luxuriating in the silky days of summer. The city was more glorious—and far more expensive—than Charlie had expected. In the two days since her arrival, she had felt like Aesop's country mouse as she gazed about her adopted city, salivating at the croissants and tarts piled high in the *boulangerie*, and the wedges of cheese that oozed on vine leaves in the windows of the *fromagerie*. But it was the *Parisienne* women who left her breathless: their impeccable suits, a felt hat tilted just so, the alluring smear of red lipstick that hinted at forbidden pleasures.

As Violet and Charlie talked, their glasses tapped against the marble tabletop. 'I *need* details from your interview,' said Violet. 'Is Lady Ashworth's hair a wig, or is it really green?'

'Every last strand. On an ordinary person it might look like a topiary hedge, but on her it's *très chic*. She's the size of a twig, yet one of the strongest and most self-assured people I've ever met. It's incredible that she had such humble origins.'

'Indeed. Now she's the modern Marie Antoinette.'

'Well, I imagine she has quite the wardrobe, but she's far more down-to-earth than her predecessor at Versailles. You should see the circus marquees going up in the garden—there's a big top just for cocktails! A sprung dance floor has been imported from England . . .' Charlie took a sip of her drink.

'I can't wait! This is the ball of the season.'

'I may be from the Antipodes, but I am *aware*, Violet!'

'Very well. Then you need the right dress.'

'I have dresses. I can't afford—'

'Shush. You *need* couture.'

Biting her lip, Charlie looked at her magnificent new friend. She was tempted, but she didn't want to spend the meagre savings she'd managed to bring with her. Her salary was adequate for a little fun in Paris, but she didn't earn enough for couture. 'I'm not sure I can afford a designer dress at the moment.'

'Understood. You have style, but what about a bit more . . . panache?' Violet kindly took in Charlie's beige suit with an approving look.

Charlie had three versions of this suit in beiges and greys, and it served her well: elegant enough for Paris, plain enough for her to disappear. She didn't want to be the story—but what would be the harm in learning a few fashion tricks for an extravagant soiree? She was in Paris, after all, and Lady Ashworth had told her to wear something fabulous . . .

'Surely it can't hurt to have a look,' she said.

Though Violet's voice was haughty Anglo, her nonchalant shrug was most certainly Gallic. 'We need something to show off this hair.' She plucked at Charlie's curls. 'Green or blue.' Pulling a pen from her purse, she sketched on a notepad. 'I'm seeing layers in your ballgown, and a nipped-in waist. Something a little saucy'—she winked—'like this.' She tapped her drawing of a pretty dress. 'We'll be in masks, so we can get away with more skin. I'm . . . *friends* with one of Paris's best ateliers, Aleksandr Ivanov.' She leaned in conspiratorially. 'He serves Perrier-Jouët Belle Epoque champagne while he fits you. I'll take you there after lunch.' Judging by her reddened cheeks, she very much enjoyed her fittings with him. She immediately changed the topic and regained her composure. 'How did your meeting with the photographer go?'

'Very well! Conrad Mackenzie's folio is with George, and we'll draw up a contract. You're right, his work is impressive.'

'Isn't it just? Keeps to himself, but then still waters run deep. Lady Ashworth *made* him. He shot her houses for *Vogue*, from New York to Boston. Now he's her . . .' Violet paused, as if uncertain about how much to give away. She seemed to know everything about everyone in Paris, which made her a perfect assistant for a newspaper office.

'Lover?' Charlie couldn't imagine it: although there was respect and affection between the two, their connection seemed more familial than romantic.

'Anything's possible! Lady Ashworth has broad and eclectic tastes.' Violet arched an eyebrow. 'She and Lord Ashworth occupy separate rooms in the villa, and they keep separate apartments beside the Luxembourg Gardens.'

In Sydney, such matters were clandestine and spoken about in hushed whispers; here, Lady Ashworth was free to be herself. In Paris, emotions were amplified, abstract ideas and dreams revered, and conventions shrugged off with French nonchalance. Charlie thought it was wonderful.

She had come to Paris to reinvent herself in the city that flouted rules. Break news. Break stories. Break with her past.

'And what about your tastes, Charlie?' Violet asked slyly. 'Now that you're no longer attached . . .'

'A lady never tells,' Charlie said with a laugh as she knocked back the last drops of her martini and was soothed by the dry gin burning the back of her throat.

She noticed a black town car pulling up by the kerb. A tall man in his forties got out of the back seat and buttoned up the jacket of his naval uniform; he had the stocky physique of a rugby player, with broad shoulders and strong limbs. A second man emerged, middle-aged with pink cheeks and a matching nose that suggested he was partial to port and bordeaux.

Violet spoke out of the corner of her mouth, her voice lowered. 'Perfect timing! They sometimes have a late lunch here on Thursdays.' She stood and politely waved the men over. 'Lord Rupert Ashworth,' she nodded at the older gentleman, 'meet our newest *Times* correspondent, Charlotte James.'

'Charlie James,' Charlie gently corrected, giving Violet a grateful look as she also got to her feet. Not only had the fashionable young woman set up the interview with Lady Ashworth, but now she'd delivered the primary object of George's interest right into Charlie's hands. Would Violet have done the same for Charlie's male predecessor? Perhaps the idea of working with a woman held a certain appeal.

Lord Ashworth shook Charlie's hand. His demeanour was polite but languid, very patrician.

Then the well-built Royal Navy man took Charlie's hand, holding it for a moment longer than Lord Ashworth had. She noted his grizzled short back and sides with curls slicked down on top, the sharp pleats in his trousers, and his upright carriage. His dark-blue uniform was perfectly fitted over his muscular biceps and thighs, and his chest was highly decorated.

He removed his hat and tucked it under his arm. 'Commander Edward Rose-Thomas, military attaché to His Majesty's Embassy.' He had the weather-beaten face of an experienced sailor, with a scar above his left eye that crinkled when he smiled. It was . . .

very attractive. Charlie met his brown eyes and wondered if he was married; not for the first time, she wished that wedding rings were commonly worn by men.

She remembered her ex-husband's cheeky face at the last cocktail party they had attended together—his lopsided smile and open laugh, and his unmistakable scent that had made her drag him into a storeroom to unbutton his shirt and press her nose to his chest. When she couldn't bear to wait any longer, she'd unbuckled his belt as he'd lifted her onto a stack of boxes against the wall and hoisted her silk dress past her thighs. She'd pulled her husband close and wrapped her legs around him so tightly that he'd groaned as the bricks had dug into her bare back.

Their marriage had ended outside on the footpath one hour later.

Charlie let go of the commander's hand and stepped back as conflicting emotions stirred. She had thought she was done with men for a while, but as she caught a whiff of his aftershave and admired his athletic frame, she wondered if she should make an exception. A fling perhaps . . . something that did not involve secrets and broken hearts.

Violet turned to Lord Ashworth. 'My colleague here met with your wife this morning,' she said brightly.

'Ah, no wonder you are drinking stiff martinis! She cuts quite a pace, my good Lady Ashworth. I suppose you discussed her Circus Ball? It will be the talk of the town.'

'I'm very much looking forward to it!' said Charlie. 'What brings you to Café de Flore today, Lord Ashworth?'

'It's livelier than the club. One overhears gossip, chatter about politics, and the odd smattering of philosophy. And I like seeing the workers in their natural habitat.' He sniffed pompously. 'Perfect spot to keep one's finger on the pulse. We're here to meet Monsieur Maxime Marchand.' He peered past Violet. 'That's him, at the far table.'

Violet turned to Charlie. 'Monsieur Marchand is Paris's most prominent merchant banker and philanthropist.'

'Yes, he has business everywhere,' said Lord Ashworth, sounding bored.

Charlie remembered that Lady Ashworth had said Maxime Marchand was a fellow patron of the Louvre. She followed Lord Ashworth's gaze to see a fit man, with excellent cheekbones, in a cream linen suit. Reclining at a corner table, he chatted to a blushing waitress. His sandy hair brushed his collar, almost raffish, and was swept back from his tanned face; he looked as though he'd just sauntered off the beach. Ostensibly he was the very picture of an easy-going, benevolent philanthropist, but his black eyes suggested something darker as he scanned the room, narrowing them when he studied other patrons. For a moment his gaze fixed on something—or someone. Then he laughed in response to whatever the waitress said, his lips peeling back to reveal a row of slightly jagged teeth, and Charlie felt she was staring into the mouth of a wolf. She shivered.

As Violet made chitchat about Marchand with Lord Ashworth and the commander, Charlie craned her neck to survey the far reaches of the restaurant, looking for whatever or whoever had transfixed the banker. Patrons had gathered on leather banquettes around marble tables laden with wine and platters of scampi, oysters, fresh tomatoes and basil. Then Charlie saw her: a curvaceous woman with glowing brown skin and glossy dark hair, who had clearly just emerged from the powder room and was dabbing at the corner of her immaculate red lips. She was dressed in a navy bouclé suit and killer heels, and it seemed she was deliberately keeping to the shadows. She shot a long sour glare at Marchand's table—and perhaps at the waitress. Sighing, she slipped on her kid gloves, then startled when she noticed Charlie staring at her from the footpath. The brunette's eyes narrowed—seemingly because she'd noticed the two gentlemen beside Charlie, who were still distracted by Violet—and she pressed back against the wall. Quickly, she tugged on her hat and veil, squared her shoulders, turned on her heel, and slipped out a side door without a backwards glance.

As though Marchand sensed the party gathered outside on the footpath, he swivelled in his chair and faced his audience. If he was surprised to see two young women and two Englishmen staring at him, he did not show it; instead, he raised his martini glass and, with a smile that did not reach his cold black eyes, mouthed, 'Santé.' Charlie wondered why the warm, quirky, gregarious and strong-minded Lady Ashworth would co-host any event with this man.

Violet reached for her purse and signalled a waiter. 'Gentlemen, I'd ask you to join us for a drink, but I'm afraid I must drag my friend here away for a dress fitting.'

The women put on their hats and gloves as they said their goodbyes. Charlie's cheeks felt flushed from the martini and the sun, and she turned her face to catch a breeze that licked its way around the corner. The flowers in the window boxes started to dance, and a second gust hit the brim of Charlie's blue hat, whisking it from her head. It rolled off the footpath onto the cobblestone road.

The commander raised a hand to stop an oncoming car before it could flatten the still-rolling hat. He took a couple of swift steps and retrieved the hat, waving it casually as he made his way back to the footpath.

'Thank you,' said Charlie, smiling when he handed it to her. She tugged it hard onto her head, pushing some curls into the band to force it to stay.

'Always the knight in shining armour,' joked Lord Ashworth. 'Although that's the most action you've seen for a while. Good to see those reflexes are still in working order! God knows you might need them soon enough.'

'Pleased to meet you, ladies,' said the commander. 'We look forward to seeing you at the ball.' To Charlie, he said, 'I suggest you hold on to your hat—Lady's Ashworth's parties can take some wild turns.'

A short taxi ride later, Violet and Charlie stood outside Mainbocher Atelier. Violet rang the doorbell, and a butler in a blue velvet tuxedo let them in. 'Mademoiselle Carthage, welcome to your appointment.'

He ushered them through a waiting room painted duck-egg blue and filled with overstuffed silk sofas. Charlie's shoes sank into the plush carpet as she and Violet were led down a corridor past private fitting rooms. They glimpsed the back of a curvaceous woman with a mane of dark hair; she was standing on a red velvet pedestal while the seamstress pinned her hem and spoke at an impressive pace through a mouthful of pins. The client wore black silk taffeta with a fitted V-back bodice. She lifted her hair for the seamstress to pin some darts, revealing thousands of tiny glass beads and gold sequins that shimmered under the lights.

This was Charlie's first time in such a fancy fashion house, and she felt giddy with excitement. Though her work clothes were plain, she loved dressing up for evenings out, fixing her hair and applying a bright red lip—it made her feel vibrant, strong and attractive.

'Violet! *Ma chérie!*'

'Aleksandr!' Violet threw her arms around the tall blond designer with searing blue eyes and chiselled cheekbones. 'This is my new colleague, Charlie James. She needs a beautiful dress for the ball.'

Aleksandr Ivanov kissed Violet dramatically on each cheek and held her close for a moment before he greeted Charlie with air kisses. 'This hair! Titian! A goddess!' His thick Russian accent was studded with exclamation marks. Stepping around Charlie, he ran his fingers through her cropped wavy hair. 'Hmm.' He tilted his head and studied her face. 'Bring me the green crepe,' he snapped at one of his minions in the hallway, who took off on tiptoe and came back carrying a roll of fabric. Another minion carried a silver ice bucket containing a bottle of Belle Epoque, with its dreamy botanical label, and three coupes. 'Ladies, I insist,' Aleksandr said as his butler poured the bubbles.

'*Merci*, Sascha, so thoughtful,' said Violet, batting her eyelashes.

Charlie smiled to herself. It was lovely to see this playful side to her new friend.

Aleksandr waved the bolt of silk over Charlie's shoulder and tugged it in at her waist.

Violet reached for her drink. 'Well, look at you! Green is your colour.' She looked like the cat who ate the canary.

'You were right, darling—beautiful bosom, tiny waist. Her skin is like buttermilk.' He was eyeing Charlie's neck. 'Long lean lines . . . Violet said your mother is French, *da*? You can tell—high cheekbones and fine shoulders. We'll keep the bodice tight, then make tiny pleats at the waist, front and back. For the goddess you are.'

Charlie couldn't help but be flattered by this charming man. She eyed herself in the mirror and had to agree that the green set off her hair and eyes. But while her salary was sufficient for a comfortable life on the Left Bank, there would be no spare francs left at the end of the week for this couture dress. 'I can't afford it,' she mouthed at Violet over the designer's shoulder.

He stepped back as if he'd heard her—perhaps he'd seen her in one of the mirrors—and he muttered something in Russian. 'Oh, I know *that*. But you need the right people to notice you at this party. If you are dressed like one of them, all of Paris will open up. And if you wear *those shoes* . . .' He pointed at them and let the words hang in the air as he mimicked slashing a knife across his throat. 'Violet here is a dear friend.' He picked up a crystal flute. 'I'd like to help her. It would make me happy.'

Violet blushed.

'You and I, Charlie James, are in the same business. People tell us their secrets. I see diplomats' wives, aristocrats, even royalty. I came to Paris to meet such people, *da*. *Interesting* people wear my dresses. *C'est compris?*'

Violet said in a low voice, 'Aleksandr has been setting up a small showing of some dresses—something on the side. You're invited, of course.' She glanced at him, adding in a firmer tone, 'It's a line of his own, with his own name attached. He's hoping

The Times will cover it exclusively, and he has invited all of *le tout-Paris*. The Ashworths have already confirmed their attendance.'

Violet was handing Charlie a scoop wrapped in green silk. Charlie replied, 'I'd love to attend your showing, Aleksandr, and report on it with George's permission. But I can't accept a free dress. I'll pay the first deposit this week.'

'She's as stubborn as that red dirt they have down in *Australie*,' said Violet with obvious pride. 'But *I'm* grateful, darling.' She kissed his cheek, and it was his turn to go pink.

He looked at Charlie and said warmly, 'This dress is a welcome gift. You can't go to the ball without couture! You'll just be seen as an ordinary member of the press. In my dress, you'll stand out and also attract attention to my design, so I benefit too. I'll be there—I can introduce you to some of my clients, if you like.'

'That's kind, and an offer I'll gladly take up. Thank you.' She ran her fingers across the soft silk. If she was going to report on Parisian society, she needed to look the part. She knew the transformative power of a beautiful dress—it was like the French lingerie she always wore under her sensible work clothes: not to please someone else, but to make herself feel magnificent.

There was movement in the hallway, and Charlie turned to look. It was the woman they had passed earlier, walking out of her fitting room. Charlie recognised her as the mysterious beauty from Café de Flore.

'Who's that?' Charlie whispered to Violet. 'She's spectacular.'

'A woman from Uruguay,' said Aleksandr softly. 'Very closed, that one.'

'Her name is Mercedes Rose-Thomas,' Violet told Charlie.

Charlie gave a half-hearted nod, her thoughts already returning to the cafe and the commander's laughing eyes and the feeling of his warm hand around hers.

'She's the commander's wife,' Violet added.

Chapter 4

Charlie had been to masquerade balls in Sydney, but she'd never seen guests arrive on the backs of elephants. The Indian maharajas dazzled, their turbans studded with rubies and emeralds, bright silk robes billowing in the summer breeze. The grand driveway at Villa Trianon was humming as excited guests in couture dresses and tuxedos spilled from town cars. They grabbed martinis and gasped in delight at the avenue of fairy lights that beckoned them past manicured lawns to the striped tents and jazz band on the park-like garden in front of the villa's main terrace.

With her notebook on her lap, Charlie scribbled details in shorthand as she craned her neck for a better view out her taxi window. Sydney was still on its knees after hobbling through the Depression—many shopfronts remained empty, and many families were patching clothes, resoling shoes and cooking endless pots of broth. But Paris was dancing in her finest.

A butler in a black-and-white uniform quickly helped Charlie from the taxi to make room for more important guests in the turning circle. He thrust a coupe of champagne into her hand and nudged her towards the lawn.

Violet bounded over, her silver dress hitched up in one hand and silver-sequined purse tucked under her arm. 'Good evening, Charlie James! You look fabulous. You've got your brooch on.' She tapped it with admiration. 'Looks perfect.' Violet dropped her hem and smoothed the tasselled peplum over her hips. She looked like a movie star: the sheer diaphanous silk hugged her body in all the right places, thin straps showing off a warm glow across her shoulders and décolletage before the material plunged at the bust. Walking in a cloud of Chanel No. 5, she seemed oblivious to the admiring glances of nearby guests.

'Thanks, you too!' said Charlie. 'Sorry I'm a bit late, my driver got lost. It's quite the hike from Paris, and there was so much traffic.' She looked around. 'Is George here?'

'Sends his apologies, I'm afraid. His wife, Daphne, had a rather bad fall this morning. She's just had an operation on her ankle.' Violet winced in sympathy.

'Sounds serious, poor thing. Is she expected to be in hospital long?'

'Unsure. She's tough as old boots.'

'I imagine, given her husband!' Charlie chuckled. 'No matter, I was going to introduce him to Conrad Mackenzie but I'll do it when Conrad drops off tonight's negatives on Monday. I sent him the list of people George wants photographed along with his contract, which he sent straight back with his signature.'

'Wallis Simpson and the Duke of Windsor . . . Lord and Lady Ashworth . . . Maxime Marchand and his wife . . .'

'Exactly, plus some ambiance and character shots. Shouldn't be too hard for such a talented photographer.'

Violet gently took Charlie's wrist. 'Let's get moving. We should have travelled together . . . I could have kicked my delicious designer out of bed half an hour earlier. It's not like he needed the time.' Violet rolled her eyes, and Charlie tried to avoid choking on her bubbles. After less than a week in Paris, she was still trying to keep up with her colleague's candour.

'So,' she said, 'where is your handsome Russian?'

'Over by the big-top bar.' Violet pointed. 'He's in hot demand tonight—let's go rescue him.' She looped her arm through Charlie's and whisked her under a rose-covered archway to where the red-and-white big-top cocktail tent was set up around a large oak tree.

Charlie stared at a collection of men in matching red-and-white sequined jackets and painted clown faces. Beside them, standing a head taller, was Aleksandr Ivanov, debonair with his slicked-back hair, black Zorro-style mask and black tuxedo with a cream rosebud buttonhole. His blue eyes glistened like sapphires through the holes in the mask. He lifted a champagne coupe in the air to greet Charlie before air-kissing her on both cheeks. 'The two most beautiful women here tonight,' he said, beaming.

'Best dressed, at the very least,' said Violet, shimmying her hips.

As the trio marvelled at how the party had come together, performers walked through the crowd juggling knives, pulling coins from behind guests' ears, and tugging white doves from top hats.

Then Charlie noticed movement on the large ornamental lake that took up the rest of the parkland: a handful of black swans were paddling together. The sight of their curved necks and red beaks made her stomach knot. Strange how the most obscure things could trigger homesickness.

'Are you okay, Charlie?' asked Violet, sounding concerned. 'Come, we need to get you another drink and introduce you to *important people.*'

Aleksandr laughed softly. 'Go. Mingle. But make sure you tell them *I* designed this dress.'

'Noted.' Charlie smoothed the green silk crepe over her hips. As she looked up, her eyes caught on a man in a top hat who was leading a tiger through the guests as though he were walking a puppy. Charlie pointed this out to Aleksandr and Violent, her hand trembling in shock. 'Look!'

The crowd parted, oohing and aahing at the tiger. One tipsy lady with chandelier diamond earrings held out a gloved hand to stroke the tiger's ear as it slinked past, only to retract her arm quickly when the animal bared its teeth and growled.

'She's a pussycat, really! Aren't you, Princess?' The trainer laughed as he stroked the sleek coat, then he and the tiger kept strolling.

Charlie stared at the couture-clad guests, who were almost as exotic to her as the tiger. She wanted to shake off the shoes Violet had lent her, run over and release the tiger into the woods of Versailles beyond the high stone wall the bordered the garden. The animal had no place here, and perhaps neither did she.

Still, tonight she had a job to do. The next hour was a blur of handshakes, curtsies and double-cheek air kisses as Violet introduced her to a viscount, a market-gardening heiress from Philadelphia, one of the Indian maharajas who'd arrived on elephants, and many others. After each introduction, Violet whispered commentary in Charlie's ear. 'Shy to the point of rude. Will inherit the Singer sewing machine fortune. Grandfather's a German duke.' 'Brought a trainload of luggage from India. Nobody has more diamonds.' 'Embassies are a lonely club for second sons.'

Starting to feel a little overwhelmed, Charlie asked Violet if they could take a short break, so they headed to the edge of the big-top crowd. The summer breeze caressed Charlie's skin as she drew the scent of jasmine and roses deep into her lungs. She looked across the lawn to where acrobats and fire-twirlers danced to the beat of a drum. The terrace was awash with light from thousands of candles, and the humid air pulsed with laughter as well as gossip in a variety of tongues. Slim ladies clad in Chanel, House of Worth, Schiaparelli and Mainbocher were dripping with diamonds and their décolletages sparkled in the light. Many guests had pushed their masks up onto their foreheads or dispensed with them altogether. Charlie sympathised; it was a muggy evening, and sweat was gathering under her own mask.

She thought of the parties she'd attended on the Sydney foreshore, where parochial women had shot her suspicious glances while they'd clutched their boorish husbands close. She'd thought them ridiculous. If only she'd known she should have been the one doing the clutching.

It hurt, still. The betrayal. The humiliation.

Hollow promises that it would never happen again . . .

Charlie looked at the brightly striped marquees and the crowd of dazzling guests, and listened to the murmur of drunken conversations, the rhythm of the drum and the trill of laughter. She held her breath. Part of her wanted to toss her crystal coupe against the smooth bark of the oak tree and watch it shatter—it would echo how she felt about the end of her marriage.

'Here she comes!' hissed Violet out of the corner of her mouth.

'Who?' As Charlie spoke, she noticed the confident stride of a willowy brunette in strapless, bias-cut aquamarine silk and a peacock-feather mask.

The striking woman drew closer and held out a gloved hand. 'Amelia Goldsmith,' she said in a husky American drawl. 'Please, call me Milly.'

Charlie felt as though she were meeting a young Vivien Leigh.

'Milly is the Paris correspondent of the US magazine *Harper's Bazaar*,' Violet explained. 'And Charlie James is *our* new Paris correspondent.'

A narrow eyebrow shot up above Milly's mask. 'Welcome to Paris, Charlie James.'

Charlie pulled up her green mask, while Milly's remained in place. The American was a fellow journalist—what was she playing at? Still, Charlie shook her hand. 'Pleased to meet you, Milly. No doubt we'll often find ourselves at the same events.'

Milly gave Charlie a probing look with her piercing green eyes for a beat too long—as if at this very moment, she was deciding if Charlie was friend or foe.

Charlie wanted to smooth over the awkward silence; she needed as many friends in Paris as she could get. It wouldn't do to get off on the wrong foot on her first assignment. 'Have you covered many of Lady Ashworth's parties?'

But Charlie spoke too softly; her question was absorbed by the music and chatter just as Aleksandr wandered over to join them. 'Mademoiselle Goldsmith.' He took Milly's hand and encouraged her to twirl around, showing off the lines of her dress. 'The blue looks lovely.'

Charlie felt Violet stiffen a fraction.

'This dress fits my body perfectly, Aleksandr.' Milly cocked her head, sassy and coquettish.

They were interrupted by Maxime Marchand. He'd sauntered over from the bar, bow tie loosened, hair still in that raffish style. He wore a white dinner jacket, and his mask was tugged haphazardly above his tanned forehead. He reeked of money.

Violet's neck was slightly flushed as she hurried to make introductions.

'*Enchanté.*' The banker coolly raised Charlie's hand to his dry lips. He stepped back, still holding her hand, and his shrewd eyes took in her emerald dress, lingering at her waist, then her bust, before he continued in French, 'Magic! This green—Aleksandr, you get it right every time. Genius.'

Charlie felt that she'd been evaluated, and that her outfit had passed. She secretly wiped the hand he'd kissed on the back of her dress, wishing she could also wipe away the discomfort he'd given her.

'M-Monsieur Marchand.' Aleksandr shook the older gentleman's hand, then they stared at each other for a moment before the designer stepped back. 'Glad you approve,' he said in a neutral voice, his usual smile absent.

'Monsieur Bocher tells me he is very impressed with your output,' said Marchand, in a tone clearly intended to seem encouraging. 'Sales are rising exponentially since you took over the Paris atelier.'

'You know they are Monsieur Bocher's designs,' said Aleksandr, batting away the compliment. 'I merely execute them.'

'*Non,* we both know that's not entirely true!' growled Marchand as he slapped Aleksandr on the back, lips parting to bare his uneven teeth. He looked as though he might pounce on the Russian. 'My wife and I are looking forward to your fashion showing.'

Aleksandr swallowed nervously and shot a glance at Violet. 'Thank you, monsieur, but that's just a side project. At the atelier, I honour the history of Mainbocher. In fact, Miss Goldsmith's dress is a direct descendant of one that Monsieur Bocher designed more than a decade ago.' His voice sounded a little hoarse, his accent slightly rougher. He was doing his best to be polite, but the banker had clearly touched a nerve.

'Russians.' Milly rolled her eyes. 'Loyal to the end. Even if it sends you broke!' She shot a defiant look at Marchand before leaning closer to Aleksandr. 'Think about it. *Aleksandr Ivanov* embossed on your card. Brass plates outside your atelier. But I wonder where you could find a worthy backer . . .' Tapping her lips, she glanced at Marchand, who clenched his jaw and narrowed his eyes.

Violet threaded a protective arm through Aleksandr's and rested her cheek against his sleeve. Judging from Violet's tight frown, Milly was pushing a little too hard.

Charlie couldn't help feeling curious, so she decided to probe the connection between Aleksandr and Marchand. 'Are you currently in business with Monsieur Bocher?' she asked the older man.

'Monsieur Marchand is one of the finest bankers in Paris,' said Lord Ashworth, appearing from behind Marchand and slapping his friend's back as he praised him. 'He manages funds for *everybody* who counts.'

'You are kind, Rupert—but *everybody* is an exaggeration. Besides, a gentlemen never tells.'

Lord Ashworth guffawed, but Charlie noticed a flash of annoyance in his eyes. The Englishman was surely unused to being corrected.

Marchand turned to Milly. 'Is that American photographer not working with you tonight, Mademoiselle Goldsmith?' The slightest edge had crept into his voice, though his dark eyes looked amused.

'Mr Mackenzie has only shot for *Harper's* on two occasions. We'd like to offer him more work, naturally.' She gave Marchand a defiant look.

'Mr Mackenzie is actually working for us tonight,' said Charlie.

'Better watch your back, Rupert, before these pretty reporters lure your wife's assistant to work for them full-time,' teased Marchand.

'Oh, that has nothing to do with me. My wife champions Conrad Mackenzie every moment she gets. And he did a great job helping her with the party planning, as you can see. She has a nose for these things! Seems to think Mackenzie's the next Cecil Beaton.'

'But he's not!' Milly exclaimed. 'Conrad . . . Mr Mackenzie is far more imaginative than Beaton. He finds beauty in all his subjects. Or at least truth.' For some reason she looked at Marchand, who seemed bemused.

Lord Ashworth held up his champagne as he pompously quoted the poet Keats. '*Beauty is truth, truth beauty.*'

A pale, very petite, fine-boned woman in royal-blue silk appeared at Marchand's side.

'Please meet Maxime's wife, Claudette, whom he most certainly does not deserve,' said Lord Ashworth with a chuckle.

'No, I most certainly do not,' Marchand responded with surprising good humour.

Claudette Marchand was introduced to Charlie, and they politely shook hands.

Marchand said, 'We are very pleased to meet the newest correspondent in town.' He took a leather case from his pocket and handed Charlie a thick cream visiting card. 'Call my office if I can help you with any stories, or any introductions . . .' He raised his eyebrows and let the words linger.

Beside Charlie, Milly grew tense. Had the banker subtly propositioned her like this too?

'Thank you, monsieur, you're most kind.' Pasting on a pleasant smile, Charlie unclipped her purse and tucked the card inside. 'My first feature is on Lady Ashworth. Perhaps you'd care to be interviewed for comment?'

'Eleanor is an open book!' he said smoothly. 'I'm not sure what I could add, but call my secretary and we'll set up something next week.'

At his shoulder Madame Marchand sipped her champagne, her face neutral. Charlie studied her: impeccable skin enhanced with a hint of makeup, coiffed hair, tailored couture. In her late fifties, she looked her age, and Charlie admired that—she hated hollow compliments, and none was more irritating than the suggestion that a woman who looked less than her age was to be feted. Madame Marchand's amber eyes studied everything but revealed nothing, and Charlie wondered what lay beneath. Monsieur Marchand ran hot and cold; his wife was polished and closed.

'Hello, Charlie James,' said a deep voice from beside her. She looked up to see Commander Edward Rose-Thomas standing next to his elegant wife, her curves hugged by layers of bias-cut black silk. 'May I introduce my wife, Mercedes.'

The two women shook hands, then Mercedes rested a possessive hand on his forearm. There was a flicker of recognition in her eyes when she looked at Charlie, but all she said was, 'Lovely to meet you.' Her words rolled out in a rich Portuguese accent.

She exchanged air kisses and compliments with the rest of their group before returning to stand at her husband's shoulder. As she removed her mask to sip champagne, Charlie thought back to her furtive behaviour in the cafe, and the way Marchand had fixed his gaze on her.

Aleksandr politely excused himself to mingle with Mainbocher clients, while Violet and Charlie continued to chat with the Marchands, Milly, Lord Ashworth and the Rose-Thomases. Others wandered in and out of their circle, usually people who coveted the attention—and patronage—of Marchand, even though he always remained aloof.

The commander was mainly talking to Violet and Madame Marchand, but at one point Charlie noticed him follow his wife's gaze. When he saw she was looking at Marchand, his face fell for a second before he regained the rhythm of his conversation. If the banker was aware of this scrutiny, he didn't show it.

An unlikely couple in ornate Venetian masks strolled towards the group. The small woman had the wiry body of a dancer, while the man was young, tall and blond. The woman's green hair gave them away. The pair pull their masks away to reveal their faces as they approached the group.

'Ellie, you've outdone yourself again,' Marchand crooned. 'What would Paris be without your parties, your elan?' He held his champagne in the air as a greeting and kissed the hostess on both cheeks.

'My pleasure!' she said.

'This is truly an incredible evening,' said Mercedes. 'There will be no better party on the Continent this summer!'

Beside Lady Ashworth, Conrad quietly snapped photos of the group, his mouth a tight line. Clearly, the young American was used to being ignored in this circle.

Lady Ashworth smiled at Charlie before turning to the others. 'I see you've all met our newest correspondent. Gosh, there are so many international reporters arriving every month now. It's hard to keep track of them all!' She dropped her voice. 'Let's hope the Boches don't do anything silly so you can stay here, nice and safe, writing about our soirees. I almost put INW on the invitations instead of RSVP.'

'*If no war,*' explained Lord Ashworth. 'But, my dear, there's nothing to worry about. Chamberlain won't have it, and Hitler and his cronies don't have the gall to take on Britain—not after the drubbing we gave them last time.' He threw his head back and laughed, apparently untroubled.

He's never been to war, Charlie realised. Sure, he might have had a junior job in a cushy war office somewhere, but he had never set foot in a trench or on a warship. Meanwhile, a look of deep concern was creeping across the commander's face.

Lady Ashworth clocked the sombre mood and dragged her guests back into the party spirit. 'I'll have to come up with something even more spectacular next year! In the meantime . . .' She clicked her fingers at a row of waiters in black aprons, who topped up everyone's glass with Krug. 'Conrad, I hear Miss Goldsmith has your photos in the next *Harper's.* Congratulations!'

The photographer paused in his work to give her a soft smile, then kept snapping pictures.

Lady Ashworth leaned closer to Milly. 'My dear, he showed me the portraits he shot in your study. Quite magnificent!'

The young woman cast a quick glance at Conrad before looking at Marchand. 'They're really something. Conrad sees the truth . . . no need for my copy.' Her laugh was on the cusp of icy.

Charlie was again puzzled by Milly's attitude to Marchand, and unsure what to make of these young Americans: the prickly journalist and the shy budding photographer. They were from the same continent, but they were clearly from different worlds. Milly interacted easily with *le tout-Paris*—so easily that if Violet hadn't pointed out that Miss Goldsmith was press, then Charlie would have mistaken her for a wealthy guest. Conrad, on the other hand, looked as though he'd prefer to be anywhere else, even though he wore a professional expression and had helped plan the party.

Everyone exclaimed as white doves were released overhead. The birds looked like hundreds of stars disappearing into the darkness.

As she lowered her eyes, Charlie jumped at a sound behind her. She turned to see that it was just Conrad, camera poised as if he were about to take a photograph of her. He whispered, 'Oh, I hope I didn't frighten you.'

'No, not at all,' Charlie reassured him. 'I hope you've been getting some interesting shots for *The Times*?'

'Yes, yes,' said Conrad, 'but not one of you. Your dress is mighty fine.'

She batted him away, laughing with embarrassment while struggling to sound stern. 'Thank you, but that's not necessary. I'm not the story here, so keep circulating, please.' She motioned that he should follow the crowds.

He grinned and shrugged in an almost childlike way. 'I promise you, I'll get you when you least expect it!' He patted his camera.

Out of the corner of her eye, she noticed Marchand fixing her with his crafty eyes. She swallowed, her arms prickling with goosebumps.

Chapter 5

Charlie took deep breaths to settle her nerves as she stepped away from Lord and Lady Ashworth and their tight-knit clique. She suddenly wanted to put as much distance between herself and Maxime Marchand as possible. There was also something a little unsettling about Conrad—it was as if he held a mirror up to people, rather than merely capturing an image. Charlie wasn't ready to have her shadows outed by her new American colleague.

As she moved solo through the crowd, making contacts and collecting name cards, she was surprised by how natural it felt to be communicating in French. Around her, waiters poured top-shelf whisky and magnums of Krug into the glasses of those guests who weren't holding fancy cocktails from the bar, while other staff carried silver trays loaded with creamy lobster brioche rolls, caviar blini and shucked oysters.

Charlie's head began to spin amid the whirlwind of laughter, chatter and jazz. It seemed as though she were surrounded by happy couples, young and old. She adjusted her mask and took a deep breath, realising she needed a moment alone. Her problems had travelled to Paris with her, and no amount of couture—and no mask—could hide them.

She looked past the terrace, the lake and the lights to the far corner of the walled garden. Towering oaks and elms beckoned. She chose a path and was guided by a line of cast-iron lamp-posts towards high hedges, which she presumed concealed a smaller garden.

Once the bright lights and music had faded, she stepped off the path, her heels sinking into the lawn. Fairy lights dangled from tree branches, swaying with the breeze. The clearing revealed a small rose garden, reserved perhaps for picking—arcs of pink, red and white rose bushes were either side of her now, their sweet scent tickling her nose. Up ahead she saw a simple wooden bench lit by a lamp. Violet's high heels made her wince with pain, and she thought with longing of running barefoot in her backyard as a child. When she sank down onto the bench, she removed her strappy sandals—her mother would have been horrified. Relieved, Charlie rubbed the soles of her feet on the plush grass.

She thought of the invitation that Marchand had extended while his wife was watching. Charlie supposed Madame Marchand was used to hearing such propositions, but surely that didn't lessen the hurt. Charlie couldn't help but feel a kinship with the banker's wife.

Pulling her notebook from her purse, Charlie pressed Marchand's thick card into the spine. The man was a creep, but he was well connected. Who knew where his connections might lead? She was pleased with how her feature was coming along, but there was no getting away from the fact that she needed to prove her skills to George in the long term—especially if she wanted to work on the banking and finance pages, along with criminal investigations.

She was jotting down notes when she heard a twig snap behind her.

'Who's there?' she said, her voice sharp to disguise her fear as she twisted to look around.

Approaching her wooden bench was a tall, broad-shouldered man in a tuxedo and plain black mask; a man with slicked-back hair and a confident smile.

Charlie swallowed. She was alone with Edward Rose-Thomas.

He glanced uneasily over his shoulder.

'Are you looking for someone?' she asked.

'No,' he said a little too quickly. 'Quite the opposite.' He tugged at his collar with his forefinger and loosened his bow tie. His right shirt cuff was stained with droplets of what appeared to be blood.

'Are you all right, Commander?' she asked, sitting up. A navy man wouldn't have come to a party with a stained shirt.

'I beg your pardon?'

'Your cuff. It has blood on it. Have you cut yourself?'

'Oh.' He lifted his arm to examine his sleeve. There was a distinct blood-smeared scratch down his wrist that he quickly pulled his cuff to hide. 'I must have brushed against a rosebush.' He smiled reassuringly. 'Lady Ashworth's arbours are lethal!'

Then he noticed Charlie's bare feet, his eyes widening, and she tucked them back under the seat with an embarrassed laugh.

Stepping closer, he looked at the open notebook on her lap. 'May I join you, or are you hard at work?'

'Please, do sit.'

She held her breath as he sank down close beside her. His muscles strained in his tuxedo pants, and she did her best not to imagine running her fingers along his leg. She clenched and unclenched her fists, something she often did under tables to force herself to focus in interviews.

'What *are* you writing about?' the commander asked.

'I'm making a list of contacts and possible sources for down the track.' She realised she was stroking the gold edge of Marchand's name card, a gesture that gave her a strange comfort. 'I might have trouble putting faces to names, though, given so many of them were masked!'

The commander leaned back against the bench. 'If you manage to get an invitation, you'll see them all again in a week at Lady Ashworth's private gala at the Louvre. She's hosting it with Maxime Marchand this year. Last year she and Miss Goldsmith hosted a dinner among the Egyptian mummies at the Louvre to raise some funds for the antiquities division. Lady Ashworth has a list of worthy causes as long as my arm.'

'Mummies! Sounds spooky.' Charlie pulled a face. 'Forgive me for being crass, but how could a reporter fund a party on par with this?' She had already worked out that Milly was from wealth, but she wanted the details.

'Miss Goldsmith just covers fashion for a ladies' magazine.' He laughed. 'Her father owns most of Michigan. The Goldsmiths are the largest private traders of agricultural commodities on the Chicago Stock Exchange.'

'Oh!' said Charlie, irritated. 'Miss Goldsmith may come from privilege, but that doesn't mean she can't have her own ambitions, does it?'

'True,' conceded the commander.

'Maybe she writes about fashion because those are the stories women tend to be given. Had you thought of that, Commander Rose-Thomas?' Even though Milly had been cold to Charlie, she didn't deserve to be belittled by a man who knew nothing of how hard it was for a woman to land a position on a news desk.

'I'm sorry, I didn't mean to insult Miss Goldsmith, or you, Miss James.'

'Thank you, but it's Mrs James,' Charlie said quickly, feeling churlish. She sighed as she thought of the signed divorce settlement papers sitting under briefing notes in her apartment. *This week!*

'My apologies again.' He glanced at her left hand. 'I assumed . . .'

Charlie shrugged.

'Is your husband here in Paris?'

'He stayed in Sydney. We—I—' She took a deep breath. 'Well, I'm divorced. Or will be, soon enough.'

In less than a year her happy life had been destroyed. She closed her eyes and remembered pressing her cheek against her ex-husband's bare chest. She couldn't help thinking of his easy laugh; his gentle Irish lilt when he told her about funny things that had happened in court. As the warm memories swirled and regret pawed at her, she opened her eyes and straightened up.

She would also never forget the sour scent of whisky coming out his pores when he stumbled in their front door at dawn, excuses falling from his mouth about having to work late on a case. An unfamiliar perfume lingering in his hair, on his shirt . . .

'Divorced.' The commander seemed to mull over the word. Apparently sensing Charlie's discomfort, he apologised again as he looked her directly in the eye. His gaze was warm—he meant it. Putting his hands on his knees, he seemed about to stand up. 'I'd best be moving on. I can see you were seeking out a quiet corner to be alone. I'm sorry to have interrupted you.'

Charlie softened. This man was perceptive, and she found herself liking him more than she should have. 'No, honestly, you aren't interrupting anything. I just have a lifetime habit of crowd avoidance. Ran away from my own fifth birthday party! In my defence, I did take the strawberry sponge cake with me and share it with our terrier, Bessie.'

The commander's eyes disappeared when he laughed. Remaining seated, he pulled a silver Cartier cigarette case from his pocket, took out two and lifted an eyebrow as if to say, *Would you like one?* Charlie nodded, and he lit them between his lips before passing one to her.

'Thank you.' Usually she hated smoking, but in this instance it made her feel like a different person—Parisian, almost. 'You must think me strange, a reporter who hides from crowds, but I find it is easier to observe people from the edges.' She and Conrad had this in common.

The commander drew on his cigarette and exhaled. 'Understood.'

They smoked in silence, gazing at the bright lights of the party. When Charlie finished her cigarette, the commander took it from her and stubbed it out on the lawn beneath the toe of his shoe. He did the same with his cigarette before he turned to face her.

'Permit me, Charlie James, to offer a new acquaintance some advice.' He glanced at the name card in the open notebook on her lap. 'Stay away from Maxime. He's charming. Intriguing. Wealthy. Handsome, I'll grant you—'

'Those hardly sound like reasons to stay away, Commander.' Charlie tensed up. Why was this Englishman—a stranger— warning her away from Monsieur Marchand?

'I mean it.' He leaned closer, eyes imploring. 'He's . . . not what he seems.'

Charlie was annoyed at this overstep. 'Commander, we've met twice. You've just told me to stay away from a man I've met once. Would you care to elaborate?'

The commander clenched his jaw. 'Maxime is not a good man.'

'Oh? Maybe he prefers to keep his private life private. That's hardly a crime.' Charlie looked the commander in the eye, thinking of Milly and Mercedes, and of Marchand's wife.

'That isn't what I'm talking about,' said the commander, sounding a bit frustrated. 'Maxime is . . . dangerous.'

'How so?'

'I'd rather not say more.'

There was an awkward silence. She wondered if he knew that his wife had been at Café de Flore at the same time as Marchand. Even if not, surely the commander's dislike for the banker was based on jealousy. But Charlie hadn't the slightest romantic interest in Marchand. There was more than a hint of cruelty lying beneath his handsome, carefree façade.

Despite her better judgement, Charlie was attracted to Edward Rose-Thomas. His athleticism brought out something visceral in her. She hadn't been with a man since she'd separated from her husband, and while she didn't want to launch herself into another relationship, she missed being touched. But there was a line Charlie would never cross—she did not wish the hurt she felt on another woman. She would have to content herself with imagining her hand on the commander's thigh.

A gust of wind rustled the trees around them. Distant horns started to play, then a gong rang—a signal to guests that it was midnight, and the main show was about to begin. Charlie had promised Violet they would sit together on the lawn, so it was time she made her way back.

'I shall have one last cigarette,' said the commander, as she put on her shoes and got to her feet. 'Lovely speaking with you, Mrs James.'

Charlie watched an acrobat walk along a tightrope. She was sitting beside Violet and Aleksandr, her notebook open again on her lap. Guests were lolling about on cushions, enjoying the main event—an orchestra, the acrobat, and bare-breasted dancers on horseback—when a gust of wind blew out the arena lights for a few moments. Soon after they came back on, and Lady Ashworth had commanded the orchestra to play again, a piercing scream cut through the wind and music.

The orchestra's conductor waved his baton above his head and stopped the music. The scream continued.

Charlie looked at Violet. 'Is that . . . *human*?'

Violet's normally composed face crumpled into a frown. 'I'm not sure.'

Charlie twisted her neck, trying to work out where the sound was coming from. Her first instinct was to run towards it, to swallow her fear and help. Some of the guests were fleeing the noise and darkness, the villa's lights beckoning them like a safety beacon, while Charlie and Violet remained seated, calm among the chaos.

The scream cut off.

Charlie took a deep breath, then gathered up her purse and notebook. Kicking off her heels, she was about to head to where she thought the scream had come from, when Milly Goldsmith staggered out of the trees along the edge of the performance area. Her blue silk dress was hoisted above her knees with one hand and muddied at the hemline. She'd lost her heels, and her face looked hollow. Ghostly.

When the spotlight fell on her, Milly didn't even blink.

'Oh my goodness, she looks awful,' whispered Violet, her voice full of concern as she clutched Charlie's wrist.

'Yes, she's very pale.' Charlie gently prised Violet's fingers from her wrist. 'Let's get closer.'

As they approached Milly, so did Lady Ashworth. Violet put a hand on Charlie's arm, and they hung back discreetly, away from the spotlight, as they listened in.

'Milly, my dear, whatever is the matter?' Lady Ashworth asked. Her cobalt cape was gone, and her black Chanel ballgown rippled in the breeze. Her voice was soothing, as if Milly might rear up at any moment.

Milly turned to face her hostess, mouth pressed shut, eyes wide, and she shook her head, trembling with fear. 'It was too late. I . . . I tried . . .' Her words were laboured—it seemed she was very drunk.

'Dear Milly, let's go and sit down, shall we?' Lady Ashworth's voice was a fraction sharper now; she was clearly keen for her guest's indiscretion not to play out in the spotlight. 'Come, my dear.'

As she touched Milly's elbow and tried to usher her away from the glare, Lady Ashworth shot Charlie a look that said, *Please don't write about my drunk guest.* The rules of *le tout-Paris* could be ambiguous, but in this case Charlie was certain that reporting Milly's bizarre, intoxicated behaviour would ensure that another gilded invitation never came her way, and that she could say goodbye to her feature article—and her future in France.

Milly refused to budge. She stayed in the spotlight, clutching the hem of her dress to her thighs, shivering. Then she lifted her right hand from behind her back. It was sticky with blood.

Gasps. More screams.

For in Milly Goldsmith's hand was the unmistakable shape of a knife.

Chapter 6

Charlie's head whirled with questions. Whose blood was dripping off that knife? Why was Milly brandishing it?

The remaining guests lingered on their cushions for a beat, perhaps uncertain if this was part of the performance. After all, who could forget the faux-murder party hosted by Tilly Munro on the Riviera last year? The guests looked around at one another, clearly unsure what to do.

Her eyes wide with horror, Lady Ashworth lurched back from the weeping and shivering woman. This was no prank.

The wind lowered. Frightened guests tensed.

'Where did she get the knife?'

'Who did she stab, more like it?'

'Is that *her* blood?'

Everyone rose to their feet, shouting and pushing each other out of the way. Masks were torn off and discarded. Eyes were bloodshot and makeup was smeared after hours of freely pouring alcohol. They were all desperate to put more distance between themselves and the knife.

Charlie, Violet and Aleksandr didn't move as Milly dropped the weapon and sank to her knees, sobbing. Lady Ashworth tentatively approached her and coaxed her to her feet, then finally led her out of the spotlight.

Over her shoulder, Charlie noticed Conrad standing at the rim of the circus, camera lowered, face ashen.

The crowd gathered on the driveway and the terrace, pressed together in the sticky summer night. Over the din, Lord Ashworth spoke in a loud but calm voice as he stood in front of the terrace. He waved his hands, palms down in a soothing gesture. 'We'd much appreciate it if you'd remain where you are. The police have been called and should be here within the hour.'

He rushed across the lawn to his wife's side and put his arms around her, and she pressed her tears into his chest. Perhaps what Violet had said about their marriage was true, but it seemed clear that whatever their circumstances, they cared for each other.

Lord Ashworth stroked his wife's hair and murmured into her ear. With two fingers, he motioned for Conrad to come closer, then he asked the young man to guide the two women away from the prying eyes of the crowd, the snap of cameras and clamouring journalists into Villa Trianon. He added, 'Please get Miss Goldsmith upstairs with a cup of tea.'

'Brandy,' corrected Lady Ashworth, as she gently placed an arm around the sobbing Milly. Charlie could see why Lady Ashworth had made an excellent nurse during the war.

Conrad walked just ahead of them, ignoring a visibly shocked Mercedes Rose-Thomas, then Claudette Marchand and some equally elegant but distraught friends. He lead Milly and Lady Ashworth away from these women to the villa via the secluded picking garden, his camera banging against his chest, and Charlie felt a flicker of irritation. While she appreciated his chivalry and obedience to Lord Ashworth, she needed him to take more photos.

Lord Ashworth continued to speak calm instructions to the guests and his staff. 'Everybody needs to remain here until the police arrive. Stay near the lights! Don't do anything that might disturb a crime scene! Anyone who does so may face legal consequences. Close the front gates and make sure nobody leaves until the police arrive. Is there a doctor in the house?'

Charlie had assumed that Commander Rose-Thomas would be the type to take charge of an agitated crowd, but he was nowhere to be seen.

In a distant part of the walled garden, beyond the hedged picking garden where Charlie had sat to rest her feet, Charlie watched police set up cordon ropes and battery-powered lamps. A handful of local journalists were trying to get as close to the officers as possible, shouting at each other while they jostled for position. Bulbs flashed as photographers held their cameras high in the air and pointed them towards the crime scene, snapping and hoping for a decent shot.

Of what, Charlie wasn't yet sure. She was annoyed that Conrad still wasn't here among the throng; he wasn't cut out to be a news photographer if he was willing to miss the scoop.

A line of young uniformed police were keeping an impatient crowd of guests at bay. They hadn't been interviewed yet, and they all wanted to flee to their town cars and waiting valets and the safety of their apartments. Most of them were in the villa and on the terrace, but a substantial number had gathered at the crime scene, and some were demanding answers. Heads dipped and craned, angling to see what was going on. Charlie overheard some of the whispers that spread from the front of the crowd.

'I can't believe he's dead.'

'Such a charismatic man!'

'A leader of men.'

'Mademoiselle Goldsmith held a knife—it was clearly her.'

'I heard her tell the police she found it on his body.'

Charlie's stomach clenched. *A leader of men . . . a charismatic man . . .* She'd looked in vain for the commander during and after the performance.

Shoulders tense, she decided she could no longer wait for Conrad. With a deep breath, she pushed her way into the crowd. She could have asked around for the victim's name, but for some reason she felt the need to find out for herself.

She'd sat with the commander on the bench not far from this spot. Had someone stabbed the Englishman as she'd walked back through the trees to the circus performance? Had he been given the chance to smoke one last cigarette?

Quickening her pace, she elbowed past the gossiping guests as police continued to secure the area. An older officer had joined them, and he was yelling at the crowd in a mix of French and very angry English. '*Va-t'en!* Stay back!'

As she reached the police rope, she finally saw the body.

It wasn't the commander lying there in his tuxedo, sprawled on the lush green lawn, jacket open, white shirt slashed and stained crimson, powerful neck mutilated.

It was Maxime Marchand.

The blond charismatic banker who had oozed confidence lay in a black sticky puddle of his own blood.

Charlie sucked in her breath and counted to five. She'd seen a handful of murder victims while investigating homicides back in Sydney: both cold and clean in the morgue, and still warm on footpaths or sprawled in beds, life gurgling from the wounds. But blood-soaked dead bodies were always a shock—always nauseating. She turned her head and pressed the back of her hand to her mouth, trying not to gag at the cloying, metallic smell of blood, or the jagged chunk of flesh dangling from the neck. She couldn't see the number of wounds because of the blood and the position of the body. Revulsion and adrenaline churned in her stomach, and she pulled a handkerchief from her purse to dab at the sweat beading her forehead.

Conflicting emotions flickered in her chest: shock that Marchand was dead, but also a sliver of relief that the commander was not. Of course, Marchand was a husband and possibly a father. He was the head of Paris's leading bank. His death would leave a hole in the lives of many. Charlie pictured Claudette Marchand's glowing face and felt sick for the woman.

Taking deep, even breaths, Charlie pushed her feelings aside and turned away from the body. She had a job to do.

The whole of France—indeed Europe, and perhaps the entire world—would be interested in this news. Here was her chance to prove to George and his seniors in London that she was an excellent news reporter. If she handled this story right, she would stay in Paris permanently.

Charlie grabbed her pen and notebook from her purse. Her mind raced as she wondered who had committed the crime, and she was scrawling her thoughts across the page. Could it really have been Milly? Perhaps the murderer was someone else Charlie had spoken with that night . . .

She froze as she remembered the blood on the commander's cuff. The scratch on his wrist. Had their chat on the bench been a ploy to distract her from the murder scene? The commander clearly loathed the banker. But why would he have warned Charlie to stay away from someone he had murdered only minutes earlier?

Charlie spotted Violet a few feet to her left. She put away her pen and notebook and went over to the young woman. The pair hugged, then exchanged sad looks. Charlie squeezed her colleague's arm. 'Are you okay?'

Nodding vigorously, as though she were trying to convince herself, Violet gestured through the crowd to where Aleksandr stood. He lifted his hand in a small wave, his brow furrowed.

Violet turned back to the crime scene. 'I just can't believe it. Marchand! He's such a force—*was*. This is a *huge* story!' She held Charlie's gaze. 'What do you need?'

Charlie scanned the crowd for Conrad, thinking of the state-of-the-art Leica camera slung around his neck. 'We need photos. Fast. *Before* they cover up the body. Please go to the villa and give Conrad my order to come out here and take some photos. If he refuses, tell him his contract is broken and ask if you can at least borrow his camera.'

While Violet fetched Conrad, Charlie held her spot near the corner of the police rope. Beside her, a balding reporter about her age kept waving his press card above his head and calling out, '*Le Monde! Le Monde!*' while making a frantic effort to push past the rope. The police were having none of it, shooing him back as though he were a pesky toddler.

Charlie didn't introduce herself to the local press as she wanted to chase this story solo. Besides, these male reporters would surely be as unwilling to share information as her peers in Sydney had been. She needed to find a way to break this story first—she needed to connect with the police.

From her new vantage point she could see there was just one deep, gaping wound in Marchand's neck. Flipping open her notebook to the page where she had wedged his card, she recorded details: what the victim was wearing, how he was lying, and the nature of the wound. His eyes were open, and he looked surprised rather than terrified.

Violet finally appeared beside Charlie, Conrad at her shoulder.

Charlie gave him a sharp look. 'Good to see you decided to stay with *The Times*, Mr Mackenzie. Please get to work.'

He was pale, his eyes haunted, and he was uncomfortable and fidgety—as though he'd rather be anywhere else but here—but he went ahead and reached for his camera.

Police were studying and photographing the body. Someone elbowed Charlie in the hip, and she winced as she shifted to make room for Conrad. 'Right-oh, let's get the shots before they cover the body.' She waved him towards the rope. As he moved beside her, she said in a softer tone, 'Before you look at Marchand, I just need to prepare you. It can be a shock to see a dead body— especially a mutilated body—for the first time.' She needed to appear professional, even as she gulped down her own nausea. 'Are you feeling up to this? I realise it's an unexpectedly difficult first assignment.'

Conrad's face remained still.

'I'll take that as a yes,' said Charlie. 'Go, get some pictures. And ignore the loud French reporters, bloody pains!'

Conrad knelt beneath the rope so he was as close as possible to the body and wouldn't be blocked by any of the frantic guests. He adjusted his lens and the bulb started flashing.

Violet was peering through the crowd towards the driveway. 'They've taken Milly in for questioning.'

Conrad's head snapped up.

'Look!' Violet pointed.

Milly was hunched over and draped in a thin grey blanket in the back seat of a police car.

'No!' said Conrad, getting to his feet. 'They can't arrest her!'

Chapter 7

Conrad started to make for the police car, but Charlie stopped him by placing her hands on his shoulders. 'Conrad, we had a deal!'

His face contorted with frustration. 'But she's innocent!' He spoke in a whisper between clenched teeth, his amber eyes hidden behind his fringe as he tucked his head low and tried to step around Charlie.

How could he be so sure of Milly's innocence? Charlie would get the photos first, then the answers. 'Conrad,' she said, sounding stern, 'I *need* more photos. Quickly, before the police cover up the body.'

'But—'

'And I'm sure I don't need to tell you that confronting police at the start of a homicide investigation never helped anyone.'

'Understood.' Conrad turned from her, his cheeks slightly flushed.

Charlie studied Milly's slim frame. Part of her wanted to believe Conrad. But Marchand had the stature of Napoleon—it wasn't a stretch to think Milly could have overpowered him, especially if he had been intoxicated.

On first seeing Milly with the knife, Charlie had wondered if the young woman had stabbed someone in self-defence. But the depth and position of the wound suggested someone had been determined to kill Marchand.

'I'm going to head back to the villa and try to reach George,' said Violet, and Charlie nodded and murmured her thanks.

Conrad was crouched down again, contorting himself to get the best shots. Relieved she would have some decent images, Charlie took out her notebook and walked to the outskirts of the crowd. Leaning against the thick trunk of an oak, she jotted down impressions of the party. She recalled the tension between Monsieur Marchand and a few of the guests—Milly, the Rose-Thomases, Aleksandr—along with the dignified composure of Madame Marchand, as Lady Ashworth had smoothed the way with entertainment, canapés and Krug.

Charlie cast her gaze over the crowd, who shuffled their feet on moist grass, beads of sweat gathering at their brows in the humidity. How many of these members of the Parisian elite had their money invested with Marchand? What did his death mean for them? She eyed the diamonds and sapphires glinting at wrists, ears and necks, and thought of how unwilling any of them would be to part with such treasures. These women wore them like a second skin, but Charlie knew all too well how precarious life was, and how quickly one could lose something precious.

Violet gently touched her arm to get her attention, then spoke in a whisper. 'Claudette Marchand was watching the performance with a few of her husbands' clients. She saw everything! She was whisked into the villa and taken upstairs for a cup of tea and a rest until she was ready to talk to the police. I tried to check on her, but Lord Ashworth has stationed his butler and a few other staff at the bottom of the stairs to keep everyone out. Members of the press are allowed one short phone call each.'

'Did you manage to leave a message for George?'

'Yes, with his housekeeper, who told me he's still at the hospital with his wife. I gave her the salient details and promised you would file first thing in the morning.'

Charlie was really back in the game now—in Sydney she'd grown used to working through the night on big scoops. 'Of course! Thanks.' The beautiful new typewriter in her apartment was going to earn its keep. Her story might even make the front page in London.

As Violet and Charlie walked back to Conrad, he was straightening up, his face composed. 'There's something about our new photographer that I can't put my finger on,' said Violet, shaking her head as he began getting some snaps of the officers at the scene. One of them was carrying a rolled-up white sheet.

'Hmm, I know what you mean. He's a real mix, isn't he? Shy but mature.'

Charlie caught a last glimpse of Marchand's sprawled body before police unfurled the large white sheet over it. Given the frantic state of the crowd, she thought it was far too late for that.

'Violet!'

Aleksandr was beckoning her over, and she cast a guilty look at Charlie.

'Go on,' said Charlie with a fond smile. 'Be with your handsome Russian. And thanks for all your help!'

Violet blew her a kiss and practically skipped off into Aleksandr's arms.

Charlie made her way back to Conrad, and he acknowledged her with a nod between snaps. She was hoping she might speak to the police now they had finished examining the body in situ. Other journalists and press photographers had made it to the edge of the crime scene, jostling with Conrad for good positions. The balding man from *Le Monde* was speaking quietly to a uniformed officer over the rope, gesticulating at the body and trying to coax his way in. Judging by the frown on the officer's tired face, the reporter was getting nowhere.

Charlie was the new reporter on the beat, an Australian and a rare woman in the field—a novelty—so she thought she might have more luck. She gestured to a uniformed officer to indicate she wanted a word. The young man gazed at her, apparently a bit stunned, and nodded slowly.

But just as Charlie lifted the rope, she was stopped short by a tall man in a sharp three-piece suit. Charlie had spotted him earlier. He was clearly the most senior officer at the scene, judging by the deference the uniforms paid to him. Amid flashing bulbs, panicked guests, demanding journalists and exasperated policemen, he remained calm.

'*Où allez-vous?*' He was at least a decade older than her, with dark hair greying slightly at the temples and a strong jawline. His face was tanned and open, and his eyes were quite green. Square wire glasses were perched on his nose.

'I was hoping to get past and speak with your officer,' Charlie replied in French.

He seemed curious now, perhaps because of her accent. In a polite yet firm voice, he responded in English. 'I'm sorry, this is a crime scene. We cannot let you through. No more photographs!' He waved his hand at Conrad and the others. 'No more!'

The man from *Le Monde* groaned and threw his hands in the air. '*C'est le bordel!*' he exclaimed as he signalled to his photographer that they should leave.

The senior policeman brushed off this comment with a shake of his head and an exasperated grin, tiny laugh lines appearing around his eyes. He watched *Le Monde*'s disappearing back with visible relief. '*C'est comme ça,*' he muttered under his breath before he again turned to Charlie. 'Go back to the circus ring, and my officers will be over to interview you as soon as they have finished.

If you do not wish to speak with them now, they will take your details and arrange a time in the coming days.'

His English was clipped but very clear, yet Charlie heard his weariness. She glanced at her wristwatch: 2 a.m. It would be impossible for a dozen officers to interview a couple of hundred people before sunrise.

She pulled her press card from her purse and passed it to him, and he took it with a raised eyebrow. 'Charlie James, *The Times*, London,' he read before looking up. '*Anglaise?*' He sounded as though he'd tasted something rotten.

'*Australienne*,' Charlie corrected.

'*Bon*, much better,' he quipped with the tiniest of smiles.

'This is one of our part-time photographers, Conrad Mackenzie.'

The young man nodded hello but looked as though he wanted to hide behind a tree.

'Inspecteur Benoît Bernard. I'm running this investigation.' He slowly took in Charlie's couture dress and the crumpled mask in her hand with her notebook. 'I take it you were here to write about Lady Ashworth's party.' His tone was neutral as he neatly folded her press credentials and handed them back. 'Go home. There is nothing beyond a dead body to report at this stage.'

'Inspecteur Bernard, could I perhaps meet with you tomorrow? I could come to the station at a time that suits you.'

He sighed again. 'I'm not in the habit of making arrangements with the press,' he said cautiously.

'That may be so. *We* are not in the habit of making arrangements with the police. But instead of making you jump through hoops to obtain a warrant, we'll quickly print duplicates for you of all Mr Mackenzie's photos from this evening and hand deliver them'—Charlie smiled sweetly and held up an index finger—'as long as you agree to share some information about the case.'

There was a faint smile at the corner of his lips again.

Charlie took this as a positive sign. His first impression of her was not altogether negative—she could build on this. 'So, you agree?'

'*Non!* I'll agree to no such thing,' he said, shrugging as he started to turn away. 'I will simply wait for the warrant. Now if you'll excuse—'

Charlie powered on, determined to find a chink in his armour. 'What has Miss Amelia Goldsmith told you?'

'No comment, *laissez-tomber*, let it go.' He pursed his lips. 'All right, one thing. We have not yet spoken with Miss Goldsmith. She has chosen to wait until we reach the station.'

Smart girl, she's probably waiting for legal representation. 'And the knife? Where did she get it?'

'Uncertain. We are looking into this, and we will release a statement to the public.'

Charlie remembered something. 'Could the knife have been part of the circus? There was a knife juggler.'

Inspecteur Bernard jerked his head up. 'Is that so? *C'est possible.*' He told a couple of his men to find any knife jugglers and ask them to wait for questioning. *'Merci,* now I must go.'

'Miss Goldsmith didn't do it!' Conrad said abruptly.

The inspecteur ran his eyes over the young American as if truly noticing him for the first time.

'She didn't do it.' Conrad's voice was softer now, imploring.

Inspecteur Bernard cocked his head and said wearily. *'Comme ci, comme ça.* Do you have something you want to share with me?' He squared up to Conrad and stared into his eyes.

Conrad didn't blink. 'I'll destroy my photos unless you agree to keep Charlie here in the loop.'

She gasped. 'Conrad, your contract—our articles—'

He turned anguished eyes to her, and she realised he was almost certainly in love with Milly.

'Comme vous voulez, as you wish,' said the inspecteur, who clearly would not concede to the young American. 'You will face charges of obstructing an investigation.' He turned as though about to walk away.

Charlie remembered the blood on the commander's cuff. 'You might want to speak with Commander Edward Rose-Thomas, Inspecteur. I sat smoking with him in the garden not far from here, either right before or right after the murder. He had a deep scratch on his wrist—he said he had snagged it on a rosebush.'

Conrad gave Charlie a confused look, which she ignored.

The inspecteur did not seem to judge her for spending time alone with a man who was not her husband. He merely seemed grateful as he wrote down the commander's name in his pocket-book with a lead pencil. 'Blood, you say? And you sat with him at what time, and for how long?'

'Just before the gong rang for the performance at midnight. We spoke for ten minutes, maybe fifteen. I'd come out here to clear my head and take some notes, then he approached me. We made polite chitchat.' Charlie tried to keep her voice steady as she knew how her actions would be perceived. It didn't matter if it was Sydney or Paris, it was her reputation that would be in tatters, not his.

'*Merci*. Commander Edward Rose-Thomas.' The inspecteur turned to speak quietly to a uniformed officer, who proceeded to move off through the crowd, presumably in search of the commander. For the first time, the inspecteur gave Charlie a genuine smile. 'You are being very helpful, Mademoiselle James—unusual, in my experiences with the press.' He smirked at where some younger male journalists were still leaning over the ropes, desperate for his attention with their notebooks and cameras out.

'It's . . . Madame.'

'*Très désolé.*'

Charlie blinked and moved on. 'The commander is with the British Embassy on secondment.'

'Of course he is,' the inspecteur said, throwing his hands in the air. 'Just what I need, a British diplomat implicated in a murder on French soil.' He scratched his head. 'I'll look into it, *merci*. It could be circumstantial. It could be coincidence. Sometimes a rose is just a rose.'

Charlie smiled at the joke, and his eyes crinkled with amusement. He was warming to her—it was a start.

He tightened his silk scarf around his neck. '*Excusez-moi.*'

'Milly didn't do it,' Conrad pleaded, as though he couldn't help himself. 'I know she didn't!'

'What makes you so sure?' asked the inspecteur.

Charlie stared at her photographer.

'Because I was watching her,' he confessed.

The Times, June 1938
Charlie James, Paris correspondent
Photography by Conrad Mackenzie

American heiress released without charge due to alibi

US *Harper's Bazaar* magazine correspondent Miss Amelia Goldsmith has been released with no formal charges being laid for the murder of Maxime Marchand, heir to the Benjamin Marchand Bank.

Marchand was found stabbed, with his neck and chest mutilated, in a darkened corner of the grounds at Villa Trianon, Versailles. He had been among two hundred guests at Lord and Lady Ashworth's annual summer ball.

Miss Goldsmith seemed to be the primary suspect, as she appeared in front of the crowd clutching a blood-smeared knife just prior to the body being discovered. Her innocence was determined with the help of a key witness, photographer Conrad Mackenzie from Birmingham, Alabama, who placed Miss Goldsmith with him at the estimated time of the murder.

Mr Mackenzie said that during the circus performance, he had gone into the garden for fresh air and a cigarette when he saw Miss Goldsmith stumble across Marchand with a knife in his neck. She pulled out the knife in an attempt to save him. When blood spurted onto her hands and silk dress, she fled the scene. The witness followed her to the edge of the circus ring, where she revealed the knife to startled onlookers.

Miss Goldsmith was held for questioning at the Metro Police Station before being released once the alibi was established. Inspecteur Benoît Bernard, the chief investigator, would not be drawn for comment. The investigation is ongoing.

Maxime Marchand is survived by his widow Claudette and their son Jacob, who recently joined the family firm after he graduated from the Wharton Business School in the United States.

The Marchands have accepted President Lebrun's offer of a state funeral.

Chapter 8

'Grand,' said George Roberts graciously as he tossed that day's edition of *The Times* onto his desk. 'The lads in London particularly appreciated the pics of the stiff. But they want us to run who bloody committed the crime before anyone else does. You need to stay ahead of this story, James.' They were sitting in his poky corner office with the door open, letting in the whirr and clack of typewriters. 'Well done, though.'

Charlie smiled. 'Thanks, sir.'

For those who hunted news, homicide stories presented a fascinating challenge—how to describe the crime scene, what to make of the limited facts from police, how to talk to witnesses while picking through facts and rumours. Homicide stories were shifting puzzles.

As a child Charlie would fold herself into the sofa at the far corner of her father's office, sketching his face or practising the French verb conjugations her mother insisted on, while he pieced together criminal cases for the Crown. One of Sydney's leading prosecutors, he hunted convictions, raking over the coroner's reports and witness statements that he spread across his cherrywood desk. He would prise them apart and examine each one from every possible angle, building his prosecution cases piece by piece. He'd often discuss them at length with his eldest daughter; he encouraged her input—long after she was supposed to be tucked up in bed—and challenged her to help him step through evidence. The most studious of her siblings, she preferred to be inside with the smell of linseed oil on wood, leatherbound books and tales from afar than outside wrestling, climbing trees and kicking footballs. Later, her father encouraged her to put her name forward as a cadet journalist. Her father's mentorship and mother's support had given Charlie all kinds of notions. Namely that she was as capable as any man—a career should not be ruled out just because Sydney society said ladies like Charlie were best off at home.

Sitting across from George, she took a deep breath, relieved he was keeping her on the case. 'Is your wife recovering well?'

'Well enough,' he said stiffly. 'Daphne did a real number on her ankle. The doctor thinks she'll be on bed rest for a couple of weeks, poor love. I might have to head home early today. God knows,

I have a few sick days owing—haven't had one in twenty years.' He softened a little as he looked at Charlie. 'Thanks for your concern, James. It's a relief for me to know this case is in good hands.'

'You can call me Charlie, sir.'

'What's the difference? You have two first names, doesn't matter which one I call you.' He chuckled to himself as he tapped her article. 'Back to the Marchand case. So, Goldsmith has a very convenient alibi—and I suppose her daddy made some calls and the girl walked.' Scoffing, he shook his head. 'Typical French: authorities roll over at the first nudge. So, did she do it?'

'I have no idea, sir.' Charlie paused, comparing the sassy correspondent to the translucent waif crying in the back of a police car. 'Conrad is certainly very insistent that she's innocent.'

George rolled his eyes. 'Bloody hell, the Yank's hiding something, James. And I think he snuck off to follow the girl when he was meant to be taking photos for us! It seems bloody fishy to me. Maybe they were in it together.'

'Maybe.' Charlie knew better than to speculate this early when reporting a homicide; the public got angry if you fed them a story then needed to backtrack because it had holes or was simply untrue. 'Miss Goldsmith . . . seemed familiar with Marchand. They're part of a tight circle.'

'How *familiar*? You were there, James. You must have a hunch?'

'I find that facts are better than hunches, sir,' she retorted. Hunches could break your heart, if you weren't careful. 'All I can say is that I sensed she personally disliked him, or that he made her emotional in some way, but perhaps I was wrong.'

'And the police? Will they cooperate with you?'

'I think so,' said Charlie brightly. 'I've spoken to Inspecteur Bernard, and I'm hoping he'll swap information for all of Mackenzie's party photos and my ongoing cooperation. I've made an appointment with him for early this afternoon.' She remembered his look of gratitude when she'd given him the information about the commander. 'Violet has prepared a cheque for Mackenzie, and I've asked him to bring me the rest of the party photos this morning. We'll have a little chat before I go to the police station.'

'Understood.' George signed the cheque and whistled before he pushed it across the desk. 'You're good, James. That Yank's got the pics we need—possibly key information too, if you play your cards right. Whatever he's guilty of, we need to keep him on side—and keep our exclusive access to his work.' He cleared his throat. 'As for your plan with the inspecteur . . . You can try, but I wouldn't bet on getting much from him. Can't trust a Frenchman. Can I give you some advice, James?'

Charlie leaned back in her chair and nodded.

'Inspecteur Bernard wants to catch whoever did this. Marchand is a famous and well-connected man. The higher-ups will be breathing down his neck for results.'

Like they're breathing down yours. She kept this thought to herself.

'You need to think like a detective.'

Or a prosecutor. She also kept this thought to herself.

George knocked his knuckles against the desk. Her allocated time was up.

A few minutes later, Violet presented Conrad Mackenzie at Charlie's messy desk.

'Thanks for showing him in.' She gave her colleague a grateful smile, then watched her clack away on her red heels.

Conrad eyed Charlie's desk, and they shared a grimace.

'We'll go to the main meeting room to look at your photos. Better light. Bigger desk.' She beckoned the young man down a corridor and into the room, flicking on the light switch. His fringe was stuck to his forehead, the tip of his collar stained with sweat. 'Water?'

Conrad nodded, and she poured two glasses from a silver jug Violet had left on the table. Beside it was a crisp white envelope with *Mr Conrad Mackenzie* typed across the front. If the American noticed the envelope, he was too polite to say.

'Mr Mackenzie—'

'Conrad, please.'

'Conrad, I appreciate you coming in so soon—especially on a hot day. Did you walk here?' Charlie wanted to know if he lived at Villa Trianon.

'I used Lady Ashworth's town car. I have some errands to run for her and her husband after we finish here.'

'So you live at the villa?'

'Not exactly.' He coughed softly and took a sip of water. 'I live in some small rooms by the gatehouse. It's at the original entrance, on the far side of the garden by the lake.'

'Near where Marchand's body was found?'

Conrad shifted in his seat. 'Not far. A hundred yards, maybe.'

'Were you planning to discuss work there with Milly? Is that why you left the performance you were supposed to be photographing?'

'I . . . told you and the police. I just went for a short stroll to get some fresh air. I wasn't intending to be gone long. I was standing nearby when Miss Goldsmith pulled the knife out of Marchand's body. She was screaming, really upset.' Sweat beaded above his brow. 'Then she ran off.'

'She's a small woman and you're a tall man, but you couldn't catch up with her? You couldn't help her or raise the alarm? Milly walked into the arena distressed and alone.' Charlie waited a few seconds for her words to sink in. 'That all seems strange to me.'

Conrad's jaw clenched, and he looked at her with pleading amber eyes. 'She didn't do it.'

The kid definitely has a crush on Milly.

Charlie studied his flushed, sweaty face and the well-cut suit draped over his slightly hunched shoulders. Conrad was well out of his league: she was a beautiful heiress, he a photographer on the make. At home in America, this pairing would be almost impossible—but here in Paris, the city of open hearts and open minds . . .

'You love her,' said Charlie kindly.

Conrad shrugged and winced, but said nothing. There was no point in denial—it was written all over his face.

Charlie pushed some more. 'Does she know?'

Another boyish shrug.

As gently as possible, Charlie asked, 'Are you . . . lovers?'

Conrad's silence and deep blush gave it away. He nodded.

Silence.

He shifted in his seat and studied his shoes.

'Were the two of you in the woods together?'

'No!'

'The police aren't going to leave you alone, not until all their questions are answered. And if your story doesn't match up with Milly's . . .'

'Alrighty. I guess it can't make things worse if I tell you that I was nearby, behind a tree.' Conrad looked sheepish. 'She went wandering off into the garden—I didn't know why! And I followed.'

It was hard for Charlie to hide her surprise, but she managed it. 'You were jealous?'

His fist clenched and relaxed. 'I guess.'

'Aside from that, what were your impressions of Marchand? Lady Ashworth was planning to co-host the Louvre gala with him, so you must have encountered him.'

'Unfortunately, yes.' Conrad gritted his teeth. 'Swanned about as if he were bigger than the Mississippi. Treated most people real bad, unless they had proper money. Paid no attention to the likes of me.'

'But he paid attention to Milly.'

'You met Milly—she's kinda hard to ignore.' Cherries appeared on his cheeks.

Could Conrad have stabbed Marchand moments before Milly stumbled across the body? He certainly had a motive. Charlie had covered plenty of homicides in Sydney where lovers had killed for less.

As if Conrad could read her thoughts, he looked her square in the eye. 'Milly tried to save Marchand. *That's* your story.'

'So help me, Conrad. Help me, help Milly. Did you see—'

'I've told you everything I know.'

Charlie didn't believe the young man for a second. He seemed corn-fed and wholesome, but he was hiding something underneath that fringe. Perhaps George was right—perhaps Milly and Conrad were in it together. She decided at this stage it was best to play along until she could speak with Inspecteur Bernard. She would also need to speak with Milly.

Leaning forward, Charlie spread her hands out on the table, palms down. 'Well, let's look at these party photos and see if they give us any leads.'

'Okay.' Conrad was visibly relieved as he reached into his briefcase and pulled out a fat envelope. 'Here they are. I have a second set here, for the police.' He took out another envelope and set it on the desktop.

'Thank you.' Charlie pulled the first envelope towards her. 'We'll have a look in a moment. In the meantime, this one is for you.' She slid the cream envelope towards him with two fingers.

Conrad picked it up and pulled out the cheque with a gasp. 'This is double what Mr Roberts put in my contract,' he stammered. 'And I failed to capture the whole circus performance.'

'True,' said Charlie. 'But that fee was for some party pics, not photos of a homicide. Everyone at *The Times* is very keen that we have exclusive access to these images, and that you continue to work for us.'

Conrad nodded as he studied the cheque again. 'Thanks, Charlie.' He stuffed the envelope into his blazer pocket, exposing a sweaty armpit as he did so.

Charlie topped up his water glass, and he sipped gratefully before he stood and started to spread the photographs across the desk. Charlie sucked in a breath as she took in the riot of feathers and jewels amid the bright lights and striped marquees. 'The Ashworths told me you did a lot of the party planning. It was very impressive.'

'I helped out, but it's Lady Ashworth who has the knack for it—and the stamina! Her interior design work takes her all over the world, and I kind of tag along, offering second opinions. I help her choose flowers, I dress tables, I take measurements . . .'

'You procure elephants!'

'Exactly!' Conrad gave a soft laugh, his amber eyes smiling.

Charlie picked up a photo of Lord and Lady Ashworth standing in a prim pose, shoulders almost touching, with an elephant raising its trunk behind them. In the next pic they had turned to each other with bemused laughter.

'That's early in the evening, before everyone arrived.' Conrad flicked Charlie an uncharacteristically cheeky look. 'I got there first thing to take the best shots, because I knew that many photographers would be coming.'

'Nice work.' Charlie studied a candid shot of Maxime and Claudette Marchand, gregarious and full of life. 'This is incredible. We'll definitely be printing it.'

Conrad blushed, nodding his thanks. 'Well, ma'am—Charlie, not all the photos are good enough to print. But you will be interested in a few of those shots. Wait a moment . . .' He was nearing the bottom of the pile, layering photos over the table.

Charlie's breath caught when she saw two people leaning towards each other on a park bench, backlit by a garden lamp, her own pale, freckled back laced with a dark silk.

When she looked up, Conrad was staring at her, but all he said was, 'Found them!'

He handed her a stack of four photos. The first image was askew and slightly out of focus. A lipstick-painted mouth pressed against Marchand's cheek, the hint of a dark dress in the frame, a distinctive jawline: Mercedes Rose-Thomas. There was something in the background. As Charlie held the photo directly under the light, a pale ghost in the corner took shape. It was the commander, his face contorted with fury.

Chapter 9

Straight after her meeting with Conrad, Charlie headed to her appointment with Inspecteur Bernard. When she'd telephoned the police station, the officer at reception had told her she needed to arrive before 1 p.m. She took a taxi to the Cité Metro Station on Place Louis-Lépine, but it pulled up at a giant sandstone quadrangle used as a flower market, with the station on the opposite side. The driver indicated that Charlie must walk through the flower stalls to get to her destination. Although she very much doubted this was true, it was a warm day and a magical forest beckoned.

She marched through avenues of pink and red roses spilling out of metal buckets, pails of blue irises and white lilies, hanging bushels of rosemary and sage, and armfuls of wildflowers in every hue. Her nose tingled with all the sweet and heady scents, and she resolved to get armfuls of roses and herbs to fill her apartment.

The Cité Metro Police Station stood like a chateau at the far end of the quadrangle. The huge arches of former garrisons flanked the entrance, with the Paris-standard grey tiled roof above. Charlie jogged up the grand marble steps into the foyer, her satchel banging against her thigh.

She was about to approach the imposing reception desk when Inspecteur Bernard appeared to one side. '*Bonjour.*'

'*Bonjour, ça va?*' said Charlie politely.

He was fastening his trench-coat belt and holding a beret. 'I appreciate you bringing me the photos so quickly. This is a big story for you, and it is also a huge investigation for us. I do not want to deal in rumours. So, I've changed my mind—I think we should share information. Facts. After all, we want the same thing, *oui?*'

'The truth?'

'*Oui.* A conviction.'

'Well, I can't run stories by you, but I will check facts with you. I'd like to start off by discussing a few of these photos.'

'I hoped as much. But it is 1 p.m.' He shook his head at her and looked at his wristwatch.

'I'm sorry I'm late! The taxi just dropped me off on the other side of the flower market.'

'*Ah, ce n'est pas grave.*' He waved a hand and smiled, his eyes crinkling attractively. 'I take lunch at a nearby bistro—they keep a table for me. Would you care to join? We can discuss the case. *Kill two birds*, I believe you say in English.'

Ten minutes later they were seated at the back corner table of a classic bistro, with a half-carafe of white burgundy and a basket of sliced baguette sitting on a red chequered tablecloth. Orders were taken, wine was poured, and Charlie smeared her bread with salted butter and devoured it in three bites. This was a huge step up from the lukewarm half-pints and stale bowls of peanuts in the Sydney dive bars where she'd met her local police contact to exchange information on criminal cases.

The inspecteur had removed the photos from their envelope. '*Merci. Le Monde* and the other papers are going through the official channels as usual, so I appreciate having these now. I have also asked Mr Mackenzie for all his films and photographs. We have a warrant application to search his premises and the dark room where he processes his photos . . . this is a good start.'

Charlie kept a neutral face, but her stomach churned. Surely her colleague would not conceal evidence—not when a murder investigation was underway?

'I also have something for you.' The inspecteur pulled an envelope out of his satchel and handed it to her. 'A copy of the report *l'autopsie*.'

'*Merci*. Anything in particular I should know?'

'The wound to the front of the neck was the only one.'

'Marchand probably knew the murderer. And he wasn't a large man, so it could be a woman?' Charlie tested a theory. 'Marchand was comfortable enough for them to be standing close by, not threatened by them.'

'So it seems. It is also clear, from the depth and precision of the wound, that this is someone who really wanted Marchand dead.'

'The knife used, was it the one in Miss Goldsmith's hand?'

'*Oui*. A knife that did belong to one of the performers, as you guessed—a Russian, Vladimir Sidorov.' The inspecteur pointed to a line in the autopsy report, and Charlie transcribed the man's name into her notebook.

'You've interviewed him?'

'*Naturellement*. His fingerprints were all over the weapon. He actually came forward and claimed the knife—said he'd put his three knives away for safekeeping in his allocated storage space, then couldn't find this one when he went to retrieve it.'

'You believe him?'

'Not sure.' The inspecteur sipped his wine. 'Our discussions are . . . ongoing.' He gestured to the report. 'There is something else. We found an empty tobacco pouch in Marchand's pocket. His widow said she had not seen it before, and that her husband did not smoke.' The inspecteur dropped his voice, 'The pouch contained traces of white powder.'

Charlie sat up. 'Cocaine, perhaps?'

'*Oui*, perhaps. We cannot yet confirm what type of drug. The lab will need to do a test.' The inspecteur frowned as he fiddled with his glasses. '*La cocaïne* is very popular in jazz clubs. Hardly surprising for a man like Marchand. Paris is awash with it, comes from Berlin. He could afford as much as he wanted, I am sure. It was a party . . .' He shrugged.

'Did Madame Marchand know that her husband used cocaine?'

'We haven't asked her, not yet. First we need the results. Something conclusive.' He sighed. 'A man like Marchand—many people would like to see him dead. But who would actually *do it*? They are two different things.'

'I tried to make an appointment with Marchand's secretary at the bank. To see if any clients were angry—'

The inspecteur sucked in his breath and said at once, 'Please hold that line of questioning. My staff are looking into Benjamin Marchand et Fils financial records. It requires warrants and, as you can imagine for a bank of this magnitude, it will take some time. Also, because we are dealing with the financial records of some of the most prominent individuals and institutions in France, my superiors have insisted on discretion. No confidentiality laws must be crossed.'

'Understood.' Charlie nodded as she slid her fork to one side on the chequered tablecloth, while she tried to focus on what further information she could glean from the inspecteur today.

He held his wine up to the light. 'So vibrant,' he said, smiling to himself before he sniffed it then took another sip.

Charlie found the gesture strangely endearing: the man was investigating France's biggest murder case, yet here he was taking time to enjoy his lunch with a glass of wine—savouring a precious moment. Inspecteur Bernard clearly relished details.

Charlie focused back on the autopsy report. 'Is there any chance that the murderer was a stranger? Could the juggler have been quick enough to surprise Marchand, even if he had taken cocaine?'

'*C'est possible!*' said the inspector. 'But I can't think why a Russian performer living on the breadline would kill one of our most successful bankers. Where's the motive?'

'It *could* be a paid hit. The Russian would be the fall guy. Do you mind if I interview Mr Sidorov about the party, the atmosphere?' They both knew she wasn't really asking permission, merely being polite.

The inspecteur half-smiled. 'Please, hold off for the next couple of days. We are looking to see if he transferred money to Russia. Next week it will be okay to speak with him. I recommend you take a translator—his French is rough. Zero English. Unless you speak Russian, of course?'

Charlie chuckled self-deprecatingly and shook her head. 'But I know someone who can help me.' She'd take Violet.

The inspecteur swirled his wine and took another sip, closing his eyes to appreciate the flavour. 'You can almost taste the sun in this—it is ripe, but not so much that it is too sweet. Good acidity.' He put his glass on the table as a jovial waiter served plates of salmon terrine and a pretty summer salad of beets, radish, chevre, parsley, lentils and dill.

After enjoying a few mouthfuls, Inspecteur Bernard turned his attention to the photographs. He glanced at Charlie over the top of his glasses after he examined the first one in the stack: Commander Rose-Thomas looked furious in the background as his wife studied Maxime Marchand's face.

The inspecteur glanced up. 'By the time my men located the commander for questioning, he had been allowed upstairs in the villa and changed his shirt. A laundress had scrubbed out the stain.' Inspecteur Bernard looked to the next photo, which showed the commander standing between his wife and Marchand. 'Circumstantial evidence, but of course there's a possible motive here.'

Charlie nodded, her face warming as she remembered the commander's leg pressed against hers on the garden bench. Had he been flirting with her, or distracting her?

She stared as the inspecteur flicked to the next image: it showed the commander raising a threatening fist to Marchand. In the fourth image, the Rose-Thomases had turned and were nearly out of the frame; Marchand was straightening his collar with a smirk. Inspecteur Bernard raised his eyebrows but said nothing; instead, he polished off the terrine.

Charlie lifted her fork and tried the salad, which was delightful. 'Have you interviewed Mercedes Rose-Thomas?' she asked.

'Not personally.' He grimaced. 'I took some time speaking with the commander—a certain temperance is required when dealing with foreign officials on French soil.'

Good, thought Charlie. *I'll get to her first.*

The waiter bustled over, cleared the plates, and returned with sliced salmon, fries and a green salad. As the waiter topped up their glasses, the inspecteur studied Charlie, looked at the photos, then stared directly into her eyes. '*Et vous*, Madame James, did you believe the commander's tale about the rosebush?'

She shifted in her seat. 'Yes. I mean, I had no reason not to. It sounded innocent enough.'

'Are there any other of these photos I should look at immediately?'

'Not that I know of.'

The inspecteur slid the pics back into their envelope, then pulled a large yellow notepad from his satchel. '*Merci*. I appreciate you sharing this information with me. Usually I find it is a one-way exchange with the press.'

Charlie recalled the arrogance of *Le Monde* at the police cordon ropes. 'That's unfortunate. In Sydney at times, police and prosecutors were my greatest allies.' *Until they weren't.* She quickly drank the rest of her wine, wanting to get the image of her rake of an ex-husband out of her head.

While Inspecteur Bernard took meticulous notes with one hand and forkfuls of salmon with the other, Charlie picked at the fries and looked out the window, promising herself an after-lunch constitutional in the shade of the row of plane trees along the perimeter of the park.

The inspecteur made neat bullet points down the page as they swapped information about the Circus Ball, and Charlie finished her share of the salmon, which was coated in a light bechamel sauce that melted on the tip of her tongue. The inspecteur stopped writing, tucked his notepad under the photos and devoured the rest of his food, thoughtfully leaving a few fries for Charlie. When he was finished, he put his knife and fork together, dabbed at his lips with the linen serviette and pulled a ring binder from his bag. He tapped it with his knuckles and studied Charlie, as though trying to make a decision. Eventually, he sighed and opened the file as he asked, 'How well do you know Monsieur Mackenzie?'

'I first met him at the villa last week when I was interviewing Lady Ashworth for a feature. Mr Roberts and I approved of Mr Mackenzie's folio, and he signed a part-time contract with us. The Circus Ball was his first job.'

'And you were informed that he attended the Rhode Island School of Design?'

'Yes, my colleague Miss Carthage told me it's a prestigious institution.'

His lips pursed. 'Not only prestigious—the art school most difficult to enter in America, it seems.' He held up his hands and rubbed his fingers together as though there were banknotes between them. 'Also, *très cher*. But you see, Monsieur Mackenzie obviously does not come from money. People from huge wealth—Mademoiselle Goldsmith, the Marchands, the Ashworths—they carry themselves differently. Almost with a lightness. They are different to us.'

Charlie noted the implication in what Inspecteur Bernard had just said, and the respect and honesty in his tone. He had accurately profiled her as an educated member of the middle class. *Us.* He was letting her know she was an equal.

'So, I asked myself, how did Monsieur Mackenzie pay for such a college? My office booked a short call with their dean of admissions, and I spoke to him late last night. He said that Mackenzie's spot was paid for by a generous benefactor. According to a confidential source, that benefactor was the good Lady Ashworth. She set up a means-tested scholarship when she became successful in New York. Conrad Mackenzie was the first recipient.'

'Impressive!' Charlie wrote this fact in her notebook, pleased to better understood the connection between Lady Ashworth and Conrad at last. She added a note about the confidential source, vowing to track down their details. 'But what does this have to do with Marchand's death?'

'Mackenzie seemed very keen to clear Mademoiselle Goldsmith. Enough to reveal the breach of his contract with *The Times*. Why do you think that is?' The inspecteur leaned a little towards Charlie and peered at her.

'I wondered the same thing. To be honest, I think he has a crush on Milly. I got the strong impression they are lovers.' Not the complete truth, but Charlie wanted to keep Conrad close and also keep the inspecteur on side.

Inspecteur Bernard gave a slow nod. 'Interesting. Thank you, Madame James. We are looking into the background of all our suspects.'

'Suspects?' repeated Charlie cautiously. 'I agree that Conrad's story has holes. But why would he be so eager to help the police if he was guilty?'

'To clear Mademoiselle Goldsmith—and himself. I cannot help but think he may not have been so forthcoming with the photos otherwise. If indeed he has given us all of them.' The inspecteur watched Charlie closely. 'Monsieur Mackenzie began his studies at twenty-two, but the only academic records the college had were from his . . . what the Americans call "middle school" in Birmingham, Alabama.'

'Alabama!' Charlie shook her head as she tried to imagine the chic young man growing up in that sleepy Southern state. 'What was he doing instead of his final years of school?'

'Well, after our confidential source told us a fascinating story, we called in a contact at police headquarters in Birmingham. I spoke to them just before you arrived at the station today.'

'You have police contacts in Alabama?' exclaimed Charlie, failing to hide her surprise. This lunch was taking a strange turn.

'*Non!* Of course not. I'm a *metro inspecteur*.' He gave Charlie a bemused look. 'But I know someone in New York who might have had a contact—turned out he did. I wanted to see if there was a file on our friend Mackenzie, given the missing years on his college application. I sent a telegram with some questions.'

'And?'

The inspecteur adjusted his glasses. 'Mackenzie was charged with driving a getaway car after a robbery at a local hardware store, then released on bail. His older half-brother Michael had talked him into it, apparently, and took the blame—and the charge. Mackenzie has cleaned up his act. He went to college, moved to Paris, followed his dream of becoming a photographer. He cuts a very fine figure . . . But soon after the robbery, he was put away for a more serious crime.'

'What crime?' Charlie leaned forward.

'*Homicide involontaire*.' Manslaughter. 'Conrad Mackenzie stabbed a man in the neck.'

Chapter 10

Charlie blinked twice as her head started to spin. *Find the facts
. . .* Her father's words echoed in her thoughts. *More than likely,
the killer is someone close to victim. They know them.* This had
often been the case in her father's prosecution trials, and Charlie
had found it to be true when she graduated to the news desk.
It seemed likely that Marchand had recognised his killer.

She shivered. 'Are you sure it was *this* Conrad Mackenzie that
killed someone?'

'He didn't kill a random *someone*. He killed his half-brother
Michael, who had been released on parole that very day. Stabbed in
the neck by dinnertime—quite the welcome home.' The inspecteur
folded his hands in his lap, leaned back in his chair and waited for
her reaction.

'Manslaughter,' repeated Charlie. She thought of how her father had combed over the details. *Check your facts,* he'd say, peering through his half-moon glasses at Charlie, who would be curled up reading a novel in the giant leather sofa. *Be brave, my little one. Be truthful. Check your facts . . . then check them again.*

'*Oui*, an accident. Apparently, Michael turned up unannounced.'

'Hardly a reason to stab someone—not quite the welcome home he was expecting. But how do you accidentally knife someone in the neck?' Charlie pictured Marchand's torn skin, his oozing blood, and felt sick.

Something niggled. When she'd checked with Conrad at the cordon rope to see if he was willing to photograph a corpse, he had looked at her with steady eyes. She had prepared him for the shock, yet he hadn't displayed the usual responses to a mutilated body.

'*Exactement.* How *do* you accidentally knife someone in the neck? Mary Mackenzie—Conrad's grandmother—testified that it was an accident. But Conrad's own lawyer argued differently.'

'Makes sense. There are plenty of protective families in the world.' Charlie wanted to keep the inspecteur talking. 'And the parents?'

'My contact couldn't find any reference to Conrad's parents in the files, other than the grandmother's statement that she had raised Conrad since he was an infant, as both his parents spent time on the road as back-up musicians and whatever other itinerant work they could get.'

Charlie was taking notes in shorthand as fast as the inspecteur was speaking. She was weighing up the photos of the commander against this shocking news about Conrad. She resolved to contact the photographer's grandmother as soon as possible.

'How long was Conrad in prison?' she asked.

'Two years, before he was released on parole for one year due to exemplary behaviour.'

Charlie frowned as she considered this. 'So how did he get a visa with his criminal record? How did he travel the world and enter Europe?'

'*Bref*, I asked myself this same question. It is hard for criminals, *non*? Unless—'

'Unless they have good connections.'

'*Exactement*.'

Charlie chewed her lip. Lady Ashworth and Milly were both wealthy, well-connected Americans who could be relied upon not only for employment but also for greasing the palms of administrators, should it be required. And Lady Ashworth was married to an especially well-connected man.

Inspecteur Bernard signalled for the bill by pretending to write on his palm. 'Allow me to pay, Madame James. Thank you for bringing me this material. But I would like to be very clear about one thing: the killer is probably still walking around Paris. I can tell that you are an experienced reporter, but . . . be careful.' Behind his glasses, he wore a look of concern.

'Conrad Mackenzie is now the main suspect,' said Charlie as she sipped her cup of Earl Grey tea. She was sitting opposite George again, his messy desk between them. 'Which means Milly Goldsmith is still in the mix, because Mackenzie indicated to me that they're more than colleagues, so he has a reason to give her an alibi. But I'm assuming that because of Goldsmith's family connections—and our desire not to be sued—I should focus on Mackenzie until we know more.'

In George's hand was a draft article that Charlie had put together after her lunch with the inspecteur: it outlined Conrad's criminal history. She would have to wait for the police to give her documents confirming the facts before she sent the final version to the subeditors.

'Nice work, James.' George grunted as he placed the draft on his desk. He leaned back in his chair, pressing his fingers together. 'What a car crash. We get our hands on a great photographer, now he's the prime suspect in our biggest story?' George thumped the arm of his chair. 'Run this by me again . . . why would Mackenzie have followed Goldsmith? Why wouldn't he have walked with her if they were lovers?'

'Mackenzie admitted to me that he was jealous. Maybe she set out to rendezvous with Marchand, although Mackenzie may have made a false assumption.'

'But if Mackenzie and Goldsmith were a couple, why didn't they attend the party together?' George asked. 'Why keep it a secret?'

'There could be any number of reasons. But if Goldsmith was having or breaking off an affair with Marchand, or was personally connected to him in some other way, then that might provide a motive—for her, for Mackenzie, or for the two of them.'

'James, you just might have got your scoop.'

She returned his smile. 'Well, I'm going to do some digging into Mackenzie's criminal history in America. I've tried to track down his grandmother, but she's moved on from her last known postal address. And of course, I'll speak to Goldsmith at the first possible opportunity, as well as Claudette Marchand.' Charlie paused. 'There's something else, sir.'

Earlier in the day, she had asked Violet to pass on the Circus Ball photos to George, but she'd kept four of them aside: the images of Commander Rose-Thomas threatening Marchand. She brought them out of a folder and explained the whole story, including her chat with the commander on the secluded bench.

Her bureau chief started to cough and splutter. 'Jesus Christ, James. The bloody commander? Seconded to the British Consulate? That would keep London cartwheeling for weeks. Did you give those photos to the inspecteur?'

'Yes, of course, I had to—'

'Oh, bloody hell. Nothing can be done about it.' He sighed. 'Look, James, we need iron-clad facts, not some photos and a bloody rosebush.'

'Yes, sir,' she said, taken aback.

'Keep at it! Now what else do you have?' He rapped his knuckles on his desk.

She glanced down at her notebook. 'Inspecteur Bernard mentioned that Marchand had a tobacco pouch with traces of white powder in his pocket. Apparently he didn't smoke.'

'Cocaine?'

'They haven't been able to establish that yet, sir.'

'Too much bloody money, this lot,' George muttered. 'Can't publish that until you have evidence—Marchand's lawyers will bury me.' He clicked his fingers in frustration. 'We need to run something pronto. What can you give me about Wallis Simpson? Mackenzie may be dodgy as hell, but the photos he took of the Royals are gold.'

'The Duke and Duchess have fled to the Riviera—the palace can't handle another scandal. They've put some distance between themselves and the Marchand story.'

'Got anything to link them to the murder, James?'

Charlie shook her head. 'Not suspects at this stage.'

'Pity. Royal scandals mean double the print run. And the Duke and Duchess are partial to little love-ins with the Boches, I hear.' He screwed up his face with distaste. 'Choose the best pic of the Royals and give me a par on why they've gone to the Riviera for tonight's edition.'

'You want a piece on people who are *not* suspects?'

'Exactly. With two of those pics. Give it to the subs in an hour.'

'Yes, sir.'

Charlie got to her feet and was about to leave when he cleared his throat and said, 'Sir Roberts was my father. Call me George.'

'All right, George.' Charlie gave him a smile.

He just shifted uncomfortably. 'When are they burying Marchand?'

'The state funeral is tomorrow afternoon.'

'I have to take Daphne back to the hospital, otherwise I'd come myself. Surgeon needs to check the sutures.' George winced. 'Make sure to grab Miss Carthage and take her along—get extra eyes on whoever turns up. Chances are the killer will be there.'

It took Charlie just twenty minutes to type up the piece about the Windsors. She selected a few of Conrad's photos as options before passing the copy and images to the subs and getting back to the murder case. Tapping her pen against her desk, she read through bits and pieces of Alabama court documents and newspaper articles that a policeman had delivered to *The Times* office during her meeting with George. The quotes and summaries had been dictated over the phone; it would take a while for the full documents to arrive.

She would thank the inspecteur next time she saw him, and perhaps even suggest a reciprocal lunch. He had only given her material on the public record, but he had tipped her off: none of the other journalists investigating this story would have had time to gather this background material on Conrad Mackenzie.

At Conrad's trial, his lawyer had tried to argue that he had not used excessive force against his half-brother, who had provoked him:

Conrad Mackenzie believed that he was about to be killed or to sustain grievous bodily harm. Over the course of the struggle, the defendant thought that the victim, Michael Mackenzie, posed a threat to both his life and that of his grandmother Mary Mackenzie. The victim had held a knife to Mary's throat and threatened to murder her; he had also struck her three times on the back of the head to render her unconscious. Conrad Mackenzie believed that the only way he could walk out of the house alive was to kill his attacker.

Conrad had been protecting his grandmother from a vicious assault—or at least he had claimed to be. On the next page, Charlie found a summary of a newspaper report confirming that Mary had suffered concussion and significant bruising to the skull and neck. The coroner's report confirmed cause of death for Michael as stabbing. He had been a habitual drug user, and his behaviour was known to be erratic. Yet based on evidence from the crime scene, the prosecution had successfully argued that Conrad had used excessive force and had not needed to kill Michael, so he'd been convicted of manslaughter and sentenced to gaol time.

Charlie fed a fresh piece of paper through her typewriter and started to redraft her article: *New suspect in Marchand murder case . . .*

She leaned back in her chair and thought of her father. One day, as he'd been laying out the charge sheet for a manslaughter case, he'd removed his glasses and said, 'The thing is, Charlotte, that a person rarely has enough time to consider other options before responding.'

'What do you mean?' she'd asked as she'd looked up from her mother's daily list of French conjugations.

'Well, if someone is coming at you with a knife or a pistol, then you have very little reaction time. In a perfect world you might try to coax them to stop, or to step away. But when you're panicking, emotions can overwhelm you.' He'd sighed. 'You make the wrong decision—one mistake in the heat of the moment. You may not usually be a violent person, but you're angry. Afraid. Acting on impulse, not reason. That's how, Charlotte, good people sometimes find themselves in trouble with the law.'

She was sorely missing her father's wise counsel. She imagined him in his office chair, sorting through his papers, scratching his beard and puffing on his pipe while Sylvie tried to tidy up around him and cajole him to quit smoking. He agreed to do this every year on 31 December—by 2 January, the smell of tobacco filled his study once more.

Charlie rubbed her eyes. To protect himself and his grandmother from harm, Conrad had knifed his half-brother in the neck. Perhaps he had assaulted Marchand out of a desire to protect Milly, rather than jealousy. Horrible deeds from a noble place.

But why would Conrad have seen Marchand as a threat to Milly?

Charlie's typewriter pinged as she reached the end of the row, and she realised that she needed to check on something. With a yawn, she stood up and wandered over to Violet's reception area. Her friend was at her desk, dressed in a chic slouchy navy pantsuit that made her look as powerful as Katharine Hepburn. She was drinking a cup of tea, with half an egg sandwich on greaseproof paper at her elbow. Sipping with her left hand, she used her right to flip through a handful of pastel silk fabric swatches.

'I thought you hated English food?'

'I do, mostly.' Violet grinned with perfect red lips.

'Choosing your next season's gowns?'

'I wish! Aleksandr gave me these.' She blushed. 'Wanted to know what I thought of these colours . . .' She held up the mint, sky-blue and lemon swatches. 'I think they're utterly divine—can't you just imagine the folds?' She wiggled her hips and shoulders playfully.

'I'd be happy with any of them. But I can't accept another free dress!'

'Understood. Mainbocher dresses are . . .' Violet rubbed her thumb and forefinger together. 'But Aleksandr might be able to work something out for you—in the mint silk, I imagine!'

'Let me think about it,' Charlie said with a laugh. 'Anyway, back to business! I'm just wondering if you've found out how we can get in touch with Conrad's grandmother Mary Mackenzie.'

'Not yet, but I'll keep trying.' Violet pulled a face. 'Might take some time.' She smiled. 'Here, take the mint.' She thrust the silk into Charlie's hand, just as the elegant black phone on the desk rang. Violet picked it up, and a few seconds later her eyes widened. She covered the receiver with her hand and turned to Charlie. 'It's Inspecteur Benoît Bernard. He's taken someone into custody for the murder of Maxime Marchand.'

The Times, **June 1938**
Charlie James, Paris correspondent

American photographer insists he is not guilty of murdering French banker

Up-and-coming American photographer—and sometime assistant to Lady Eleanor Ashworth—Conrad Mackenzie was taken into custody this evening for questioning over the murder of Maxime Marchand.

It has recently come to light that Mr Mackenzie was convicted and gaoled for the manslaughter of his half-brother Michael in Birmingham, Alabama. The victim, like Monsieur Marchand, was slashed across the throat.

The homicide investigation is ongoing.

Chapter 11

The next morning, Charlie decided to take the forty-minute walk to Avenue Montaigne from her apartment. The short article on Conrad Mackenzie had gone to press in London overnight on page two, and she needed to get ahead of the story by speaking with Marchand's widow, whose staff had refused to take Charlie's calls until Inspecteur Bernard had let her know about Conrad being taken into custody. Charlie also wanted to speak with Mercedes and Milly, but they were proving to be harder nuts to crack.

Charlie needed fresh air to clear her head and time to prepare for the interview. The summer sun, already high, warmed her back. Rows of plane trees arced over the boulevards, throwing dappled light on the road.

Paris was an easy city to walk through, and she liked to explore the arrondissements and learn their personalities. That morning she took the long way around the Palais-Royal gardens, past burgundy and green awnings overhanging elegant shopfronts for all the couture houses: Chanel, Lanvin ... She read the brass nameplates discreetly placed beside each atelier's door. Then she gasped at the bias-cut diaphanous gowns in the window of Vionnet, wondering who other than the very rich or Greek goddesses could get away with such beauty. Violet could, of course! The young woman would layer it up and make it her own with diamond cuffs, long gloves, and lashings of pearl necklaces. Charlie had noticed that Violet's desk was scattered with sketches of garments and accessories drawn while she was on the phone or when George was out for lunch.

Charlie stopped in front of the grandest building on Avenue Montaigne and checked the address Violet had scrawled out for her. This was it. She drew a deep breath and eyed the topiary as large as Christmas trees either side of the front steps. Madame Marchand's butler buzzed her in and led her to his employer, who stood halfway down a grand marble hallway, wearing a black Chanel suit with gold buttons and ballet flats.

She took Charlie's hand and shook it, saying, '*Bonjour*, Madame James.'

'*Bonjour*, Madame Marchand. I'm sorry for your loss.'

Madame Marchand looked frail and wan, despite her emerald baguette earrings and the dab of rouge on her cheeks. Grief was etched in the lines of her face. 'Please . . .' She indicated that Charlie should step inside the library.

And what a library it was! Huge two-storey sash windows flooded the space with light, and the end wall contained a gallery of paintings. Charlie couldn't help gazing at them, wide-eyed.

'This is an impressive collection,' said Charlie, opening the conversation.

Madame Marchand's French accent was as sharp as her suit. 'You didn't come here to discuss art. You want to speak with me about Maxime.' She clasped her hands together in her lap, and her shoulders tensed. 'I'm not in the habit of speaking with the press. We are a private family and this is a private matter. It is particularly distressing for our son, Jacob.'

'Yes, of course, again please accept my sincere condolences.'

Madame Marchand nodded graciously, the corner of her lips tightening.

'But you agreed to meet with me,' said Charlie. 'Why?'

'I wanted to learn what gutter stories are being passed around about my husband now the matter is close to being resolved. I wanted to have my say.'

Charlie gave her a polite smile. 'I'm looking at all leads.'

'But they've taken that man into custody.'

'Yes, but only for twenty-four hours at the most. They have to release him if they don't find enough evidence.'

'But you ran the story?' She wrinkled up her petite nose, confused.

'I ran the facts to date. It's not a *fait accompli*.'

'Well.' The woman shrugged as if that were Charlie's oversight.

'Perhaps you could help enlighten me as to why Conrad Mackenzie was—'

Madame Marchand's face contorted with contempt as she almost spat out her words. 'Do not mention that *plouc* under this roof again. He came with that Goldsmith woman to take a portrait of my husband. After it was done, and they were leaving, he *threatened* my husband. Threw him against the wall and held his forearm to Maxime's neck. He only stopped because I walked in.' She pursed her lips. 'I wanted to call the police, but Maxime said it was nothing, just a *plouc* wanting money. He said he'd sort it out with Lord Ashworth.'

Suddenly, Charlie felt wary of Madame Marchand. It seemed that she and her husband were extremely self-centred. Her only concern here was keeping the Marchand name out of the press.

Charlie called her bluff. 'Do you have any proof Mr Mackenzie tried to extort money from your husband? Any notes or letters?'

'Isn't pinning my husband to the wall by the neck threatening enough?'

'But why would Conrad have done that so publicly? And why would he have needed the money? Perhaps he attacked your husband for some other reason.'

The elegant woman's eyes narrowed. 'What exactly are you suggesting?'

'I'm saying that Milly Goldsmith was apparently wandering alone in a dark corner of the gardens, during the main circus performance, when she found your husband's body. Don't you find that strange?'

Madame Marchand pursed her lips and said nothing.

Charlie decided it was time. She pulled out an envelope, from which she slid the four photos of Commander Rose-Thomas threatening Marchand. 'These were taken not long after I met you at the ball. Do you have any idea why the commander would intimidate your husband?'

'No.' Claudette Marchand shook her head and folded her hands in her lap. For the first time, she was noticeably perturbed. 'Are you going to run those pictures?'

'We have no immediate plans to do so.' Charlie sat back and waited to see how the woman would respond.

The butler filled the uncomfortable silence as he placed a silver tray on the table between the women, then poured tea into delicate white cups and set down a plate of tempting green macarons.

Charlie thanked him as she took her cup and sipped the tea. She reached for a pistachio macaron and bit in, noting that Madame Marchand was leaving her own cup and the treats untouched. Charlie salivated as the biscuit melted in her mouth.

Buoyed by the tea and macarons, she decided to keep pushing ahead. 'I have reason to believe that Mercedes Rose-Thomas took lunch with your husband last week—alone—at Café de Flore.

Is there any reason why that would have aggravated her husband, the commander?'

'I can't go into details,' Madame Marchand said sharply. 'My husband aggravated many people in business—and made many wealthier. That's his gift . . . was his gift.' Her face remained stony, eyes cold.

'So you're saying the commander could have been frustrated with your husband because of bad blood over an investment that involved his wife?'

'That's all I'm prepared to say. My son will be taking over the bank and reviewing all relationships with our clients.' She picked up a macaron and daintily nibbled the edge. 'I doubt very much you and I will have cause to cross paths again, given the culprit is in custody. Now, if you don't mind, I have a state funeral to finish arranging.'

Charlie slipped the photos into her satchel and started to stand. 'I appreciate your time, madame. Again, my condolences.' As the butler led her from the room, she turned slightly. 'Just one last thing—did your husband ever take cocaine?'

Madame Marchand let go of her teacup and watched it shatter across the parquetry.

Chapter 12

After a couple of hours of note-taking and eating a hasty lunch at a cafe, Charlie had gone to the office only to be told to meet Violet at Mainbocher. Now Charlie was slumped in a crimson lounge chair, nursing a glass of champagne in the corner of Aleksandr's main fitting room. Red velvet curtains draped sash windows, and Violet stood in the centre of the room, arms aloft as a dressmaker tugged at silk to pull in the darts.

'Sorry you had to come out here, Charlie,' said Violet, 'but I had an appointment that couldn't be missed—could it, Madame Hubert?'

The dressmaker snorted and shook her head affectionately, her mouth full of pins.

Violet continued. 'Two things, quite urgent. First: Conrad Mackenzie has been released without charge. The inspecteur called and asked me to tell you.'

'Did he give a reason?'

'Conrad didn't confess, and they have no other evidence.' Violet sucked in her breath for a moment, the dressmaker pinning at breakneck speed. 'The other thing is that you asked me to find out the Rose-Thomases' address so you could try to approach Mercedes . . . well, I did one better.' She fluttered her eyelashes at Charlie. 'A little bird told me she's due for a fitting'—she glanced at her wristwatch—'oh, about now.'

Right on cue, the doorbell rang.

Charlie jumped up, placed her champagne flute on the walnut sideboard and ran over to kiss her friend on the forehead. 'You are a marvel, Violet.'

She made for the corridor, where she watched the butler escort Mercedes Rose-Thomas to another fitting room. Charlie leaned her cheek against the oak door and gently knocked.

'*Entrez.*'

Mercedes looked surprised as Charlie entered, as if she couldn't place her. Unsurprising, given they'd met at a masked ball with hundreds of people—and a murder.

'Apologies, I'm Charlie James from *The Times* of London. We met at Lady Ashworth's ball.'

'I remember.' The woman's voice was rich and gravelly. Her dark hair cascaded in perfect waves past her shoulders, and her navy wrap dress accentuated her smooth brown skin and tiny waist. 'Why are you here? I need to speak with Aleksandr, so I only have a minute.'

'I just met with Madame Marchand. I showed her these four photos.' Charlie pulled the envelope out of her bag and passed the pics to Mercedes.

A clock ticked on the wall as the woman flicked through them, wincing.

'I wanted to speak with you before we ran these images.'

'You wouldn't! My husband is a diplomat.'

'Diplomatic immunity does not extend to the press, I'm afraid. But you already knew that.' In truth, Charlie was almost certain that George would never run the photos, based on what he'd told her the day before—but Mercedes and Madame Marchand didn't need to know that. 'Marchand leans in to kiss you, yet you recoil?'

'Marchand was a heinous man, calculating and cruel.'

That summed up Charlie's impressions of the banker. 'How so?'

Mercedes wavered for a moment, running her fingers through her thick hair. 'I know you saw me at Café de Flore after I had lunch with Marchand. My husband—he once suspected we were having an affair, so I told him the truth. And I will tell it to you, because those photos . . .' She grimaced. 'If I'm to be accused of murdering Marchand, I don't want anyone to think I was his lover.'

Charlie nodded, hastily taking out her notebook and pen.

'Marchand lent money to my family in Uruguay. We had always run beef farms and small abattoirs, but Marchand talked my parents into taking on a huge debt to build massive factories that would process meat and leather. He promised that other goods would come—but they haven't.'

'I didn't realise Marchand had travelled to South America.'

'Oh, he travelled everywhere. He could smell disadvantage from across oceans.'

'And the factories . . .'

Mercedes hung her head. 'Closed. Or full of broken French machines he insisted we buy that no one knows how to fix. I feel so ashamed for making the introductions.' Her voice started to break as she lifted her head. A tear rolled down her cheek. 'Marchand was a pig—he called in the debt. My parents are broken. My brothers bankrupt. The farms where my family toiled for generations have been sold from under them, and now they are the laughing stock of the country. My father, he drinks whisky to hide the pain.' Mercedes wiped her tear away with the back of her hand. 'When I finally told my husband, he offered to help—he's not wealthy, but we have enough. His position gives us a house and a driver.' She dropped her voice. 'Aleksandr sells these dresses to me for a special price, as I attend parties with women who can really afford his creations—he's a good man.' A few more silent tears slid from her eyes. 'My parents could come to Paris and start afresh, but they refuse to set foot on French soil. They think it's the land of the devil, and they are right. Marchand was evil. I'm glad he's dead.'

Charlie swallowed a gasp.

'I didn't do it, though I wish I had,' Mercedes added. 'And I believe that several wives of my husband's colleagues have provided me with an alibi.' She sniffed, and Charlie pulled a handkerchief from her satchel. 'You should also know that his death does not benefit my family. Madame Marchand has already told me that the debt is still owed in full.'

This matched up with what Claudette Marchand had told Charlie earlier that day. And as Mercedes dabbed her eyes with the handkerchief, Charlie couldn't help but believe her story.

Chapter 13

The murder of one of Paris's favourite businessmen had jolted the city out of its sleepy summer repose. As funeral bells chimed across the city, a crowd of people in dark suits snaked its way up the steps of Sacré-Coeur and fanned about the doors to await entry, murmuring in hushed tones. The suits and black town cars were at odds with the pink hues thrown across the marble steps and walls by the late afternoon sun.

'Marchand struck me as the kind of man who would appreciate the theatrics of this send-off,' said Violet as she put on her sunglasses while Charlie just raised a hand to block the sunlight. In a black turtleneck twin-set, black pencil skirt and dark red lipstick, Violet was the only person Charlie knew who could pull off provocative *and* appropriate at a funeral.

'Perhaps.' Charlie watched as onlookers, photographers, and members of the local and international press gathered at the base of the stairs. The local dailies were feeding this frenzy with headlines like *Society Murder!* and the usually nonchalant population had turned out in droves.

Inspecteur Bernard stood to one side of the crowd, observing as official mourners stepped from their cars and made their way into the cathedral. Madame Marchand was escorted by her adult son, Jacob, who tenderly held her forearm as though she might collapse. She wore a black Chanel bouclé suit and pillbox hat with a mesh fascinator that obscured her face.

The car behind waited a respectful beat before pulling to the kerb and releasing Lord and Lady Ashworth at the base of the stairs. Lady Ashworth's green hair was tucked discreetly underneath a tasteful black hat.

'Lady Ashworth really is spectacular,' Violet gushed. 'She deserves her own magazine.'

'She does.' Charlie was distracted by the Rose-Thomases, who walked arm in arm up the stairs. They were a handsome pair: tall, dark and broad-shouldered. Mercedes gave Charlie a mournful sideways glance, while the commander met her eyes before averting his gaze and ushering his wife under the archways to the entrance.

'Come along, let's go in before they close the doors.' Violet led the way up the marble steps and they slipped into the stream of people flowing inside.

As Charlie and Violet reached one of the old oak doors, a choirboy handed them both a thin candle and an order of service printed on thick stock.

'A few people held a flame for ol' Marchand,' said a familiar deep Southern voice at her shoulder. 'Church will be lit up like Christmas.'

'Conrad!' Charlie said, pausing as Violet walked on. 'I wasn't expecting to see you here.'

He stared at her, his amber eyes sad. She realised it was natural he would attend as part of the Ashworths' entourage and as the photographer who had shot Marchand for *Harper's*. But he'd only just been released from police custody—either the kid was innocent or he had a hell of a nerve.

'Thank you for the photos,' she said with a grateful smile, hoping to keep him on side.

'Not a problem, ma'am,' he whispered.

Charlie was taken aback at his apparent softness and vulnerability. Here was a man who had killed his own blood, yet she just couldn't imagine him as a cold-blooded killer. Still, if Madame Marchand was telling the truth, Charlie needed to find out why Conrad had assaulted Marchand.

She paused and decided to be direct. 'Why did you attack Marchand at his home? Madame Marchand mentioned the episode to me.'

'I'm a legitimate photographer and assistant, but he seems— *seemed*—to regard me as "the help".' Conrad frowned. 'I should be used to it by now, but he was the worst of the lot.'

'Hardly a reason to attack him?'

Now he looked angry.

Charlie spoke lightly and gave him a gentle smile, hoping to soften the words. 'Lady Ashworth wouldn't stand for any of that nonsense, would she? She's got quite the humble upbringing herself.'

'It's complicated—' he started to say but they were separated by the crowd.

She spent a few moments craning her neck to look for him. When she finally spotted him, he was already well into the church.

Perhaps the assault had had nothing to do with Milly or the murder; perhaps Marchand really had just been unbearable during the shoot—patronising, almost certainly. He was a busy, cold-hearted man forced to sit still for a portrait, and in Charlie's experience, prominent men usually took some cajoling to sit even for a quick snap. They also usually had strong opinions on how they would be represented—protruding bellies needed to be safely hidden behind jackets, second chins concealed by the correct angle. Marchand had been all ego. To emerge unscathed, his photographer would have needed the diplomacy skills of a Swiss ambassador.

Charlie looked at Conrad's mousy head as he found his seat beside the Ashworths. He did not strike her as the cajoling nor the diplomatic type.

'Charlie!' a voice hissed, and she realised Violet was standing in a middle archway, gesturing discreetly for Charlie to join her.

After walking over, Charlie leaned against the smooth marble as organ music began to bellow through the cathedral. Everyone stood to sing a stirring hymn. Over their shoulders, she could make out the black coffin beneath a colourised photograph set in a heavy gold frame.

Maxime Marchand's smile was that of a benevolent philanthropist. He looked calm and confident, with a hint of stubble along his jawline as though he were on a holiday. There was no sign of the cruel, conniving man he had been—the man who, it seemed, had ruined at least one family. Conrad wasn't a diplomat, but he was certainly a magician.

Charlie wondered what Monsieur Marchand would have made of his funeral. Except for Milly, all the prominent guests from Lady Ashworth's ball were in attendance. The sermon and eulogies were formal, dull and sombre, barely drawing a murmur or smile from the audience.

On the other side of the cathedral, tucked behind a parallel arch, stood Inspecteur Bernard. His gait shifted, and he whispered in a colleague's ear. They both nodded slightly, then turned to look towards the front pews.

An uneasiness settled across Charlie's shoulders as she realised that the policemen were staring at Edward and Mercedes Rose-Thomas.

When the service eventually drew to a close, Charlie grabbed Violet's hand, tugging her outside ahead of the crowd. Seeing the Circus Ball guests together again had helped Charlie to organise her thoughts.

'Lady Ashworth is at the crux of all this,' she told Violet as they walked out the old oak door. 'She knows all the main suspects, she knew the victim, and the murder was at her party. I can use my feature piece as an excuse to find out what she knows about everyone.'

Violet was slightly out of breath as she followed Charlie down the stairs. 'You've already interviewed her, though. I know that London would love a second part to the piece—before and after coverage of the Circus Ball murder, focusing on the hostess—but do you think she'll talk to you again?'

'Well, this is hardly the publicity she covets,' Charlie laughed. 'But I hope she'll play nice for the feature. Lady Ashworth has flirted with the press her whole life, and I'm sure she'll bet that she can sway this story in her favour somehow.'

Violet nodded. 'True! And I forgot to mention that despite the loss of her co-host, she is going ahead with the Louvre gala to launch the exhibition. Apparently it will now be held in memory of Marchand.'

'Thanks, good to know. I can use that as a pretext for the interview.'

Charlie felt that she'd connected with Lady Ashworth, and she was keen to cement their bond. If Lady Ashworth trusted her, she would speak to her instead of the local reporters who were circling. Charlie thought of the ruddy face and patronising voice of the man from *Le Monde* in the crowd of reporters straining over the cordon ropes, and she knew she couldn't let him win.

She guided Violet to the roadside, feeling excited and nervous as she thought about where she wanted to go next. 'We need a taxi, now!'

When the first taxi drove straight past, Violet sighed and stuck out her stockinged right leg—the next taxi braked immediately. As they jumped in, Violet turned to Charlie. 'Who do we need to see so urgently?'

'Someone whose usual defences are almost certainly down.'

Chapter 14

Milly Goldsmith swung open her front door, looked Charlie and Violet up and down, and tried to shut them out.

Charlie wedged her foot in the door. 'Five minutes. It's about Conrad. He's . . .' She paused ominously.

Milly gasped. 'Is he all right?' she asked, in a trembling, desperate voice.

Bingo! Charlie had just proved that Milly cared for Conrad, perhaps just as much as he cared for her. Violet made a soft sound of surprise.

'He's fine,' Charlie said, her foot still in the doorway. 'For now.'

Milly sighed, perhaps realising she'd given too much away. She wrapped her peach silk housecoat around her, then busied herself with fastening the tie, obviously to avoid eye contact.

Her hair was lank, and dark rings looped beneath her eyes. She smelt strongly of hard liquor.

'I'm sorry, Milly,' said Charlie softly. 'I know I'm probably the last person you want to be speaking to. But I'd like to help get your side out there. You know as well as I do that the press can be brutal, and I don't want you and Conrad to keep facing a trial by media. However . . . if nothing else of interest comes to light, *The Times* will publish the full details of Conrad's criminal history. I need to give them something better—fast.'

Milly shook her head and covered her mouth with her hands.

'Did you know about Conrad's record back in the States?'

The young woman nodded, brushing away tears.

'So why didn't he tell the police about it? He must have known they'd do a background check, especially when he came forward with your alibi.'

'I don't know. It was silly—he was just scared it would make him the prime suspect. I mean, both victims were stabbed in the neck.'

'Of course!' said Charlie. 'People can make silly decisions when they're frightened, I get it. So, help me to help Conrad?'

Milly's shoulders sagged, then she stepped back from the door. 'You might as well come in, make yourselves a martini . . .' Her words were slurred. She waved them down the hallway and into her salon, where she pointed with a shaky hand to a brass mirrored cocktail trolley in the middle of the room. A crystal jug of ice was already prepared, droplets of condensation gathered at the lip. Violet poured two martinis, holding the ice cubes at bay with a gold strainer. After popping an olive in each, she passed one to Charlie, who nodded her thanks.

Milly picked up her half-finished drink and gave a lopsided smile as she gestured to a chintzy sofa laden with cushions. Violet remained on her feet, while Charlie sat down and sipped her drink.

She took in the soaring sash windows, the tasteful cream-and-white décor, and the oak parquetry. Milly's family money was stamped all over this airy apartment—either that or *Harper's* paid their correspondents significantly more than *The Times* did.

'I know you've given your statement to the police,' said Charlie, 'but I'd like to hear it in your own words.'

'Are you going to record it?' Milly asked.

'Would you mind?' Charlie put her martini on a side table and pulled out her new Dictaphone.

'Absolutely not. But . . .' Milly raised a finger and waggled it. 'Except when I tell you otherwise, everything I say is *off* the record—never to be printed. I'll *sue* you if you even think about turning it into copy. I just want to tell the truth to *somebody* who'll believe me. I know the police don't, so it might as well be you. And maybe you'll help Conrad. He can't go to gaol! You'll do a better job of investigating this crime than those Frenchy police. They're not interested in finding the truth.'

Charlie reflected that the inspecteur was doing his job, just as she was doing hers. It wasn't easy trying to investigate a murder when those closest to the victim were all trying to cover up their own secrets and indiscretions. It was taking time to sort through the lies and half-truths of Marchand's inner circle.

Squeezing herself in among the cushions, Charlie elbowed one away to maintain eye contact with Milly, who had sunk down beside her. 'Inspecteur Bernard released you without charge. The police *must* believe you, at least.'

Violet cut in. 'But you did have a bloody knife in your hand . . .'

Charlie quickly shook her head at her friend: *Not now.*

Violet pulled an apologetic face and retreated to a corner of the room. Honestly! The woman was a tiger, but there was a time and place for her forthrightness.

'Perhaps'—Milly was still slurring—'perhaps it's best if you read this for yourself. It's personal. *Off* the record.' She blushed as she hauled herself from the sofa and disappeared into what seemed to be her bedroom.

Moments later she appeared with a green leather diary, locked with a gold clasp. She flipped through some pages before handing it to Charlie.

'You . . . want me to read your diary?' Charlie was stunned.

'Not all of it, obviously. Just the bits with Maxime.' Milly gulped down the rest of her drink and nestled into the pillows. 'I first met him at Lady Ashworth's ball last year.' She half smiled to herself. 'Lord Ashworth introduced me to Maxime. They had already enjoyed a few cocktails, if you know what I mean! Maxime's collar was loosened, and so was his tongue. He teased Lord Ashworth about the extravagance of the party and claimed he'd never waste money on "such trifles".'

'What a lovely man,' Violet muttered from her corner as she popped the martini olive into her mouth.

Charlie gave her friend a quelling look, then turned to Milly with an encouraging smile.

'So,' said Milly, beaming back at Charlie, 'Maxime had his little routine. You saw it at the party. He's all charm and sets up a meeting at his office. The *next* meeting is at his home.'

'His home?' Charlie was intrigued.

'Yes, so you feel comfortable.'

'Where was Madame Marchand?'

'The Riviera, of course, like most of Paris for the back half of summer. Marchand caught the Blue Train down to meet her most weekends. My interview was to take place in his front rooms. But he was delayed and had his secretary reschedule for five o'clock on a Friday.'

'Aperitifs!' Violet said with approval.

'Exactly! Or so I thought. I arrived on the hour, and he greeted me at the door. The staff had just left for the day. We had cocktails—yes, a few. I know what you're thinking.' Her blush grew deeper. 'We had cocktails in the Marchands' incredible two-storey library.'

Charlie just managed to stop herself from blurting out that she'd been there that morning. There was no need for Milly to know about her visit with Madame Marchand.

Milly continued, oblivious. 'Maxime showed me his new Rembrandt, hanging alongside a Vermeer and a Bruegel. Now, I'm from Chicago—I'm familiar with the nouveau riche. But a room full of Golden Age paintings, well, that's something else entirely! There are national galleries that would have less of a collection than Maxime had. Most he inherited, but he said each generation made an addition, and the Rembrandt was his!'

'Were you there to interview him about this acquisition?' Charlie asked.

Nodding, Milly tapped the open pages sitting on Charlie's lap. 'Read.'

Maxime insisted I stay for a light supper. It was all prepared and laid out on silver trays beside a bottle of Ruinart: a small tureen of caviar and crackers, smoked salmon, and slivers of buttery grilled lobster tail. I hadn't eaten all day, and I devoured it all.

Maxime noticed and said, 'It's magnificent to see a woman really enjoy her food.' I was embarrassed, naturally, and stopped eating. He dipped his finger in the caviar, then brushed it on my lips. It was salty—caviar just tastes like crunchy seawater!

Charlie grinned at this observation, then continued.

I licked the caviar off my lips as he put his hand up to stroke my face with his thumb. Then he touched my hair and ran his fingers down my neck. I wanted Maxime to touch me. Caress me. I stepped

towards him, willed him to run his hands along my shoulders.
He was just so . . . confident.

I couldn't resist. A charismatic man like that delighting in
me! Afterwards, of course, I realised that this had all been part
of a well-worn routine. But at the time, when he was peeling off
my jacket, unbuttoning my silk shirt, kissing my breasts . . . well,
I wanted it.

I wanted it all. We made love on a Persian rug that had prob-
ably seen several revolutions. Occasionally we'd pause to have
some more champagne, or he'd feed me slices of lobster with his
fingers and then lick my lips. Kiss my neck.

Charlie's face was burning with startled embarrassment. She
was used to the candour of Violet and other friends, and to
strangers confessing their secrets, but this was something else!
The revelation of such intimate details was surely a drunken ploy
to convince Charlie that she should trust Milly.

'No wonder you're considered a first-class writer,' said Charlie,
as she tried to digest what she'd read and work out what to say next.

Milly smiled at the compliment, her eyes hazy, her alcohol-
soaked mind probably caught up in the memories.

'If your affair was over,' said Charlie, 'why meet Marchand at
the far side of the garden, alone, away from everyone?'

'I know what you're thinking! But no, it wasn't for a tryst. Our
affair had been over for some time at that point.'

'How long?' asked Charlie, adding to her notes.

'I don't know . . . maybe two, three months?'

'If you don't mind elaborating—why did it end?'

Milly closed her eyes, taking one deep breath, then another. When she opened them, there was a stiffness to her. 'It just petered out to a natural end. No doubt Maxime had someone else in thrall . . .' She swallowed and picked an invisible thread at the knee of her housecoat.

'And you?' Charlie probed. 'When did you and Conrad become lovers?'

'Around the same time.' She gave Charlie an imploring look. 'You have to help Conrad. I'm only talking because you said you'd help him.'

'Why did you arrange to meet your ex-lover at the party? What couldn't wait another moment?'

Milly hesitated. 'There was a slight misunderstanding, that's all.' Her voice was flippant, and the squeak at the end of her sentence was a tell: she was definitely hiding something.

'And you couldn't work whatever it was out in a quiet moment at the party?' Charlie was trying not to sound as exasperated as she felt.

Milly gave a small shake of her head. 'I thought'—she dropped her head as her cheeks reddened—'that everyone would be focused on the circus. I just needed to tell him something important . . . something personal.'

'Which was?' Charlie asked, perhaps a little too eagerly.

'Not relevant,' Milly slurred, an obstinate look in her eyes.

Charlie hoped she could return to this subject later. 'So, you'd ended the affair only a couple of months before Marchand was killed. It was still fresh, maybe a little raw, and you felt—'

'Jealousy, rejection, pride?' Violet asked sharply.

This time Charlie didn't mind the intervention—she wanted to see what Milly would do when she was rattled.

What happened next surprised Charlie.

Tears filled Milly's eyes. 'The knife was stuck in his neck when I got there. I yanked it out, and blood'—she winced—'spurted everywhere. I called for help, but everyone was over by the circus. So I grabbed the knife and ran across.' She eyed Charlie. 'If I were guilty, wouldn't I have *tossed* the knife? The lake was right there. *I* was the one who raised the alarm.'

'And Conrad . . . where does he feature in all this?'

'Nowhere! That's my point. All he did was follow me and see me take out the knife.'

'But how can you know for certain that he's innocent?' Violet asked.

'Because I *love* him. I trust him.'

Charlie shot Milly a sceptical look. 'Your new lover told you he didn't murder your ex-lover, and you believe him with no evidence? Even though he was jealous? Even though he'd recently assaulted Marchand?'

'No, you're not listening! Conrad *followed* me. I'd just seen him at the circus arena. He couldn't have killed Maxime just before I got there.'

Charlie suppressed a groan of frustration. 'Milly, we don't know exactly when Marchand was stabbed. It could have happened a while earlier.'

'Maxime was still warm!' Milly suddenly burst out sobbing. 'Maybe if *I* hadn't pulled the knife out of his neck, there would have been a chance . . .'

Violet set her empty martini glass on the sideboard, walked over to Milly, leaned down and took her by the shoulders. 'Milly, listen to me. The wound was simply too deep. Charlie saw the autopsy report.'

Violet looked towards her for support, and Charlie nodded, trying to seem reassuring. 'Milly—'

'Please leave,' the woman said through her tears.

'But—'

'Please! I need to be alone.'

Chapter 15

The next morning at eight, Charlie was sitting in Inspecteur Bernard's office. It was a small corner cubicle which overlooked not the main square and flower markets, but instead an oval park and some public latrines. A white dog bounded on the green lawn like a piece of cotton being tossed about in the wind.

'I trust you have come to my office for *la belle vue*,' said the inspecteur with a small smile. 'I must say, I'm surprised to see you again so soon, Madame James. Apologies once more that I am unable to take lunch with you today. Do you have new information?'

The inspecteur looked composed and confident with his neatly combed salt-and-pepper hair. He was smartly dressed in what Charlie presumed was his signature three-piece navy suit. Although he was very busy, judging by the neat piles of paperwork stacked across his desk, the only sign of his agitation was the tapping of his foot as he crossed his legs. He was clearly an organised, meticulous person. A red polished apple sat at the corner of his desk, and she found this charming.

A small typewriter in the centre of his desk had a page half scrolled through, showing she'd interrupted him mid-task. Charlie sympathised with him—she hated it when the subs came into her tiny cubicle, barking at her for a rewrite or to clarify a fact before the final copy went off to the printing press. She could only imagine how unsettling frequent interruptions would be for someone who was trying to solve a murder case.

Charlie cleared her throat. 'Yes, there's more on the Rose-Thomases. I spoke with Mrs Rose-Thomas yesterday, and she told me that Marchand extended loans to her family in Uruguay, then retracted them. The businesses, and the family, have fallen apart.'

'They are—' He waved his hands.

'Bankrupt. Yes.' Charlie paused, letting it sink in, before she told him the rest. 'Claudette Marchand gave me information that seems to confirm this. Marchand's death won't save them.'

The inspecteur whistled. 'Madame Marchand and the Rose-Thomases should have given me these details—we would have followed the paper trail eventually. Financial ruin is cause for much stress, and a motivation for murder, *certainement* . . .

Madame Rose-Thomas has a strong alibi, thoroughly checked, yet her husband has no alibi and that wound on his wrist— and we have the photo of him threatening Marchand. She may have played Lady Macbeth, or he may have acted alone. However, because he is a diplomat, it is very difficult for us to investigate him. And . . .' He paused, looking thoughtful. 'Off the record, it seems that Madame Rose-Thomas is not involved in the crime.'

Charlie nodded. 'I feel the same.' She glanced down at her notes. 'I've been meaning to ask—am I now able to interview the Russian knife juggler Mr Sidorov? I'll bring my colleague Miss Carthage as an interpreter.'

'As you wish. You should be able to reach him through Cirque d'Hiver.' The inspecteur took a document from a folder and turned it to face her. 'The initial lab results have arrived, and they are . . . unexpectedly troubling.'

'Oh?'

'Well, as we expected, Monsieur Marchand had cocaine in both his body and his tobacco pouch.' The inspecteur frowned as he fiddled with his glasses and pointed to a rectangle of the coroner's handwriting, which Charlie found illegible. 'What troubles me is that there was an unexpected substance in his blood. They are running further tests.' The inspecteur's brow furrowed. 'Marchand seemed to be in good health, and his widow insists he did not take any medication. So what was in his system?'

Charlie tapped her lip as she thought. 'Perhaps it was something that enhanced his experiences with cocaine. Or perhaps someone drugged him. Has the coroner looked for needle marks?'

'Of course! But you were all drinking alcohol, *oui*?'

She nodded. 'Anyone could have slipped something into his champagne.'

For a few moments they were silent as they considered the possibilities.

'If Marchand was drugged,' said Charlie, 'that might have made it easier to stab him. The Russian performer or another stranger might have done it, or even someone much smaller and weaker than him.'

'*C'est possible.* But why stab him? Why not just poison him?'

'The stabbing might have been a passionate act. The murderer might not have been satisfied with poison.'

His eyes twinkled. '*Vraiment*, Madame James. You almost sound as though you speak from experience.'

She forced herself to laugh. 'I'm thinking of Miss Goldsmith! Last night she gave me a . . . surprisingly candid account of her affairs with Marchand and Mackenzie—off the record, unfortunately. I assume you're also fully informed?'

'*Oui.*' His face reddened, and he tugged at his collar. 'Mademoiselle Goldsmith has a passionate way with words, and perhaps she has committed a crime of passion. But her father has engaged the best lawyer in France, a bulldog. Our prosecution team will not permit me to take anyone in for questioning now, and especially not Mademoiselle Goldsmith or anyone associated with her. We used our warrant and searched Conrad Mackenzie's guesthouse and dark room. We found nothing. He's clear. It won't be easy to get another warrant. My hands are tied until I have more evidence.'

Chapter 16

When Charlie returned to the office and walked past reception, Violet told her that she was in luck: Lady Ashworth was visiting the Louvre that morning, as she and her staff prepared for the gala. She would be happy to meet Charlie there in an hour.

Charlie arrived at the Louvre feeling flustered. Lady Ashworth gave her a calm smile, looped her arm through hers, and paraded them past the foyer into the Salon Carré, where workmen were dusting off and hanging gilded frames. Two men pulled apart a crate, peeling it open like an orange to get to the precious artwork inside. Charlie marvelled at how gentle they were, their huge callused hands using hammers to strip nails and pull at wood.

She cast her gaze over the baroque high ceilings and out the window to the grounds. The team worked quickly and efficiently, ignoring Lady Ashworth's plume of green hair but staring at Charlie; the older woman was clearly as much a fixture here as the paintings.

Above the doorway, tradesmen were erecting a sign, *Dans la Lumière de Vermeer*, and a discreet brass nameplate: *Monsieur Maxime Marchand*.

'Maxime was a major benefactor of the Louvre,' explained Lady Ashworth as she led Charlie into the centre of the room. 'I cannot believe he won't be here for opening night—he pushed for this exhibition. Loved the Dutch Masters. When you said you wanted to meet for a second interview, I knew of course that you wanted to talk about what happened to Maxime.' The older woman's eyes narrowed as she turned to face Charlie. 'So, Just Charlie, what couldn't wait? I've told the police everything I know.'

'My boss is pressuring me to finish my feature, and it can't be published without your perspective on what happened at the Circus Ball.' Charlie softened her voice. 'And I wanted to see how you are. We haven't spoken since the party, and this case is moving fast.'

Lady Ashworth shot Charlie an appreciative look. 'You are kind—for a journalist.' She huffed a laugh. 'I'm as well as can be expected. I've seen death before—not on my doorstep, to be sure.'

'Yes, of course,' replied Charlie. 'The war. All those innocent civilians alongside soldiers in hospitals you nursed, the burns . . . it must have been horrific. But if you'll forgive me, that's very different from the murder of someone at a party . . .' She let the sentence hang in the air between them.

The older woman was clearly savvy enough to know she couldn't make the story or the circling reporters disappear. There was no escaping the fact that the dead body of a fellow Louvre patron had been found on her property. Lady Ashworth had worked hard for her beautiful life—she wasn't about to let it slip away because of a brutal murder.

Charlie thought of that tiny Croix de Guerre on the mantlepiece, which she'd spotted on the day they'd first met. Charlie now understood that Lady Ashworth's beautiful life was a means to help people who were less fortunate—like Conrad Mackenzie and Aleksandr Ivanov. She leaned in and carried all the people around her—just as she had as a nurse—when others were overwhelmed or looked the other way.

'Will you and your husband remain at the villa?'

Lady Ashworth's head shot up, her mouth taut with surprise. 'Why not? I'm distraught. We all are. But running away never solved anything!' Lady Ashworth squared her shoulders and looked at Charlie, as workmen staggered past carrying a painting covered in a white cotton sheet. 'We will stay at the villa, and I will continue to throw my balls.'

Charlie's throat went dry, and she coughed, embarrassed. Was that what she was doing, running away from her marriage and life in Sydney? She studied Lady Ashworth, with her green hair wound tightly in a tall bun, Chanel suit and matching flats, and took a deep breath. No, Charlie was making a beautiful new life in Paris, one story, one party at a time.

'I've been speaking with Inspecteur Bernard,' Charlie said. 'He seems very interested in Conrad Mackenzie. Before the murder, had you known your assistant was convicted of manslaughter in Alabama?'

Lady Ashworth inhaled quickly through her nose. 'I did! I felt I had to tell the police about it when they interviewed me, because I knew they'd look into Conrad as soon as he provided an alibi for Milly. I told that handsome inspecteur to keep my input confidential, which I suppose he did. I'm not sure if it really matters.'

Charlie nodded. So, Lady Ashworth was the source the inspecteur had referred to over lunch.

'Conrad doesn't talk about those frightful experiences with me, and I've never asked. I met him when he applied to a design school, and I saw that his charge sheet was on the application. I gave him a scholarship. He had taken some black-and-white images with an old camera that a teacher at night school had lent him: a light shaft across an old barn door, a ripple of grass up a hillside, an anonymous bride drawing on a cigarette. He had an eye, but no means. Everyone needs someone to believe in them, don't they?' Lady Ashworth gave Charlie a shrewd sidewards glance.

'How did he come to work for you when he graduated?'

'I asked him to assist me with some decorating I was doing in New York. He was great at choosing exact shades of paint and speaking with suppliers. When the jobs were done, I asked him to shoot them. Soon others did too. Before me, he knew no one. I wanted to make sure my patronage was used for someone like him.'

'Like him?'

'Conrad was hungry. Still is. For success, for money . . . for a new life. And fair enough, too. If you started where he did, well.' Lady Ashworth shrugged. 'Conrad and I—we want the same thing: a *beautiful* life. He's well on the way to making one.' She turned to Charlie and looked her dead in the eye. 'Don't ruin that for him.' Her soft voice had an edge—part plea, part warning. 'Everyone deserves a second chance, my dear. And where better to start anew, find fresh energy, than in Paris?' Lady Ashworth held a gloved hand up to a large window, and they admired the avenue of plane trees that framed the Tuileries Garden and the wide boulevards beyond. The older woman dropped her voice, sounding weary. 'Conrad's worked so very hard. He did the time . . . Please, is this something you need to keep running with for the paper? It's already stained his reputation.'

'I'm sorry, Lady Ashworth, I can't promise anything except that I'm trying to get to the bottom of this.' Charlie spoke in a calm, even tone. 'How did Conrad get visas to France? That must have been difficult, given his record.'

Lady Ashworth looked outraged for a moment, before she nodded slowly. 'Of course, I see where you're going with this. My husband and I knowingly employed a convicted criminal and helped him come to France, and then someone was murdered at my party. What a scandal!'

'That's not what I . . . The police are the ones—'

'I want the killer found as much as you do, but Conrad is innocent,' Lady Ashworth said firmly. 'All of you are looking in the wrong direction.'

'Madame Marchand told me Conrad assaulted her husband.'

'Did she? That's news to me.' The older woman studied Charlie and raised an eyebrow. 'Madame Marchand is . . . a complicated woman. Do you believe her?'

'I wasn't sure what to think,' said Charlie, 'until I spoke to Conrad, and he told me it was true. He said that Marchand had treated him poorly during the portrait shoot.'

'Well! Maxime could be . . .' Lady Ashworth sucked in her breath and pursed her lips, as if she'd already said too much.

'Could be . . .'

'Could be *singular*. He was a powerful man who wasn't used to being contradicted or shown in an unpleasant light. Conrad's photos, as you know, are candid—or intended to seem that way.'

'But Marchand's portrait is quite conventional, although it's beautiful. It could almost belong in this gallery.'

'It could! Mind you, we all want to be remembered in our best light when we're dead. I should start commissioning now!'

Charlie laughed but felt as though this conversation was increasingly difficult to navigate. 'Tell me more about what he was like.'

Lady Ashworth tilted her head. 'Maxime? Well . . . you met him—debonair, benevolent, determined—'

'I mean, what was he *really* like?'

'He was very generous with his philanthropy.' In that moment, the older woman reminded Charlie of her gorgeous mother Sylvie: *If you can't say anything nice then don't say anything at all.* Lady Ashworth waved her hand around the room. 'The French, for some reason, love to collect the works of Dutch Masters. And van Gogh—he became an honorary Frenchman, I suppose. A transplant like the rest of us!' She chuckled as she pointed to a cluster of portraits labelled *Vincent van Gogh*: a self-portrait, a brunette woman leaning on her hand, and a man with a wrinkled, pinched face. He was leaning on a table while holding a sprig of foxglove— Charlie instantly recognised the purple flower, a favourite in her mother's garden.

'That man was van Gogh's physician, apparently,' said Lady Ashworth.

Charlie thought of Marchand's wolfish face and cruel eyes, and again she wondered why this remarkable woman would co-host anything with him. But Charlie supposed that only those affected had known the extent of his cruelty, so it would have been easy for others to look past his true nature while he supported the arts. Perhaps Lady Ashworth had turned a blind eye to his unseemly characteristics for an exhibition, a performance, a ball—she'd done it for Paris.

But hadn't she been concerned about the man's treatment of his wife, a woman who seemed to be a friend? Charlie wondered what Lady Ashworth had meant by describing the woman as complicated. 'How well do you know Madame Marchand?'

'Oh, Claudette!' Lady Ashworth laughed brightly, but there was something disdainful in her eyes. 'Well, she was a *very* loyal wife, wasn't she? Or so it seems. The woman is an enigma! Absolutely inscrutable.' She lowered her voice to a whisper. 'I believe that beneath that dignified front, she was being eaten alive by jealousy. But that's just my humble opinion, off the record. Oh, I must take a look at those lovely little paintings over there!'

Lady Ashworth strode across the room, Charlie at her heels. 'I assume you're referring to Milly Goldsmith's relationship with Marchand?'

'I'm not sure what you mean, dear.'

'And do you know about Conrad and Milly?'

Lady Ashworth sighed, turned her head and surveyed the green boughs framed by the oversized windows. A shaft of light cut across the room and hit the parquetry. 'I didn't know for sure, although Conrad dropped some hints. You know, Just Charlie, it's not unheard of to have an affair in Paris.'

Or anywhere, conceded Charlie as she nodded slowly, her broken heart aching.

Lady Ashworth held up an index finger. 'There are rules, of course.'

'Rules?' Charlie liked the older woman and wanted to stay in her good books, but she would draw the line at being lectured to about the merits of extramarital affairs.

'Why yes, of course! Never speak of it—even when it ends. Discretion is key.'

Charlie thought about Milly's decidedly indiscreet confession. Had she broken the rules? Did she even know they existed? Charlie certainly didn't—she'd been blind to it all. Her ex-husband's affair had made her question her judgement—she'd had no idea just how much the person closest to her had been deceiving her.

She was determined to assemble a different life in Paris. But she'd made very little time for socialising in the week since her arrival. Was she just burying herself in work to mask her heartache? She yearned for joy, for laughter, to feel another's skin pressed against her own.

Charlie needed to lean into the beauty—the freedom—Paris offered and the Louvre seemed as good a place as any to start.

'It's such a treat to see these masterpieces gathered here for the summer. It's as though this room has been waiting for these paintings to get together and have a party in Paris. Thanks to Maxime Marchand.' Lady Ashworth gave Charlie a pointed look.

They ambled past a wall of Dutch Masters. The paintings depicted everyday people doing simple, meaningful tasks: pouring milk from jugs, baking bread, sewing buttons. The subjects were relegated to storerooms, corridors and laundries, while their humble lives were celebrated: the masters had filled the canvases with a magical illumination.

'Aren't they something, my dear?' said Lady Ashworth. 'Rembrandt and Vermeer understood the benefits of excellent lighting.' She chuckled as she turned her head from side to side, illustrating her point. Then her expression turned serious. 'Now, we've dealt with the murder case for what I hope is the last time. Perhaps a Dutch Master could have shed more light on these matters, but I can't. Shall we discuss the gala?'

'Of course!' Charlie said with a smile, getting the strong sense that if she didn't agree, she would swiftly be shown the door.

'First, I would like one more moment to appreciate these paintings.'

They lingered in front of a Vermeer. A woman stood in a storeroom holding a small metal balance. On the table before her was a gold necklace, gemstones, and a pearl necklace she appeared to be midway through threading. Golden light from a high window bathed her pale face. On the wall behind her was a dour religious painting: judgement.

Chapter 17

Charlie sat across from George while he read her copy. On returning to the office after her interview with Lady Ashworth and a stop for lunch at a cafe, she'd knocked out a few hundred words on the Louvre exhibition and its link to Marchand. George said nothing while he read the draft, face blank. She always found it agonising to have her editor read while she watched.

He read the last lines aloud:

Tragically one of the benefactors who championed *Dans la Lumière de Vermeer* will not be at the Louvre to celebrate with champagne on the opening night of the exhibition, now held in his honour. The name Maxime Marchand is on everyone's lips, as the investigation into his brutal murder is ongoing.

Police will not comment on the case, but it is understood that there is more than one key suspect.

'Who's top of the list now, James?' barked George as he looked up from the page.

'The police are still looking at Conrad Mackenzie, Milly Goldsmith, and Commander Edward Rose-Thomas and his wife, Mercedes.'

As Charlie was giving George the details of her interview with Mercedes, telling him about how Marchand had bankrupted the woman's family, he cut her off with a huff and a glare. 'I told you to leave it!'

She was stunned. 'No, you didn't, George. You said—'

'Look, James, the top brass at Westminster are leaning on us to leave well alone with the Brits. They don't want anyone over here smeared. God knows Chamberlain needs people in his corner with all the trouble brewing on the Continent. This is a direct order: *don't* go for the commander and his wife.' He took a shaky breath. 'But just between us, what did Bernard say?'

'He's keeping his mind open to all possibilities, naturally. But his instinct is that Mrs Rose-Thomas, at least, is not involved.'

'Right. Well, stand down, for the moment, or at least tread very, very lightly. The government will come for us otherwise. I'll be scalped.'

'Sir—'

'What have I said about sir-ing me? Tread *lightly*, James.' The editor's face was stony for another moment, but then it softened. 'I have to say, though, bloody good work on buttering up the Ashworths. I played poker with the commander and Ashworth at the club last night. Commander's not bad, but Ashworth lost his hand, poor bugger—not that I had much more luck!' George laughed heartily, and Charlie only just managed to hide her distaste as she thought of her ex-husband's particular interest in poker. 'The commander seems a good sort. Back's as straight as a rod.'

Charlie gave George a pointed look. 'He didn't seem quite so proper when he approached me on that garden bench. Or in those photos with Marchand.'

'Well, Maxime Marchand was a real piece of work! Anyone could have done him in, by the sounds of it. God knows, the commander's in-laws have had a hell of a time.'

'Speaking of family . . . how's Mrs Roberts?'

'Nice of you to ask,' George said with a smile, clearly not picking up on Charlie's concerned tone—he'd been off playing poker while his wife was recovering. 'Daphne has some crutches and a splint. She's in pain, poor love, but a real trouper.'

'She sounds remarkable,' said Charlie. 'I'm very much looking forward to meeting her when she's up and about.'

'Right! She's a good woman. Strong. You'd like her! We'll have you and Miss Carthage over for supper when she's better— Daphne's cross I didn't ask you when you first arrived. She's wondering how you're settling in. Everything all right in your apartment?'

'Lovely. I have fresh croissants and coffee downstairs, and flowers across the road. The aspect is perfect, with a lot of sunlight, and I'm grateful for the new typewriter.'

'Well, just ask if you need anything. Daphne is fond of the flea markets and we go to Les Puces most Sundays. Never thought I'd miss being dragged through stalls looking for silver cutlery and embroidered tablecloths.' He chuckled fondly.

Charlie smiled. 'Sounds like you make a good team.'

'So, James, what else are you looking at on the Marchand story?'

She decided there could be no harm in a little speculation. 'I've realised that Claudette Marchand should perhaps be seen as another suspect.' George was already looking incredulous, so she raised a hand. 'Please, hear me out. Yes, there's very little chance she could have stabbed her husband, given her sparrow-like build and her apparently strong alibi. But off the record, Lady Ashworth believes the woman was "eaten alive by jealousy" as she watched her husband . . . conduct his affairs. What if she hired someone to commit the murder?'

'I thought the autopsy showed that Marchand knew his attacker.'

'Not conclusively. Inspecteur Bernard told me that the murder weapon was apparently stolen from a Russian performer. I now have permission from the police to speak with this man—I didn't want to put the inspecteur offside by disobeying his informal request—so Miss Carthage and I will arrange to do that as soon as possible.'

George nodded thoughtfully. 'I see. This acrobat could have struck lightning quick with his knife?'

'That's my thinking. And I just learned there was an unexpected substance detected in Marchand's blood. It might turn out to be a sedative of some kind—something that would have made him docile.'

George was now looking impressed. 'Terrific work! But don't try to speak with Madame Marchand again until that all pans out.'

'Of course.' Charlie nodded, then checked the final point on her list of notes. 'I think we should investigate Marchand's bank further. Miss Carthage and I have called his office several times— and she's paid a visit—but they will only speak with the police.'

'Absolutely! Just make sure not to drop the pressure on the Mackenzie angle. A Yank like that with a criminal record— there's a prime story there, so get it. You need to keep the column inches coming, so finish that feature on Lady Ashworth too. London's gobbling up this story.'

Charlie felt a pang of regret as she thought of Milly's desperate plea to keep Conrad out of the press. Then she recalled what Lady Ashworth had said: *Please, is this something you need to keep running with for the paper? It's already stained his reputation.* 'Can we publish the feature before the long Mackenzie background piece? At Lady Ashworth's request.' Hopefully by then, Conrad would be cleared—or arrested. 'We've also been having trouble contacting his grandmother.'

'All right, whatever her ladyship desires. We need to keep up this connection with the Ashworths.' George's mouth twitched in a half smile as he handed back Charlie's page of copy. 'Drop this at the subs' desk. Tell them to give it a better header, but it'll do for today.'

She did as requested then went to Violet's reception area, which today resembled a Montmartre florist: a box of dusty pink roses sat on the edge of the desk next to a gold pot planted with an elegant white orchid. No doubt more than one admirer was vying for her attention. She looked as beautiful as the flowers, in a lilac twin-set and matching silk pencil skirt—Chanel, judging by the bouclé. She'd finished off the outfit with ruby-red pumps and a matching Hermès handbag that lay tossed sideways on the other corner of her desk.

'Good news!' she announced. 'I've made an appointment for us at Cirque d'Hiver tomorrow afternoon with Mr Sidorov.'

'Thanks, Violet! I was just telling George about that.'

'You can thank me by shouting me lunch beforehand at Café de Flore. Oh, and this just arrived for you.' Violet handed over a thick cream envelope with *Mme Charlotte James* on the front in perfect cursive ink.

'Who—' Charlie started to ask, just as the phone rang.

Violet picked up the receiver, greeted the caller and shot Charlie a 'pity me' look. She then began to work out complicated dinner reservations for George and some French ministers, shooing Charlie away with a swoosh of her hand.

As Charlie walked to her desk, she ripped open the letter.

Mme James,

I'd be very grateful if you could meet me tonight at Bar de l'Entracte, 6 p.m.

Commander E. Rose-Thomas.

Chapter 18

Charlie weaved her way over the chequerboard paving and through the manicured gardens behind the Palais-Royal to Bar de l'Entracte. The ivy-covered bar was tucked away in the corner of an alley with pretty green wicker chairs and tables scattered all over the pavement. The chairs were filled with patrons sipping aperitifs and wolfing down bowls of moules-frites in the warm evening sun. Her stomach rumbled at the scent of garlic, white wine and herbs as she stepped inside to look for Commander Rose-Thomas. She found him at the zinc-coated bar, nursing a whisky.

The commander wore a crisp white shirt and sharp beige linen suit that had a holiday look to it. His normally slicked back curls were slightly messy. He was so attractive . . . Charlie immediately admonished herself for thinking along those lines.

They greeted each other with an awkward handshake, and he pulled out a wooden stool for her. She smiled, sat down and got the attention of a bartender.

'*Oui?*' the woman grunted, her hands on her ample hips.

'*Kir Royale, s'il vous plaît.*'

As the bartender poured the thick purple blackcurrant cassis into the bottom of the glass and topped it with champagne, Charlie glanced around and noticed that most of the patrons were couples, leaning in close, speaking in low tones, clasping hands under tables.

The commander cleared his throat and said, 'You look uncomfortable, Mrs James. I assure you, I won't keep you long.'

'Sorry, I've just had a long day,' she said, annoyed with herself for being jittery. When the bartender slapped the drink down in front of her, she took a grateful sip.

George had been concerned about her meeting the commander alone. He'd wanted to accompany her, but Charlie had assured him she didn't need his protection. She'd interviewed suspects in Sydney under similar circumstances. They were in a crowded bar, not an alley or the dark corner of a park. She wouldn't leave with him or accompany him to another venue. Besides, he was more likely to be uncommunicative if she brought her boss along—after all, he'd reached out to Charlie, not George.

The bar was charming, with marble tabletops, watercolours on the walls, and candlelight. 'Is this your local?' asked Charlie, wondering why the commander had chosen such a quiet bar—a bar full of lovers.

'Sort of. I'm not a regular, if that's what you're wondering.'

Charlie's cheeks grew hot, and she reached for another sip of her drink. 'I wasn't . . .'

The commander smiled. 'I'm not being serious, of course.' He pulled his silver Cartier cigarette case out of his pocket and offered one to Charlie; she refused. He struck a match and held it to the cigarette, inhaling then exhaling a long plume of smoke. 'So, what do you want to know?'

'Pardon?'

'I had another visit to my house yesterday, from Inspecteur Benoît Bernard. He's visited three times now—twice for me, once for my wife. You've also spoken with her. I want to put an end to this, Mrs James. I have nothing to hide.'

'Did your wife tell you about the photos of you physically threatening Marchand?'

He nodded. 'Yes, but—'

'How did you really get that scratch on your wrist?'

'I told you, I got caught on some rosebushes. Do you think I lied?' He looked her in the eye.

She stared right back. 'I'm not across all the facts yet. I have no idea if you're lying to me—and the police. What I don't like is the way your people have put pressure on *The Times* to keep your names out of the paper. It's meddling. And undemocratic.

I would not have picked you as the type . . .' Her voice was sharp with irritation.

The commander's eyes widened. 'I know this looks self-serving, but the fact is, I'm innocent. And Mercedes is innocent.'

Charlie was not going to be distracted by his charm or good looks, or his apparent loyalty to his wife. 'Why did you threaten Marchand?'

'He insulted my wife. Suggested that if she needed money she could earn it in other ways . . .' He sucked in his breath and studied his hands.

'Let me get this clear: Marchand suggested your wife prostitute herself. You threatened him. He was dead within the hour.'

'Yes, but Marchand's death had nothing to do with me.' He kept gazing at her, his eyes dark. 'I imagined killing him. Of course I did—I imagined many scenarios. So if I *had* done it, I would have done a rather brilliant job. I would not have been wandering around with a bleeding scratch.'

A shiver ran down her spine at his intensity. 'It's understandable you wanted to protect your wife. Her honour.' Charlie's voice softened.

'He ruined her family. *Their* honour. Their name is mud in Uruguay.'

'Are you covering for Mercedes? Did *she* kill Marchand?'

'No. My wife has a solid alibi.'

'She could have hired someone to do the job.'

He gave a huff of frustration. 'You seem intent on implicating us.'

'I'm a reporter covering a homicide that implicates you.'

'I am well aware of how all this looks,' he said crisply.

Charlie waited for him to add an explanation or justification, but he remained silent, breaking eye contact and smoking his cigarette.

'You specifically warned me away from Marchand at the party, just minutes before he was killed. Why?'

'Marchand was screwing everyone, in both romantic and business affairs. He was a right bastard. My wife's factories were not his first foray into foreign industry—he invested heavily in Russia, Poland and Finland before the war, then after. Huge money, as I understand it, in St Petersburg. There might be something in that.'

Charlie finished her drink, thinking about the Russian performer she would soon be interviewing.

The commander added, 'It was a rotten way to be killed. But believe me, Marchand was rotten to his core.'

'So everyone seems to think—except his wife.'

'Ha!' He gave her a cynical look. 'Do you really believe that?'

'I have no reason not to,' she said. 'Do you?'

'That woman is no fool.'

'And Lady Ashworth is? She was happy to work with Marchand.'

'Lady Ashworth.' The commander looked surprised. 'Nothing gets past her. She just made sure to channel his money into worthy causes—the Louvre, a women and children's hospital. No one could persuade him to write a cheque faster than she could.'

'Did she know about Mercedes's family?'

'Not the extent, I'm sure. She knew my in-laws had invested with him, but he managed money for many people at that party. He had tentacles everywhere.' The commander stubbed out his cigarette, finished his whisky and signalled for another. 'I wish I'd been the one to chop them off.'

Sensing him grow more maudlin, Charlie slid off her stool. 'I should go. Thanks for the chat.' His eyes were startled as she picked up her satchel and walked outside, but he didn't call after her.

She needed to take a long walk and digest that conversation. At this point, she couldn't afford to believe anyone was innocent.

Chapter 19

The evening sun had turned the sky a hazy pink. After the dim, smoky bar Charlie needed to get some fresh air into her lungs and steady herself. She decided that she'd walk home along the Seine, so she meandered past the artists selling watercolours and portraits, while jazz music spilled out from bars and pretty girls in red lipstick walked the streets in two and threes. As she strolled past a young couple kissing passionately on a bridge, she contemplated the last happy night she'd spent with her husband, Finn.

Summer in Sydney, the year before, there was a celebration dinner party at the grand harbourside mansion of the barrister with whom her husband shared his chambers. Golden light streamed in the windows, kookaburras laughed in eucalyptus trees, while guests sipped champagne on the veranda overlooking the water. The early supper of snapper and grilled leek was being gobbled down greedily so guests could sit outside to catch the evening breeze and drink the night away. The warm humid air was bloated with triumph and expectation.

The celebratory dinner, while generous with portions, came with a side of talk that bored her: the administration of filing a brief, then compliments over the new Wedgwood set. As the matronly ladies licked their lips over the peppermint creams, Charlie knew what to do. She turned to Finn and raised an eyebrow, asking him a question only he could answer. Then she slowly turned away, giving him ample time to take in the line of her navy gown where it plunged into a V, revealing her bare back. Minutes later, her back was pressed against the cool bricks of the storeroom.

Afterwards, she fastened her stockings to her suspenders, and Finn smoked a cigarette, his hair dishevelled, bow tie undone. 'That's unlike you, kid. Was it something I said?'

Charlie scowled at 'kid'. It galled her when he called her that—he was almost two decades her senior. She straightened and looked him in the eye. 'Don't call me that.'

As she eyed the hessian flour bags stacked on the floor and the pellets of rat poo gathered in the corner, their stolen moment in this dingy storeroom suddenly felt sordid. The stale air made her claustrophobic, and she moved quickly to the door.

As she reached out to pull it open, he placed a hand on her wrist. 'Stop! I'm sorry. I'm a pig, and I don't deserve my beautiful wife.' He slowly kissed her neck, and she had to stop herself from turning around and peeling off his shirt again.

She grinned. 'Agreed. You really don't deserve me.'

His curls had flopped over one eye like those of a naughty toddler. She brushed them away with her fingers, kissed his forehead and opened the door.

Charlie made her way to the powder room, pulled a red lipstick from her purse, and leaned over the marble bench close to the mirror to apply a fresh coat of matt tint. She pulled a tissue from a nearby box and placed it between her lips to blot any excess before she applied a second coat. Opening her mouth, she dabbed at the corners.

When she looked at herself, she smiled. Her husband's scent still clung to her skin under the sheath of silk he'd slid up her thighs. She shivered as she ran her hands over her hips to smooth down the dress, thinking of his hands gripping her in the storeroom just moments before. He had nuzzled her breasts out of their brassiere cups, his lips circling her nipples, then moved lower . . .

Her stomach fizzed, and her skin felt electric. Although they were soon to celebrate their second anniversary, their chemistry matched that of newlyweds. He hadn't been her first, and for that she was thankful. It had allowed her to dispense with any awkwardness; allowed her to lean into her own kind of bliss.

Each kiss felt charged. When he'd blown on her neck and traced his tongue across her skin, she'd shivered, willing him on. With Finn, she was never shy or coy. Instead she'd breathed his sandalwood scent deep into her lungs and adjusted her body, arching her back, tilting her pelvis, clutching at his back and shoulders.

Tonight was the first time their lust had spilled over at a party. He'd been flirting with the hostess—Audrey, the wife of the barrister he shared chambers with—during the main course, spurred on by her reddening cheeks and high-pitched giggles. Charlie was used to her husband flirting; he was an attractive man, after all. But lately it had started to take a toll.

At first, Charlie hadn't minded his cocktail hours and work dinners, and all the cases and briefs that left him working long into the night, sometimes at this house. It was the drinking and gambling that followed each case's win that upset her, and the ebbing and flowing bank accounts, the second mortgage, then the third. She was too embarrassed to tell her worried parents; instead she told herself she could fix it all, fix Finn, if she worked hard to pay down the debts and steady their ship. He was always apologetic, always kind, and he knew how to soothe her brow, rub her back, her thighs . . .

Charlie had recently been promoted to the news desk and intended to stay there. Most working women were expected to resign when they married, but thankfully her editor hadn't raised this with her, and she intended to keep working news for as long as it kept breaking. She loved it, and frankly they needed her—her pieces sold papers.

Laughter and conversation rolled over her like a wave as she rejoined the party, walking past the kitchen and sweeping into the room, losing herself among the guests. Her husband would make his own way in—from a separate door, she hoped. As she strode towards the drinks table, she noticed that their hostess, Audrey, was staring at her. The older woman's lips were pursed, as if she found Charlie wanting.

'Audrey! That dress is . . . a good fit. Enjoying the evening?' She forced herself to give what she hoped was a sprightly smile.

'Not as much as you, it seems,' said Audrey, arching her eyebrows. 'I take it you found our storeroom?' She brushed some flour from Charlie's arm.

'Oh, I . . . we . . .' Her face grew hot. 'Finn had a rather big week, with the case and all. Awfully good of you to feed him and give him your dining room these past few weeks, and so kind of you to offer your spare room last week. Let's hope they win.'

'Indeed! I'm not in the business of backing the losing horse.'

Short and stocky, Audrey had a strong nose like the statue of David. There was a magnetism, an attractive confidence, that came with the onset of middle age. Audrey knew exactly who she was, and Charlie envied her that.

'Enjoy the rest of the party,' she said. 'I'm glad you had the chance to see the storeroom—it's his favourite part of the house.' She turned on her heel, leaving the faintest scent of sandalwood hanging in the air.

Finn's shaving balm contained sandalwood. He had it specially made at the local apothecary, and Charlie would have recognised it anywhere. The gambling she had tried to fix, infidelity she would not.

An hour later, all of her dreams were shattered on the footpath.

'Please, Charlie, I'm so sorry I hurt you.' Finn's dark eyes were pools of sorrow.

Fighting back tears, she said, 'It's over. I'm leaving.'

As she climbed into a taxi and it pulled away, she left her marriage. But it was only when she was slumped in the back seat, the dark harbour disappearing behind her, that the tears started to flow.

The couple on the bridge had stopped kissing and were gazing at each other with open, hopeful faces. They batted eyelashes, teased each other and laughed like only the young and unbroken can.

Charlie had been carrying her signed divorce papers in her satchel, where they lurked under autopsy results and case notes. Walking past the bridge, she resolved to send them back to Sydney immediately. Only then could she fully move forward with her new life in Paris.

As she turned the corner of the Jardin du Luxembourg, a postbox came into view. Without breaking stride, she pulled out the addressed envelope with the divorce papers, then shoved them into the box.

She went straight to her apartment, where she poured a glass of water and sat at the little desk she'd shifted under the window to catch the breeze, blushing as she remembered reading the novel *Dangerous Liaisons* as a young woman and sliding her hand beneath her nightdress until, tentatively, softly, she had explored between her legs.

She closed her eyes, dipped her fingers in the cool water and traced them over her breasts, circling her nipples before she let her hand stroke lower. She pictured Finn's face, his body pressed against hers, his lips on her neck, her breasts, between her legs.

Charlie's body thrummed. She'd missed this desire, raw and powerful. Selfish.

Groaning, she saw the face of Commander Rose-Thomas. She blinked and opened her eyes, wanting to finish as the waves became more intense. The last image in her head was of Inspecteur Benoît Bernard.

Chapter 20

Charlie arrived at Café de Flore before Violet did. After sitting at an outdoor cane table, she ordered a gin martini. While she waited, she pulled out her notebook and ran over her theories about the murder. She'd been working through them and typing up copy all morning.

Violet arrived fifteen minutes late. Charlie didn't mind—the gin had kicked in, and she was contemplating another. Violet kissed her cheeks, and Charlie breathed in Chanel No. 5, admiring her friend's diaphanous silk shirt and gold chains studded with precious gemstones.

As Violet signalled for the waiter to bring her the same drink, Charlie said, 'You should be doing the fashion pages, or modelling for one of the boutiques I just walked past.'

'Stop it.' Violet blushed. 'I love my job. I get to meet interesting people, mostly men.'

Charlie rolled her eyes. 'That's newsrooms for you,' she said, although she had never felt attracted to anyone she'd worked with—until she'd met Finn in the throng of journalists camped on the Federal Court steps after a major murder verdict had been handed down. He'd agreed to an exclusive interview only if she'd agreed to have a meal with him across the road. Over steak, salad and white wine, he'd discussed the intricacies of his case, making sure she got the scoop. After he'd finished, Charlie had stayed for more white wine and the story of his wild, rural childhood in Cork. His Irish lilt was mellifluous, his skin milky-white and freckled, like hers. He had the slim, strong hands of a pianist and curious, intelligent eyes. An intellect. A dreamer. A traveller. By the end of the night, Charlie had known she was going to marry this man. The next night she'd been in his bed.

At that very moment her divorce papers were on their way to Sydney. She swallowed, trying to soothe her dry throat, and pushed all thoughts of her ex-husband aside. She ordered the steak frites while Violet opted for the *rouget barbet* special.

'Seriously, though,' said Charlie, 'you really should consider working in fashion.'

This time Violet didn't brush the idea aside. 'Maybe. One day. Aleksandr has worked towards this his whole life. As a little boy he dreamed of coming to Paris, walking the boulevards. His parents died when he was young, and his grandmother raised him. She's the one who taught him to sew. She was a dressmaker for wealthy women before the revolution, and she and Aleksandr lived in a single room—can you imagine?' Violet's pretty face fell.

'I can't,' said Charlie honestly as she wondered how cold it would have been. 'You make a good team,' she added, reflecting on her conversation with George about his wife.

'No,' said Violet with a grin, 'we make a great team!'

Charlie needed to forget about Finn and move on with her life. There were good men out in the world who championed the women beside them: Charlie's father, Commander Edward Rose-Thomas, George Roberts, Aleksandr Ivanov. Perhaps Lord Ashworth too, although he gave the impression he was hanging on for dear life. Who could blame him?

Charlie stood with Violet on rue Amelot and gazed up at what looked like a Second Empire-style colosseum. Over an arched door was a painted sign: *Cirque d'Hiver.*

The doorman greeted them with a big smile. '*Bonjour, bienvenue!*'

'*Bonjour,*' said Violet. 'Charlie James and Violet Carthage. We have an appointment to see Vladimir Sidorov at 3 p.m. We were told he'd be finished rehearsing by then.'

They followed the doorman to the circus ring, which was covered in red carpet. Beneath a pitched ceiling hung with chandeliers, half a dozen bejewelled elephants paraded the perimeter of the ring.

'Wait over there,' the doorman said quietly, gesturing to the first row of seats. The arena had been built for nearly a thousand audience members, but at this time of day the stands were empty.

Charlie and Violet watched the daily life of the circus unfold around them. A strong man in a leotard, his arms covered in tattoos, ambled past and shot the women a curious look as he started to rub his hands in a bucket of powder then bandage them. Higher up in the stands, dancers stretched their long legs. The elephants finished their rehearsal and were herded out.

Eventually, two men in striped shirts walked over, juggling knives and talking at a bullet's pace in Russian. They looked relaxed, as if it were the most natural thing in the world to throw knives ten feet into the air. One was so close that Charlie felt the draft lift her hair.

While the taller juggler kept walking along the ring, the shorter one came up to them, put down his knives and nodded hello. '*Bonjour*,' he said before introducing himself in Russian.

Violet translated into Charlie's left ear. 'This is Mr Vladimir Sidorov. His knife, the murder weapon, was confiscated by the police.'

Sidorov shook his head, looking forlorn.

'He doesn't know when he'll get it back, if ever. It was his grandfather's knife and his father's before that.'

The man's words were pouring out, and Violet squinted slightly as she tried to keep up her staccato Russian.

'That night, nobody asked him for the knife. When he had finished his first set of juggling in the crowds, he rolled his three knives into his leather pouch, as he always did, then went across to the house for the lavatory.'

'Where exactly did he keep the knives?'

Violet relayed the question, then the response. 'Lady Ashworth was very clear about where all their equipment and costumes should be kept. Each performer had an allocated wicker basket under bench seats, because she didn't want any mess on her lawns.'

'I can imagine.' Charlie laughed as she pictured the manicured lawns and flowerbeds.

Violet continued translating. 'The first he knew his knife was missing was when Milly appeared in the ring with it. Now he's saying again that the police won't give it back, and—oh . . . he hopes you can get it for him.'

'Please tell him that's impossible,' said Charlie, giving him a polite smile.

As Sidorov complained to Violet, Charlie watched from the corner of her eye as the strong man flexed his arms then stretched them behind his head. In the ring, the dancers unfurled their legs. Drums rolled, and horses entered the arena, followed by a line of tumbling men in black, each kicking impossibly high. Pretty acrobats in sequins and tulle spun like spiders on ropes overhead.

The juggler still looked disappointed, but Violet said, 'He's told me that he understands. He is just upset.'

'I wish I could help, and I hope he gets it back.' Charlie waited for this to be conveyed, then asked, 'Did anyone ask him to *see* the knives that night? Or hold them? Or was there anyone who just took an interest?'

The juggler pursed his big red-painted lips and scratched his black stubble before he spoke.

'There was one man,' Violet translated. 'Tall and wearing a black mask, a black tuxedo and a white shirt. Slicked-back hair— Sidorov couldn't see the colour in the light. The man spoke in French, but Sidorov is far from fluent and the party was loud, so he didn't understand much. Something about how training with knives is like being in the military. And the man mentioned being away from family.'

'Why didn't Sidorov tell the police about this?' Charlie asked.

'He did!' translated Violet, as the juggler threw his hands in the air. 'They said the man fits the description of almost every man at the party. They showed him a few photos of different options, but he didn't recognise any of them.'

Sidorov impatiently shifted from leg to leg and looked over his shoulder at his fellow juggler, who was beckoning to him.

'He apologises, but he has to go to work now,' said Violet.

The juggler nodded his farewell, and Charlie nodded back.

'Thank you ever so much,' said Violet brightly, 'and see you tomorrow night!'

He beamed at her before he went to join his colleague.

Surprised, Charlie shot Violet a puzzled look.

'Oh, when I was on the phone arranging this interview, I booked some of the circus dancers to model dresses for Aleksandr's fashion showing tomorrow night. He'll pay them, and of course there will be champagne! I invited Sidorov as a guest in exchange for him talking to us.'

'What a brilliant idea!' Charlie said, marvelling at her friend's ability to kill three birds with one stone.

'I know,' said Violet immodestly. 'Thank you, though.'

Charlie smiled, but then it faded as a troubling thought entered her mind. Which party guest best fit the description of a tall, dark military man with slicked-back hair in a black tuxedo and a black mask?

Chapter 21

The next morning Charlie's head was a little foggy, so she was grateful for a cool breeze as she set off to attempt an interview with Lord Ashworth outside his Luxembourg Gardens apartment. George had been playing poker with him again the night before and he'd tipped Charlie off that Lord Ashworth would be staying there. Who better to provide some colour for the Lady Ashworth feature than her husband? Charlie wanted to surprise him so that she could glean a more personal side to his wife. She'd been impressed by the way he'd taken the lead amid the chaos at the Circus Ball and had consoled Lady Ashworth. Although he reeked of the same patrician entitlement as Marchand, it was without the malice.

She weaved her way through a pretty set of alleyways known for their matching blue doors, circular parks and topiary statues, then stopped at a tiny patisserie set into a wall less than a block from the apartment and bought an *escargot* pastry. She could see his front door, and she decided to find a spot to wait. Although it was only around eight, the breeze had died down and the sun was sharp, so she stepped into the shade of a plane tree to stop her nose from burning and sweat from running down her back. Leaning against the trunk, she peeled off sections of the spiral and slipped the buttery pastry onto her tongue. As she rolled a sultana around in her mouth, she looked down the far end of the alley and saw Conrad Mackenzie slouched against a sunny wall, camera slung around his neck.

She lifted her arm up to wave, but his worried expression gave her pause. Stepping back into the shadows under the tree, she gathered her thoughts as she watched an old lady in a trench coat walk her toy poodle on a pink lead at a glacial pace. Charlie took a deep breath, scratched her head and glanced back at Conrad.

She was surprised to realise a familiar portly figure in a morning suit was now approaching Conrad: Lord Ashworth. He must have come out of his apartment while she'd been distracted, and she hadn't been expecting him this early. She certainly hadn't expected to see him meet alone with Conrad. It was her distinct impression that the young man adored Lady Ashworth but had little time for her British husband, just as Lord Ashworth had little time for his wife's assistant.

Curious, Charlie remained tucked behind the tree as Conrad and Lord Ashworth began to speak. It escalated to an argument quickly, judging by their flailing hands, frowns and raised voices. She glanced back down the alley—no one was around, except for pedestrians near her at the opposite end of the alley. Why had these men planned a meeting in a secluded spot in such a quiet pocket of Paris?

Lord Ashworth looked peeved, while Conrad was tense, his jaw clenched. Finally, after much head-shaking and talking, Lord Ashworth reached into his top pocket and handed Conrad a small envelope.

Charlie's mind tried to wrap itself around what she was seeing. Was Lord Ashworth terminating Conrad's employment? Was he paying him for some special service, perhaps an illicit one?

But Conrad had attacked Marchand, and his widow had implied that money was involved. Inspecteur Bernard had told Charlie of Conrad's involvement in robbing a hardware store as a youth. Was Conrad somehow extorting money from Lord Ashworth, and had he done the same to Marchand? It wouldn't be the first time a man had been killed over a money dispute.

On the other hand, Lady Ashworth clearly thought the world of Conrad. The older American had made a great impression on Charlie; she struck her not only as a woman of vision and ambition, but also of excellent judgement.

Charlie shivered as the leaves rustled above her.

The conversation finished abruptly, and Lord Ashworth strode away in the direction of his apartment. Conrad slipped the envelope into the top of his suit pocket and leaned against the wall for a moment, looking towards the sky, teeth clenched as if he were making an agonising decision.

A beat. Two beats.

Charlie started to fidget, but she didn't have to wait long before Conrad strode out onto the main boulevard. She followed at a distance, using the experience she'd gained tailing story subjects back in Sydney—weaving through back alleys and avenues, pressing herself into sandstone cliffs or against the smooth bark of a eucalypt. This time she had little need to worry: Conrad walked at a cracking pace and never once looked back.

He started to approach the grander streets of the Marais, where avenues of Haussmann buildings in grey stone curled around lines of plane trees. Her eyes caught on tiny wine shops, delicatessens, and florists with buckets of perfect pink and red rosebuds. The boutiques seemed to be the kind where there were no price tags and the sales assistants kept reading magazines if they found a customer wanting.

Conrad stopped outside the Western Union Telegraph Company, and Charlie glanced at her wristwatch: 9.20 a.m. He rang the bell and was buzzed inside, climbing the stairs two at a time. Charlie waited, then tried to follow him in, but the door slammed shut in her face.

Just as she sighed and kicked the top of a cobblestone in frustration, the door opened like magic. A hunched lady in a matching grey cardigan and scarf waddled out, three pale chihuahuas tangled about her legs—it looked as though she was taking large white rats for a walk. Charlie played the good Samaritan and held the door open, ducking inside at the last minute. She walked across the empty black-and-white foyer and stared up the wrought-iron staircase. Instead of climbing it, she waited in the shadows for about ten minutes until Conrad walked down and went out the door.

Charlie's heart was racing. She strode confidently up the stairs as if she had business to attend to, combing her hands through her curls and straightening her suit jacket. A baby-faced young man in a brown suit was sitting alone behind the counter. Charlie bit her lip, tossed her hair and crossed one leg over the other, craning her neck as she pretended to look for someone.

'*Bonjour. Puis-je vous aider?*' said the man in a slightly nasal voice.

'Why yes, sir, I'm looking for my husband.' She was making her best attempt at a Southern accent. 'He was just here—Conrad Mackenzie. He was wiring some money.' Charlie had taken an educated guess: why else would he be here if not for a money transfer back to the States?

'*L'Americain, oui*, I'm afraid you have missed him.'

'Oh darn! I *told* him to wait . . . I had a little extra tucked aside. Birthday money, y'see.' She opened her purse and took out the emergency cash she carried at all times—she never knew when she might need to offer someone a small incentive, or just to catch a cab. 'I suppose y'all already wired the money.'

'*Oui, madame.*'

Charlie leaned over the counter and fluttered her eyelashes. 'You don't suppose you can send a little sump'n extra, sir. Same address. Please . . . It *is* a birthday.'

The man hesitated, then reached for the paper. 'As luck would have it I still have the details here. Let us do it quickly, madame.'

Charlie passed him the crisp notes before he changed his mind. 'Bless your cotton socks, sir. I'm gonna have words to my husband.' She leaned over to see the name, Mary Mackenzie, and memorise the Alabama address.

'Here's your receipt, Madame Mackenzie.' The polite young man folded the paper and handed it to Charlie. Bingo.

Charlie sought Violet out at her desk, where she was busy typing pages of scrawled notes. She wore a green silk shirt with a pussy-bow tie and fitted skirt. Her Hermès bag lay on the corner of her desk, as always.

'Do you have a moment to chat?' Charlie asked, peeking through George's door.

'He's out at the doctor with Daphne,' said Violet, tapping away without looking up. 'What's happened?' She paused typing and waved at the chair on the other side of her desk. 'Sit.'

Charlie's gaze caught on the pages piled up beside Violet. She leaned in as she noticed some line drawings and sketches of dresses. 'Are those your work?' Charlie glimpsed bias-cut slips with scooped backs, and details of pleating at the breasts and waist. Silk colour swatches in emerald, royal-blue and magenta were stapled to the corner.

Violet quickly put them in her top drawer as her eyes flickered around the room. 'Sorry, George was out, and I was just making a few notes.'

'Violet, you don't need to apologise to me. I told you, a career in fashion is beckoning.'

'Ha-ha! And I should have told *you* my father is beckoning— beckoning me to London to find a suitable gent.'

'Sounds like you've found one in Paris, though,' said Charlie, teasing.

Violet sighed, then leaned over the desk. 'It's becoming complicated. The truth is, I've done a lot of work with Aleksandr on his fashion showing. We've really become business partners. I'm thrilled but also terrified about what will happen tonight!'

'That's amazing news, Violet. I'm so happy for you!'

'Thank you! Aleksandr would love to design a dress for you. Truly.'

Charlie patted her short hair and said, without conviction, 'If you say so. I'm not sure a dress can help these curls . . . but I'm up for a miracle.'

'Done!' said Violet.

'My first fashion showing in Paris! Look out Elsa Schiaparelli and Madeleine Vionnet, here come Aleksandr and Violet.'

'You will cover it, won't you?' Violet asked. 'George approves.'

'Of course. And I'll have Conrad Mackenzie take the shots.'

'You're sure?' Violet sounded wary.

'Best to keep him close. Besides, he is a brilliant photographer.'

'Everyone you're investigating should be there. You'll be able to observe them in their natural habitat.' Violet winked.

'Perfect. What do I wear to the venue tonight?'

'The Gypsy Rose is a cabaret club. Picture the Moulin Rouge . . . Maybe this will help. I borrowed it from Aleksandr for you.' Violet stood up and grabbed a silk suit bag that was hanging on her coat hook.

'You did this for me? Really?' Charlie's hands trembled with anticipation as she started to unbutton the bag.

Violet reached over to stop her with a gentle tap. 'Not now. Everyone would wonder what was taking place, whereas this way it seems as though I've collected your laundry for you. No one will blink, because I pick up everyone's laundry around here.' She rolled her eyes. 'Except yours.'

'Oh, Violet, but—'

Violet's phone rang. 'Sorry, Charlie, I have to take this.'

Charlie took the suit bag back to her desk and sat down, feeling terrible that Violet had to do so much running around for all the men in the office, not just George. It seemed her guess had been right: Violet had been yearning to work with a female journalist.

As she picked up a sheet of paper and rolled it through her typewriter, she realised that in the excitement she'd forgotten to share her news about Conrad and Lord Ashworth, and about Conrad's grandmother.

She checked the time difference between Alabama and France, learning she would need to wait a few hours to call. She got some work done, then after her packed lunch of a baguette, ham and cheese, she picked up the phone and asked to be directed to the address and phone number on the Western Union receipt.

'Hello, Mary?'

'This is she, ma'am. Who is this?'

Charlie took a deep breath. 'I'm a friend of Conrad's. Charlie James. I'm trying to help your grandson.'

'Conrad!' The elderly woman's frail Southern drawl was threaded with pain and concern. 'What's happened now? Hasn't m'boy been through enough?'

'He has, ma'am. I just have some questions for you about him, because your answers might help.' Charlie rested the tip of her pen on her notebook and hoped she'd booked enough credit.

'Go ahead, then, ma'am. He's the apple of my eye! Sends me money every month, did y'all know that? That's how I get to live in this grand old place.'

Charlie's mouth dropped open, but she quickly recovered. 'Yes, Conrad does a lot to take care of you, doesn't he?'

'Praise the Lord, my word he does. He's put me up here in this fancy home for old folk, right on the banks of the Mississippi.' She sniffled. 'M'boy's done me so proud.'

Chapter 22

Charlie was fashionably late when she pushed open the door to the dimly lit club. She wore a fitted crimson tassel dress cut low in a V at the back and finishing just above her knee. As she checked her coat, she glimpsed her reflection in the bronzed mirror and did a delighted little twist, watching the tassels swirl. Her matching sequinned headband had a dark red feather that curled over her left ear.

Charlie studied her reflection. She only had a tiny hand mirror in her apartment and was unprepared for the young woman staring back at her. She looked relaxed and fresh, and she felt strong and simply gorgeous.

'*Magnifique!*' The ancient man in the coat-check box winked before he asked for her name and crossed it off the guest list.

'*Merci.*' She ran her fingers over her hips, smoothing the tassels, then stepped through heavy velvet curtains into another world.

The air was thick with cigarette smoke, perfume and anticipation. A jazz band dressed in tuxedos supported a sylph-like singer who seemed like a blonde version of Gloria Swanson. The bar had been widened, with a catwalk splitting it down the middle. Fairy lights shimmered across the ceiling.

Charlie's jaw dropped when she noticed a woman in a leopard-print corset bathing in a giant coupe glass. Several other women in burlesque outfits of heels, fishnet stockings, suspenders and ruffled bustiers playfully danced to the music while topping up champagne coupes with magnums of Belle Epoque. Who needed Berlin, when you had Paris?

The marble tables dotted around the bar were filling up with an eclectic mix of up-and-coming Parisian designers, art students and bohemians in striped tops and berets, and elegant middle-aged couples in tuxedos and evening dresses. Violet had agonised over the guest list, and Charlie was thrilled for her friend that it had all come together.

She ducked behind the bar and through more heavy curtains, hung with a *Privée* sign, into a narrow corridor being used as the dressing-room. Willowy models—some of them dancers from Circus d'Hiver—stood smoking in their underwear and silk robes, waiting to be fitted with dresses bagged on a small rack, while others bent over mirrors to apply makeup. Models in evening gowns viewed themselves in full-length mirrors, their pointed feet turned out just so.

'There you are—look at you!' Violet leaned back to admire Charlie before kissing her on both cheeks. 'I should have roped you in for the catwalk. Look, Aleksandr!' Her lover's head, with a mouthful of pins, popped out sideways from behind a model. 'Told you the dress would be perfect.' His face lit up, and he gave a salute before resuming his pinning.

'Break a leg,' said Charlie, because the show seemed far more theatrical than she'd expected. 'I'll let you get to it. I've got my notebook.'

Violet clapped. 'Yes! We want full *Times* coverage. But make sure to also have some *fun*.' She smiled wickedly as she nudged Charlie out through the curtains. '*Ciao, ciao,* have some champagne and introduce yourself to some interesting people. Perhaps pick one of them to take home . . .'

Charlie laughed as she stepped back into the room and almost collided with Commander Rose-Thomas.

'Pardon,' he said, steadying his drink so it didn't spill. His eyes widened as they met Charlie's, but he said nothing for an awkward beat. Eventually, he reached for his impeccable manners. 'I know very little about the fashion world, but my wife tells me Aleksandr is testing the waters for his own atelier. So, if we can help him start a business in some small way. That reminds me—' He pointed out a young blond man, the doppelganger of his father.

'Claudette Marchand is not here—to be expected as she has just buried her late husband. She is choosing to stay home for some time, Lady Ashworth tells me. But that young man is Marchand's son, Jacob, who has come back from Wharton Business School with a headful of ideas. Wants to go into manufacturing for the Yanks. Be their supply in Europe—get his ducks in a row in case the Boches . . .' His voice was drowned out as cymbals clashed and the music became louder.

Charlie recalled her interview with the Russian juggler and wondered if now would be a good time to ask the commander if he was the mysterious masked man. She tried to speak over the shriek of a saxophone, but he held up his coupe and nodded his head in the direction of a far table.

'Won't you join us, please?' he shouted. 'I can get you a drink.'

Charlie looked across to the table, and Lord and Lady Ashworth gave her cheerful waves. Lady Ashworth was in a midnight-blue sparkling dress that set off her green hair, while Lord Ashworth looked debonair in his tuxedo. Mercedes Rose-Thomas wore a fitted black dress and gave a polite nod to Charlie before she resumed talking to the Ashworths.

'I might join you in a moment, thank you,' said Charlie, who had just spotted Milly and Conrad at a separate table near the catwalk. 'I'll just—' She gestured at the Americans as the jazz beat stepped up a notch. Conrad raised his camera and gave her a smile with a big thumbs-up.

The commander spoke stiffly. 'Perhaps we will see you later. May I just say, before we part, that dress suits you. You look very elegant.' He clearly did not want to overstep, given their last encounter. 'Paris must be growing on you.'

'*Merci.*' Charlie took his compliment as a peace offering, but she would interrogate him about the Russian as soon as she had the opportunity.

She made her way over to Milly, who was now sitting alone while Conrad wandered around snapping photos. The women exchanged kisses and greetings, then Milly glanced over her shoulders as though making sure no one else was in earshot. 'I'm pleased you've kept Conrad out of your paper. Is he still, you know, the main suspect?'

'I'm not the police, Milly.'

She sighed, her eyes on her lover. 'He's kind and . . . really quite funny when you get to know him.'

Charlie nodded as she watched the photographer subtly work the room, sticking to the shadows.

'I'm sure he is, Milly,' she said, then decided to be direct. 'But he isn't always, is he? Do you know why he attacked Marchand in his own home? Marchand was smaller, but he could have crushed Conrad with a phone call. I'm not sure why he didn't. Help me make sense of this?'

'All right. But this is *off* the record.' Milly took a deep breath. 'Conrad and I were in Maxime's library—you've seen it. High ceilings, glorious light, lots of old men in gold frames . . . Anyway,

Maxime stepped out to use the bathroom. Conrad and I, we were fooling around as he packed his camera stand away, and I guess Maxime caught us kissing. Careless of us.'

'But you'd broken off your affair with Marchand, or so you told me.'

'Yes! Months before.' She was fidgeting with the stem of her glass, and her face took on a vulnerable expression that Charlie hadn't seen from her before. 'Marchand had been drinking cognac, and he was suddenly surly.' Her tone dropped. 'When Conrad took all his equipment outside to wait for the taxi, Maxime . . .' She hesitated. 'Maxime grabbed me by the throat and pushed me against the wall. He ripped at my stockings and jammed his hands down my underpants. Called me a *salope Américaine*.' Her voice was brittle, but her eyes were dry. 'Conrad walked in, and . . .'

Charlie was horrified. 'I'm sorry that happened to you, Milly. You don't need to say any more.'

Milly reached out and squeezed her hand. 'I'm trying to forget. But you can see why I don't want that printed in the papers, can't you?' She turned to look at Conrad. 'I'm just lucky I've landed a good one. If only my daddy thought the same.'

Conrad was testing the light and angles as though he were in a trance. Watching his earnest face, Charlie thought of her conversation with Mary Mackenzie. The woman's description of the manslaughter hadn't given Charlie new information, but it had emphasised the fact that Mary believed her grandson had saved both her life and his own.

Charlie imagined how he must have reacted when he'd seen Marchand hold a woman he loved by the throat. And had Marchand attacked Milly again that night at the ball? Had Conrad come to her rescue?

Charlie also had to investigate that strange, angry encounter between Lord Ashworth and Conrad. It seemed clear that the envelope had contained money, and that Conrad had somehow funded expensive accommodation for Mary over the past several months. Charlie needed to speak with Lord Ashworth in private, and she hoped to get the chance later in the evening.

After Milly excused herself to freshen up in the powder room, Charlie took a coupe of bubbles from a tray and glanced back at the stage, where three women were dancing with oversized feather fans to 'Summertime'. Her heart aching for Milly, Charlie found that she wasn't in the mood.

She got up and decided to look for the Russian juggler, and soon spotted him standing shyly in the corner, clean-shaven and dressed in a blue silk shirt with a red cravat. He nodded briefly in greeting.

'Mr Sidorov! Charlie James, remember me?' She spoke slowly and loudly in French above the music. 'Do you understand me?'

He shook his head and lifted his arms as if to say, 'I'm sorry.'

Charlie gave him a gentle smile, feeling embarrassed. Violet was busy with the show, but afterwards Charlie would ask her to talk to Sidorov and see if he remembered the commander—or if he'd recognised someone else as the masked man who had admired his knife. Charlie just needed to get a positive identification before she could share it with Inspecteur Bernard.

The main show would be starting shortly, so she introduced herself to Jacob Marchand. 'Mind if I sit here?' Marchand's son could not be blamed for the misdeeds of his father, as he'd only just stepped into the role, and Charlie had questions he might be able to answer.

'Please.' Grinning, he jumped up to pull the chair out for her. He sounded more American than French after years of college and business school. 'Is that one of Aleksandr's?' he asked, running a hungry eye over her dress.

'Certainly is. Mine for tonight!'

'You should keep it. *Très élégant.*'

Violet would be proud, she thought.

As she sat down, the lights dimmed even further and the waitresses departed through the curtains. The pianist struck the opening chords, then models burst out through the curtains and weaved between the tables, twisting and posing with their hands on hips so the audience could see the dresses up close. A leggy brunette brushed up against Jacob, who blushed.

'I believe your father loved fashion,' Charlie probed.

He laughed good-naturedly as he gazed at the models. 'What's not to love? Papa wanted to back Aleksandr—was ready to go—but the Russian refused. Strange. Maybe *I* can convince him, though.'

'I imagine tonight will give you lots of investment ideas. Are you looking for people to throw money at?' She playfully poked his lapel.

'No, actually.' He glugged his champagne. 'Papa had business with the families of people here. Bad blood. It's a mess, so shhhh . . .' He held a finger up to his mouth, the champagne making him loose-lipped.

Charlie pretended to be equally drunk as she leaned in and whispered, 'Who? Tell me . . .' Her lips brushed his ear.

Jacob blushed again and tipped his coupe in the direction of Mercedes and Edward Rose-Thomas.

He hesitated, clearly wanting to impress the glamorous woman sitting beside him. Charlie gazed at him with open eyes, willing him on. 'The truth is . . . some records seem to have disappeared. Papa's secretary told me he destroyed them himself. Burned them in his metal wastepaper bin one afternoon in a drunken fury after a long lunch at the club.'

'Did she say who they related to?'

'*Non!* It could be anyone . . . Aleksandr maybe—if he refused finance? Papa hated to lose.' Jacob shook his head, sadly. 'His secretary was barred from his office. To be honest, I think she was a little scared of my Papa. He could be . . . difficult.'

His expression was stony and Charlie realised at once why Marchand's son had chosen to study abroad for so many years. His dislike of his father was written all over his face.

She pitied this pleasant young man. Clearly, Jacob had intended on starting afresh in America, now here he was sifting through a company he was expected to take over, but found wanting.

As if he could read Charlie's mind, Jacob's cheeks reddened. 'I'm sorry. I've overstepped . . . I'm sure you can understand the nature of my work at the bank is confidential. I'd rather watch the show, shall we?' he raised a glass of champagne and nodded as a leggy model sauntered past swathed in gold silk.

Charlie exhaled, frustrated. Sitting back, she looked at the beading and embroidery across the silk dresses, and wondered how many hours Aleksandr had spent stitching into the night. He also spent his nights with Violet, and Charlie marvelled at his stamina.

She held up her glass to Jacob. '*Santé!*' They clinked crystal, and as she felt the bubbles slide down her throat, Charlie relaxed into her chair. She drew sweet perfume and smoke deep into her lungs as dress after dress paraded past, making her dizzy with pastel silks, diaphanous sheaths and gleaming beads. The designs were elegant and sensual, skimming over hips and breasts without being too revealing. She hoped the show was a sell-out. She would have bought one, except they cost more than her rent.

The audience whooped and clapped. Some even stomped their feet. Charlie was giddy with happiness and so proud of her friend.

She spotted Violet's smiling face peeking through the red velvet curtains. Beside her was Aleksandr, but his handsome features weren't beaming with triumph and elation. Charlie saw confusion and . . . fear? He was probably just very nervous.

Chapter 23

It was well past midnight. The dresses were hung in their bags backstage; the models had gone home, no doubt to soak their tired feet. Aleksandr was out the back in the dressing-room, making notes and some adjustments with Violet, his mouth crammed with pins again.

The Rose-Thomases, Milly, Conrad and Lord Ashworth sat around a pair of round tables near the grand piano. Tuxedo jackets were slung on the backs of chairs, and sleeves were rolled up, bow ties unravelled. Shoulder straps fell from thin shoulders.

Charlie had bid Jacob goodnight an hour ago when the show had ended. He'd taken his leave politely, saying he had a big day at the office tomorrow. When he'd kissed her hand and raised a hopeful eyebrow, she'd gently batted him away. 'I'm flattered, but

I need to congratulate Violet and Aleksandr.' There was no way she was going to sleep with a potential suspect, no matter how adorable—Jacob Marchand was far from a chip off the old block.

'May I join you?' Charlie asked Lady Ashworth, squeezing in beside her on the piano stool before she could get a reply. 'Please, I haven't had a chance to talk to you all evening. Wasn't the show heavenly? Could Aleksandr be your next project?'

But no sooner had Charlie sat down than Lady Ashworth's fingers flew across the keys playing 'Summertime' and 'In the Mood'. When she was done, she stood up from the piano and shut the lid, giving Charlie a rueful smile.

'Bravo,' cried Commander Rose-Thomas.

'Again, again,' insisted his wife.

'Stop it, dear people. You and I know I'm a poor man's Billie Holiday.' Lady Ashworth fluttered her faux eyelashes and held her index finger up to shush them all.

Charlie noticed that only Conrad sat quietly, letting his eyes travel from person to person, lingering on each one. She held his gaze for a moment before she glanced at Milly, who despite the late hour—and her emotional moment earlier—was looking fresh and dewy. Her golden slip made her glow in the dim lights. It was easy to see why Conrad was smitten.

Lady Ashworth's eyes twinkled. 'I have the most delicious idea.' She clapped her hands with excitement. 'How about we play a little game?'

Charlie straightened on the piano stool, curious. Lady Ashworth was infamous for her parties and games—assisted by Conrad. Charlie looked between employer and employee: one was full of energy and exuberance, the other like a still, deep lake.

'A game!' Lady Ashworth repeated. 'Let's! The night is young.'

The group, including Conrad, clapped and catcalled their agreement. They were up for more.

Charlie was wondering what Lord Ashworth really thought of it all. Clearly he was used to his wife's spontaneous parlour games, because he sat in his chair nodding at her, beaming. 'What are you suggesting, my dear?' he said in his plummy voice. The man had at least three decades on Charlie and was looking sprightly, whereas she kept suppressing yawns. To be fair, he'd been with Lady Ashworth for a good decade, so he was prepared for this.

'My darling Rupert, Conrad, Mrs Rose-Thomas and Miss Goldsmith, you'll be the first group.' She pointed to each of them as she named them. 'Commander Rose-Thomas and Charlie James, you'll be in the second car with me.'

'What about Miss Carthage and Mr Ivanov?' asked Charlie, as she looked over her shoulder at the dressing-room. This might be the ideal time for her to confront the commander about the Russian, but she wanted Violet in the other car so they could both use the opportunity to seek answers about the murder.

'Oh, I think those two will be working for hours yet, don't you? Just Charlie, may I trouble you for a pen and two pieces of notepaper, please?'

'Of course,' said Charlie, jumping up from the stool and retrieving the items from her purse.

Everyone looked at Lord Ashworth, who held up his hands and shrugged as if to say, *I have no idea what my good wife is up to.*

Lady Ashworth scribbled out a list on each page. When she was finished, she passed one to her husband, the other to the commander. 'Now, turn them over.' She clicked her fingers. 'We are going to have a treasure hunt!'

Everyone gasped.

'Read the list and pass it on. It will be a hoot.'

Charlie took the page that was passed to her and read:

Ballet slipper

Sailor's cap

Bucket of fish

Crocodile

Hair from the scalp of a redhead

Charlie blushed at the last one, and she could feel the eyes of the group falling on her.

'The rules are: there are no rules! These items can be gained in any order'—Lady Ashworth lowered her voice dramatically—'and by any means. We'll take our town cars and roam Paris. First team back to Villa Trianon with all the items wins!'

'Is there a prize?' asked Charlie.

'Yes, dear, is there?' said Lord Ashworth, leaning forward, eyebrows raised.

Lady Ashworth waggled her finger. 'Be first back to the villa, and we'll see what we can do. I'm thinking the losing team shouts dinner at the Ritz.'

The commander and his wife clapped, Milly threw her arms in the air, and Lord Ashworth guffawed as he said, 'Let's jolly well hope I win.'

But Charlie was chewing over Lady Ashworth's 'rules'. *These can be gained in any order . . . by any means.* These people of *le tout-Paris* thought the rules did not apply to them. They made their way through the summer in a haze of sequins, champagne and hope, barrelling from one spectacular party to the next. It was all Charlie could do to keep up with this frenzied energy. Paris kept on dazzling, with each night more beautiful than the last.

The others were tipsy, while Charlie was still thinking clearly because she'd only had one glass of champagne. As she looked at the group, she asked herself: who had the most to gain from Maxime Marchand's death? Was it someone present, or was it his own wife, perhaps even his own son?

Everyone stood as their chauffeurs rushed in carrying purses, shawls, stoles and coats. The chatter grew loud, the group excited by the audacious turn the evening had taken.

Two waitresses appeared, each carrying a silver champagne bucket and crystal glasses. 'I've arranged a little something to go in the cars with us,' said Lady Ashworth. 'To keep up our spirits!' She'd clearly planned this from the start of the evening.

When Charlie stood up from her chair, she felt a sharp tug at the back of her head. An index finger waved in the air beside her—wrapped around it were strands of her curly hair. She clutched her head and rubbed it, trying to numb where the hair had been wrenched from her scalp. Her head jerked up as she looked around at the culprit.

His face was low, cheek almost pressed against hers, and she held her breath, deeply uncomfortable.

'Well, that item wasn't so difficult to obtain.' He studied her hair in the light as he murmured, 'Your hair is like woven copper. Perhaps Botticelli and Rossetti were right—redheads are the most devious and sensual of all.' He chuckled as he stood up, dropped her hair into his pocket and patted it.

Lord Ashworth nodded benignly at her before he allowed himself to be pulled out the door and whirled into the chaos of the game.

Charlie rubbed the back of her head again as she and the commander bundled into the black Rolls-Royce parked outside the Gypsy Rose, with the cheerful Lady Ashworth sitting in the front seat. Taking a deep breath, Charlie ignored her stinging scalp, but Lord Ashworth's prank had thrown her. She slipped the list out of her purse and drew a line through the bottom item.

Charlie hadn't even had the chance to farewell Violet. No matter—her friend would be forgiving and full of stories tomorrow at work. Charlie would take her out to Café de Flore to celebrate and swap details. For now, Charlie had to focus on finding a way to speak with the commander alone.

'Champagne?' Lady Ashworth's cheery voice interrupted her musings. The chauffeur had placed a silver bucket in the front console, and the older woman poured a glass for each of them. 'To the opera—the Palais Garnier,' she instructed her driver. 'Back door, please, the artists' entrance.'

The three of them leaned back into the dark green leather seats, sipping champagne as the city lights whizzed by. Theirs was a companiable silence—a lull between whirlwinds, Charlie suspected.

The Rolls-Royce headed past some pretty stone buildings smothered with vines. Charlie wound down her window to enjoy the delicate aroma of star jasmine and roses, the scent of summer. Couples walked hand in hand along footpaths that spilled over with patrons stumbling out of bars.

They raced past the Louvre, then Galeries Lafayette, where she noticed the windows were full of silver slip dresses and tass-elled waterfall dresses set among snowdrops suspended from the ceiling. She smiled at the display, thinking it was only a matter of time before Aleksandr's line stood in those windows, and perhaps Violet's too.

Eventually they reached the square in Opéra, the 9th arrondissement, and Charlie leaned out the window a little to take in the warm lights and giant marble busts of Harmony and Poetry beside the main entrance to the Palais Garnier opera house. Golden Victory stood proud on the roof, waving her fist at the sky.

The car crawled to a stop outside a small entrance with a red door, and Lady Ashworth didn't wait for the driver to let her out. 'Wait here, back in a tick,' she trilled before she made her way to what Charlie presumed was the stage door.

Two menacing-looking men with three-day-old beards were leaning against the wall, smoking. Lady Ashworth greeted them with warm smiles, patted her hair, and was promptly ushered through.

Charlie and the commander exchanged an awkward look.

'Does Lady Ashworth have access to every establishment in town?' asked Charlie, trying to bridge the silence. Could this be her moment to ask about the knife juggler?

'I expect so. Let's hope she can work her charm and come back with a pointe.' He slumped into his seat and closed his eyes, looking like a man who would rather be anywhere but here, and for now she decided not to disturb him—there wasn't enough time for an interrogation anyway.

Why had he decided to play this game? To amuse his wife? To keep in with the Ashworths? The shadows were deep under his eyes—something was keeping him awake at night. Was it the sad situation of his wife's family? Perhaps it was the messy business of trying to convince the politicians in London that the Boches were gathering steam. Or was he troubled by the memory of sliding a knife into Marchand's neck?

A few minutes later, Lady Ashworth appeared in the doorway waving a set of pink ballet slippers above her head. She was so pleased with herself that her cheeks matched the shoes. 'I almost nabbed one of the prima ballerinas to come with us,' she said, laughing as she climbed back into her seat.

'Congratulations, one down,' said the commander drily, checking his watch. His sombre expression left no doubt that he regretted being a part of this game.

Charlie slipped the pen from her purse and struck the first item from the list. 'Where to next?' she asked softly.

'Why, Just Charlie, I think we'll try the Parc Zoologique.'

It had taken just twenty minutes to drive to the park that housed Paris's zoo, and another twenty to convince the guards to call a zookeeper. He arrived with his grey hair mussed up and shirt not quite tucked into his pants, doing his best to put on a straight face for the tiny green-haired woman, shimmering in blue sequins, who stood at his gates. 'Lady Ashworth, what brings you here at this hour? Is everything okay?'

'There you are, Gérald. Sorry to wake you, my dear, but it is a matter of some urgency. Everything is fine—marvellous, in fact, just having another little gathering. I wondered if I might trouble you for a crocodile, please?'

'A crocodile?' Gérald scratched his head and looked down at his shoes, apparently too polite to point out that Lady Ashworth had lost her mind.

The commander and Charlie looked at one another, embarrassed and concerned.

'It's late . . . perhaps we can continue this another time?' said the commander like the diplomat he was.

'But we'll just take the crocodile and go.' She laughed. 'I don't mean a live one, silly! That would be ludicrous. I just mean the one on display in the museum.'

'The taxidermy crocodile.' The zookeeper visibly relieved—no doubt he'd worried about having to explain to his superiors why their biggest patron and supporter had been eaten by one of the exhibits.

Charlie had to stop herself laughing. This time when she caught the commander's gaze, she grinned.

'Oh, and Gérald, while you are grabbing the crocodile, do you think I could borrow a bucket of those golden koi, my dear? My driver will return them in the morning, I promise.'

Thirty minutes later they pulled up outside Commander Rose-Thomas's apartment. On the seat between him and Charlie was a small taxidermy crocodile, while at her feet was a bucket that spilled over every time they turned a corner too quickly.

Charlie James had officially reached the peak of Parisian insanity.

In the front passenger seat, Lady Ashworth had dozed off. Though Charlie was fond of the older woman, she had been grateful for the quiet in which to watch Paris zip by like a line of fairy lights.

~~Ballet slipper~~
Sailor's cap
~~Bucket of fish~~
~~Crocodile~~
~~Hair from the scalp of a redhead~~

The sooner they got this jolly hat, the sooner she could go to bed.

'I'll just duck inside and grab it,' said the commander.

'Sure.' Charlie smiled as she swung open the door and jumped out onto the footpath to stretch her legs. It was a clear night without the hint of a breeze, and the warm air enveloped her skin. She skipped a little, watching her tassels swirl, and was sorry she had to hand the dress back. What must it be like to afford such beauty?

It was always my goal to make a beautiful life.

Charlie studied the sleeping Lady Ashworth. Her jaw had slackened, and she twitched as though in a vigorous dream; even in her sleep she jittered with energy. Her life was as carefully constructed as this game: outlandish, over-the-top, unexpected. The older woman peppered her life—and those of the people around her—with pockets of joy.

Charlie envied her. For her endless income, but more for her verve. Her confidence. Her judgement.

The commander appeared on the footpath as Charlie leaned into a large terracotta pot beside the front steps, pinching off a sprig of rosemary.

'That's not on the list,' he joked, but his smile was weary.

She held the rosemary up to her nose and crushed a leaf between her thumb and fingers, like she used to do in her mother's garden when she was a child. 'You're sick of this game,' she said.

'As a rule, I prefer not to play games like this at all.' His eyes were dark pools, shiny and sad. 'Here.' He took his British Navy hat out of its box and handed it to Charlie.

They stood on the footpath opposite one another, feet almost touching.

She gave a wry smile. 'I can't guarantee it will be returned in the same condition. You'd better give me the hatbox too, as Lord Ashworth seems determined to win.'

'He always is. Let's hope he has better luck this week at the club.' The commander handed over the box and looked up at the stars. 'I never thought I'd use it in action again. Set ships to sea. To war.' He bowed his head and swallowed. Mercedes wore the same harried look, and Charlie felt for them both. Damn Maxime Marchand, she thought, for sucking the life out of these two beautiful people. He'd whittled them away to husks.

Charlie realised that this wasn't the right time to ask the commander about the knife juggler: it would be awkward, and she would get nowhere. She squeezed her rosemary and made to get back into the car. 'Thank you,' she said as she allowed him to open the door for her and hold the hatbox while she climbed inside.

As the car drove away, she gave her address to the chauffeur so he could drop her off in Saint-Germain before the long drive back to Villa Trianon. No doubt the others would be back there soon enough, and they—along with the housekeeper—would help Lady Ashworth prepare for bed. Charlie had considered going there to speak with Lord Ashworth about Conrad, but the older man would probably have had her escorted from the premises, then called George to say that he and his wife would never speak to a *Times* reporter again.

Charlie took the hat from its box and twirled it on her index finger. So much for this opportunity. She was exhausted.

Just as she had let go of the night and fallen into a deep sleep, her heartbeat finally slowing, she was awakened by a heavy knock at her door.

Charlie reached for her cream silk kimono, staggered out of bed and switched on the light.

More desperate knocks, faster this time.

She was fiddling with the tie about her waist as she flung open the door.

'Violet! What's happened?'

Charlie took in her friend's shivering frame and bare feet—her heels were tossed to one side at the top of the stairs. She had a hand over her mouth, and all the colour had drained from her face.

Gently taking her friend by the upper arms, Charlie tried to meet her eyes. 'Come on, come inside.' She put an arm around her friend's trembling shoulders and led her in, settling her on the end of the bed with a woollen blanket and a cup of tea.

Violet's face was drawn and pale, and when she eventually spoke her voice was shaky. 'After the show, when Aleksandr was still busy, I had a little toast with the dancers—and the Russian juggler, Vladimir. He told me in private, just the two of us . . . He had recognised the person who admired his knife at the Circus Ball. He said it was the tall dressmaker, the one from St Petersburg.'

Chapter 24

Charlie poured Violet a strong cup of tea as the young woman gave her a pained look. 'If you had run into an Australian at the ball, then they would have been interested in what you were doing in Paris, so far from home.'

'Probably,' Charlie conceded. 'And that's probably all that's happened here.' She poured her own cup then sat on the bed opposite Violet. 'Do you think Mr Sidorov has gone straight to the police?'

'I asked him not to . . . I begged him to let me handle it myself, but he said he would need to call them because he couldn't afford to get in trouble. He left instantly for the Cirque d'Hiver, and he was worried—he said he shouldn't have told me. He didn't know that Aleksandr and I . . .' Her breath hitched. 'Vladimir would have made that call by now. They might already be taking Aleksandr in for questioning! We have to go to him, try to get there before the police arrive.'

Charlie sucked in a breath. 'I'm not sure if confronting Aleksandr is a good idea. I think we should speak with Inspecteur Bernard.'

'Nonsense,' said Violet, shaking her head. 'I know Aleksandr, Charlie.' There were tears in her eyes. 'He's a good man.'

'That may be . . . but why did you come to me rather than speaking to him on your own, as soon as you heard the news?'

The young woman didn't respond for a moment. She breathed in the steam from her tea. 'I suppose I did want you there with me. Just in case.'

'All right, I understand.' Charlie leaned over and patted her hand, as Violet gave her a teary, grateful smile. 'Do you know where Aleksandr is?'

'He'll have returned to Mainbocher. He was about to leave as I was giving that toast.'

'And would Mr Sidorov know that?'

She shook her head. 'Oh, I see. The police will first go to the club and look for him there.'

'Yes, and that gives us a little more time.'

'Poor Aleksandr. He won't have slept. He must think me so rude for running off while he was busy packing all the dresses into silk bags to take back to the atelier.' She sipped her tea and shook her head again. 'I suppose it doesn't matter now.'

'I'll telephone the police station and leave a message for the inspecteur, letting him know that he should meet us at the atelier. I doubt he will have gone with his men to collect Aleksandr from the club, but if he has then he will come to the atelier as the next stop anyway.'

'Charlie—'

'We shouldn't tip off a suspect or put ourselves at risk. But if Aleksandr is guilty, he would be an idiot to attack us or try to escape based on this one piece of circumstantial evidence, and with the police on their way. I know I won't be able to stop you from going in on your own if you have to, so let's both go talk to him before they arrive. Don't worry about the tea.'

Violet nodded and stood up. 'All right. Thank you, Charlie.'

She just hoped the inspecteur wouldn't be too cross with her. She was only doing what any self-respecting journalist would—and the truth was, she was doing it more for her friend than the scoop.

Framed by the atelier's doorway, Aleksandr stood in a tailored burgundy suit with a ruffled collar and sleeves. He looked a little like Charlie imagined Mozart might have on a concert night. 'Violet! Where did you go?' He seemed both confused and relieved as he embraced her, while she stood stiffly in his arms. 'Charlie, this is a wonderful surprise.' He beamed. 'Come in, come in.

Great timing, as I've just finished taking morning tea with my dressmakers—they are in every room except this front one.'

Violet wrung her hands and bit her lip as she followed her lover into the front room. Charlie felt sorry for her friend, but she was also glad that the building was full of dressmakers.

She chided herself for being melodramatic, deciding to get the difficult news out of the way. 'Aleksandr, we spoke with the juggler whose knife was used as the murder weapon, and he said a man matching your description had come over to admire his knives on the night of the ball.'

'That was me, yes,' Aleksandr said simply. 'Sit, please.' He gestured for the women to take a seat on an emerald velvet sofa. 'I wondered why you ran away,' he said to Violet. 'I wanted to chase after you, but I needed to keep working. I wondered what I'd done.'

Violet shot a nervous glance at Charlie, who nodded reassurance. It seemed a good sign that Aleksandr had remained calm while admitting to speaking with Sidorov. They both sat down.

'Tea?' Aleksandr offered, always polite.

The women shook their heads.

'You were talking with the juggler about the military?' Charlie probed. 'When were you in the military?'

'No!' He laughed. It sounded a little nervous. 'I said that he must have the discipline of a soldier.'

'And why were you speaking French to him?'

'At first I didn't know he was Russian. And then, well . . .' Aleksandr seemed ashamed, his head bowed for a moment. 'I have lived away from home for so long. My Russian is . . . not what it used to be.'

Violet stared at him, obviously willing every word he uttered to be good and true. Charlie could see this relationship was far more than a fling or a business partnership for Violet—she was in love with him. Only love could look like pain.

'I'm sorry to hear that,' said Charlie. 'It must be difficult to no longer have confidence in your native tongue.' She leaned forward. 'So, tell us about why you admired his knives.'

'Of course!' Aleksandr's shame and sadness turned to enthusiasm. 'The carving on the handles is beautiful—bears, trees, a whole woodland story. It looked Russian, so I was drawn to it.'

Charlie hadn't noticed the carving but perhaps that had all been coated in blood. No wonder Sidorov was so keen to get his knife returned.

'What about your alibi? Where were you when Marchand was killed?'

'I assume I was with everyone else watching the show. I was sitting right behind you, remember?'

Charlie cast her mind back. 'I don't actually . . .'

She turned to check with Violet, who squirmed. 'I can't remember seeing you, darling, after we walked across to the show. I was chatting with Charlie.' She gazed apologetically at Aleksandr, who was clearly offended. And he was very nervous now—he was fidgeting with his ruffled sleeves.

'Wouldn't you have noticed if I had gone off alone into the garden?' he asked, sounding agitated.

Violet bit her lip. 'I . . . I think so. I'm sorry, darling!'

Why was Aleksandr so nervous? What if he really had killed Marchand? Charlie was reminded of the awkwardness between him and the victim when they had greeted each other that night. 'Let's not worry about the alibi for now. There's something else I'd like to discuss. I understand Marchand was one of Mainbocher's main backers?'

The Russian's expression grew even more tense. 'An arrangement that had nothing to do with me. I really just run Monsieur Bocher's Paris House, as he prefers to spend most of his time at home in New York.'

'I know that Marchand approached you as a potential backer, and that you turned him down.' Charlie was hoping that Jacob Marchand hadn't lied to her about this, and one look at Aleksandr's face told her it was true.

Violet gasped. 'What? But, Aleksandr . . .'

Charlie continued. 'I assumed it was because you understandably disliked the man, but now I'm wondering, was there another reason?' She made a leap, thinking of what the commander had told her. 'Does this have anything to do with Marchand's business dealings in St Petersburg? Remember, the police can look into your background as they did with Conrad. Once they know you spoke to the knife juggler, they will research you.'

She waited, silently counting to ten.

Aleksandr put his face in his hands. 'I see,' he said, desperation in his tone.

Violet rushed over and wrapped her arms around him. 'It's all right, darling. Whatever happened, it's going to be all right.'

Aleksandr held her close and turned back to Charlie. 'I had to invite Marchand and his wife to my show. It wasn't possible for me to snub them, or no one of any import would have shown up. But I would never have taken a cent from that rat. He is the worst kind of man.'

'How so?'

'Marchand killed my parents.'

There was a knock at the front door.

Chapter 25

Charlie, Violet and Aleksandr soon found themselves huddled on thin metal chairs in the inspecteur's office, as a group of children shouted and tumbled on the grass in the park outside.

'Tea with extra sugar for you all,' Inspecteur Bernard said kindly as one of his underlings passed them each a cup. Case files were stacked neatly all over his desk as they had been on Charlie's previous visit, but this time there were three perfect apricots in a row near his pencil jar.

'Poor Aleksandr,' Violet whispered, still in shock.

The inspecteur spoke to the designer, who cupped the tea as though it was hot cocoa. 'So, Marchand financed the munitions factory where your parents both worked.'

'Yes. Conditions were terrible, and they slept in tiny dormitories, so I stayed with my grandmother. I saw my parents maybe . . . once every three or four months, the whole of my childhood. Their skin was yellow, their faces haggard, their hair like wire. All for a few measly roubles each month.'

'And they died at this factory, in what year?' The inspecteur took notes and so did Charlie—as discreetly as possible, her notebook nestled behind her coat on her lap.

'In 1916. I was eight. The chemicals caught alight, and the factory combusted, lighting up the whole city.' Aleksandr's open face crumpled. 'My grandmother and I thought it was fireworks. The Tsar's birthday or something . . .' He brushed away tears with his sleeve.

'I'm sorry,' Inspecteur Bernard said softly. Charlie was impressed by his compassion, and relieved that he didn't seem angry with her or Violet for speaking to Aleksandr without him. 'That must have taken an enormous toll. So why work for the company Marchand funded?'

'I only recently found out he was the backer when I was made head designer for the Paris house. I was drawn to Monsieur Bocher's designs, the silks . . .'

Charlie reflected that the garments were as far from a dingy factory as you could get. No wonder Aleksandr loved flamboyant clothes—it was all an escape. She thought of something Lady Ashworth had said: *It's possible to find magic here in Paris.*

Aleksandr continued. 'Nobody discusses finances with a lowly designer. It was only when I had to source fabrics from all around the world, for the entire design team, that I was introduced to Marchand.'

Charlie couldn't help jumping in. 'How did you know he was the same Marchand? You were only a little boy at the time of the fire.'

Aleksandr turned to her, his jaw clenched and eyes flashing. 'Everyone with family in that factory knows the name Maxime Marchand. There was an investigation, and the papers were full of stories from the factory. The Tsar had encouraged the investment. But when there were calls for the foreign owner to stand trial in Russia, he refused to come.'

'No one extradited him?' the inspecteur asked.

'You would know better than any of us, Inspecteur, how hard that process is. How costly. How lengthy. The Russian government wanted to wash their hands of the whole thing, and then there was the war . . . People forgot.' He scowled. 'But not me. And not the other families.'

Violet reached out and took his hand, and their fingers interlaced. 'Aleksandr didn't kill Marchand, Inspecteur, even though he deserved it.'

The inspecteur gave an apologetic shrug and pushed his glasses up the bridge of his nose. '*Très désolé*. I can see this hurts you, Mademoiselle Carthage, but the simple fact is that I have no choice but to hold Aleksandr Ivanov for formal questioning.'

Monsieur Ivanov, Mademoiselle Carthage, if you could both wait here in my office for a moment. Madame James, a word outside, *s'il vous plaît.*

Violet and Aleksandr exchanged worried glances as Charlie followed the inspector out into the corridor. He closed the door behind them and led her to a quiet section of the corridor before saying rather tersely, 'What were you thinking, going directly to speak with a suspect before you came to the police?'

'I'm sorry,' Charlie said. 'I was thinking of Violet. We had no idea of Aleksandr's homeland connection to Marchand until now. Promise.'

'But also were you not thinking of your paper? Your story?' His face was grim. He stood facing her, hands thrust deep into his trouser pockets. 'This is not just a story, Madame James. This is a murder investigation. If you have news that would benefit the investigation, I expect you to come to me first. What you did was reckless.' He hesitated before continuing in a concerned voice. 'You could have been hurt.' He removed his hands from his pockets and held his palms out as a peace offering.

'Understood,' said Charlie. 'Next time I have information I will share it with you first.' The last thing she needed was the inspecteur calling George at the office and complaining about her interference in the investigation. Still, she had a job to do and she was pretty sure George would understand her reasoning—both wanting to protect Violet and chasing the scoop.

The inspecteur gave Charlie a wry smile. 'Now you may go. No more surprises please, Madame James. I know I cannot stop you from investigating this story, but I ask that you tread very carefully.'

'Agreed,' said Charlie, swallowing as she wondered what turn this murder story would take next.

Charlie brought Violet back to the tiny apartment in Saint-Germain, giving her tea with a generous shot of whisky before putting her to bed. 'Shhh, I'll tell George you're not well.' She smoothed her friend's hair.

'You're going to go into the office now and run this story, aren't you?' said Violet, eyes wide with distress as her head sank back into the pillow.

'I'm sorry, I have to! Aleksandr's links to Marchand make it a story, whether or not he murdered that horrible man.'

'He didn't do it!' Violet sobbed, and Charlie reflected on the many times she had heard those words or something like them since the murder.

She put a jug of water and a glass beside the vase of roses on her bedside table. 'Sleep. You're in shock.'

As Charlie gently pulled the door shut behind her, she felt heartsick that her big scoop was going to hurt her dearest friend in Paris.

Chapter 26

After giving her typed copy to George, Charlie got a taxi to Villa Trianon. She wanted to stay on Lady Ashworth's good side by visiting her after their night out, and she hoped to speak with Lord Ashworth. The housekeeper ushered Charlie upstairs, where she was surprised to find herself sitting in a pink velvet chair by the sash window in Lady Ashworth's private chambers.

It was nearly noon, and the woman was still propped up on a sea of pink pillows, with pink and lilac cashmere throw rugs layered like sponge cake on the four-poster bed. The walls featured lilac *boiserie* panelling, and a giant gilded mirror reflected the walled garden and Parc de Versailles through the window. The room smelt of spring thanks to crystal vases of roses and star jasmine scattered on every tabletop among beeswax candles and dainty perfume bottles.

Though Lady Ashworth was in her cashmere house robe, she had a dab of rouge on her cheeks, and her hair was rolled in an immaculate chignon. 'Bonjour, Just Charlie. I heard the news from Madame Rose-Thomas—she was booked for a fitting. Such a shock! I'm devastated for Aleksandr.' She shook her head sadly. 'I can't see him as a killer. He's sensitive. Caring. Folds silk like no one I've ever seen before.'

'You seem to collect broken geniuses,' said Charlie softly, thinking of Conrad.

Lady Ashworth sat up a little and pursed her lips, then she deflated. She studied Charlie with a new intensity. 'I suppose I do, Just Charlie. And I guess I'm a bit of old chipped china myself— not a genius, unfortunately.' She chuckled.

'Some might beg to differ. We'll soon be publishing the feature on you, although of course stories about Aleksandr will be prioritised for now.'

'Yes, focus on Aleksandr. Tell his story. Spread word of his innocence!'

'Unfortunately, he has no alibi and a hell of a motive.'

'So do half of my party guests, it seems.' She heaved a sigh. 'Now, about the treasure hunt. Kind of you to let this old suck get some sleep. My car made it back just as my dear husband and Conrad returned. Their team won, so we'll all have to dine at the Ritz. I insist!'

'I'm still recovering from last night!' said Charlie.

'Well, you'll need to put your party shoes back on, because you are invited to the Louvre gala tonight! Bring Miss Carthage, if she feels up to it. Milly will be covering it for *Harper's*, so it seems only fair to invite you. We must all gather to celebrate Maxime's patronage of the arts.'

Charlie glanced out to the far corner of the garden and shuddered as her mind filled with images of his slashed neck and cruel eyes.

Lady Ashworth tutted gently. 'You think it's unseemly that we're having a party to honour a man like Maxime. But it's not just about him, it's about art. Beauty! Those canvases will be bringing light to people's lives, teaching lessons, long after we've all passed on.'

Charlie swallowed but said nothing. Maybe it was her dry mouth and thumping headache, but she was finding Lady Ashworth's effervescence off-putting. She couldn't stop worrying about Aleksandr and Violet.

Lady Ashworth recognised her distress. 'Charlie, we are all upset. This has been a very difficult week. But we are in Paris, darling. Have you not learned in your weeks here that Paris doesn't sleep? She glitters and shimmers, and we dance along, trying to keep up. Look at this villa—it was a decrepit mess when I bought it. Now it needs to be filled with people, celebrated and enjoyed, otherwise I might as well be the stuffed crocodile we collected last night.'

'I see,' said Charlie as she grinned, her sour mood unable to stifle a pang of affection. 'You know, I think you would have been good friends with your former neighbour Marie Antoinette.'

Lady Ashworth laughed good-naturedly, and the tension dissipated.

'You certainly have the wardrobe,' Charlie said as she gestured to Lady Ashworth's overflowing dressing-room.

'Always room for more pretty dresses—just like champagne, or ice cream!' She beamed. 'I'll write a note to Aleksandr this afternoon, and hopefully that nice inspecteur will pass it on. What a magnificent collection! He knows how to make all women feel beautiful. It's a gift, and we must support him.'

They were interrupted by a rap at the door, and Lord Ashworth entered, carrying a silver tray. 'Oh, terribly sorry!' he spluttered. 'Nobody mentioned you had company, my dear.'

He sat the tray beside her bed. It bore a silver teapot, a Limoges teacup, a slice of toast on a small plate, a boiled egg in a silver cup, and a red rose in a bud vase. A bottle of pills was discreetly tucked beside the vase. Charlie smiled at the sweet gesture.

'I'll pour the tea and leave you ladies to your chitchat. Conrad took my Rolls out first thing and is returning all the items from our little hunt. He'll be out for most of the day, I expect.'

While he busied himself with the tea, Charlie massaged her throbbing temples and gazed out to where one gardener was mowing the lawn while another clipped the edges with shears.

A pair of black swans swam in circles on the lake, leaving ripples behind them.

She realised she would need to check on Violet and tell her about the invitation to the gala that night. Knowing Violet, she would put on her most beautiful dress and bravest face.

'I'd best be off,' said Charlie, with as warm a smile as she could muster. 'I have a taxi waiting in the driveway. Thanks very much for the gala invitation! I'll let you know if Miss Carthage will accompany me.'

'I'll walk you down, my dear,' said Lord Ashworth.

Charlie walked beside him down the staircase, taking in the portraits, the shiny marble floors and the Persian carpets. When they reached the bottom, she turned. 'Lord Ashworth, there's something I need to ask you.'

'Yes?' he said, with a kindly smile.

'I went to visit you at your city apartment a couple of days ago, early in the morning. I was hoping to surprise you and get some quotes for my feature piece on your wife. But as I was waiting, I saw you with Conrad. The two of you seemed to have an argument, and then you handed him an envelope.'

'Oh!' Lord Ashworth looked as though a bolt of lightning had struck him. 'Oh dear. Please keep your voice down, my dear.' His eyes flickered from side to side, and his hands trembled as he gestured for her to follow him out to the front portico. 'Yes, well,' he said, after clearing his throat a couple of times. 'You caught me.'

'I . . . I did?'

'The Circus Ball cost a pretty penny, you see, and Lady Ashworth . . . well, she doesn't know exactly how much. Young Conrad doesn't approve of this at all, but I have supplemented the fee with some of my own funds and asked him to pay the supplier. I don't want her to be embarrassed, you see. She has a tendency to'—his voice dropped to a whisper—'go over her budgets. By a considerable sum.'

Charlie realised one question remained unanswered. 'The only thing is, I have reason to believe that Conrad transferred some money from your envelope.'

'Oh yes, I often give the young fellow a bit of spending money.'

Charlie tried not to burst out laughing at the seriousness of his demeanour. 'Thank you for explaining all of this, Lord Ashworth.'

'That's all right, my dear. I understand why you needed to ask—it must have looked very funny indeed.'

Chapter 27

Charlie and Violet stood in front of the Louvre as the pink sky stretched out above them. 'Another soiree, another fabulous dress,' said Violet, indicating that Charlie should do a little twirl on the footpath. 'You *do* look like a Greek goddess.'

Charlie wore a floor-length gold sequined sheath, nipped in at the waist and with a slash to her mid-thigh. The dress was finished with a cape extension that flowed over her shoulders and spilled onto the cobblestones.

'Thanks to your bulging wardrobe! I hope I don't trip on this.' Charlie waved the cape with her hand, watching it ripple in the late evening sun.

The dress was cut low, revealing Charlie's ample cleavage. Putting it on had made her feel like someone else—Jean Harlow, maybe, except Charlie was wearing her own brassiere, slip, stockings and knickers.

'*You* look like a movie star,' she said as she eyed Violet's bias-cut gown in midnight blue. The straps were thick at the shoulders, extending down around the pleated bustier and tied at the small of her back, leaving the rest of her back exposed to the warm summer air. 'I wish Aleksandr could see you in that.'

'Oh, I'm sure he will soon. I'm sorry I fell to pieces this morning, but I was exhausted! I'm feeling confident that he'll be released tomorrow and that they won't be able to charge him with anything.'

Charlie nodded and gave her friend a reassuring smile. She thought of the way Aleksandr had doted on Violet at the fittings: bringing her water and champagne, stroking her hair back from her face to test diamond pendant earrings, finding her a comfortable chair to sit on whenever she felt tired. He was so sweet, so thoughtful, that Charlie *almost* believed there was no way he could kill someone. He didn't seem capable of it, but the same could be said of Conrad. And of a mousy housewife back in Sydney who had shot her husband in the temple between breastfeeding their twins; when the police arrested her, she was black and blue from the waist down.

'Aleksandr seems very fond of you,' said Charlie, serious now.

'He's lovely,' said Violet, 'but we both know the rules. Make no mistake, Charlie, the day will come when my parents call me home to London. I'm heading into the peak age for suitable marriage pairings.'

'This isn't 1838! Surely you're allowed to choose your husband?'

'I am,' Violet said with a brittle laugh, 'as long as he's rich.' She rolled her eyes, and for the first time her face fell. 'And not arrested for murder.' Her lower lip wobbled.

'Oh, Violet!' Charlie hugged her friend tight.

'Shall we go in, Charlie James, Paris Correspondent?' Violet composed herself and held out her arm to escort Charlie into the Louvre.

They were guided by a line of waiters in morning suits and top hats into the baroque Salon Carré and down to the long hall lined with Dutch Masters in gilded frames. At the far end were the small van Goghs—paintings of a different era and style— and Charlie's eye caught on the portrait of the physician and his handful of foxgloves.

A group of people stood swilling champagne as Lady Ashworth rushed over to greet them. 'Miss Carthage, what a treat! I put on my finest for you.' She winked as she kissed the young woman on both cheeks before moving on to Charlie. 'I'm sorry Aleksandr's not with us tonight, but I'm sure he'll be released soon. They made the same mistake with Milly and my Conrad.' Her brow furrowed with concern. 'Aleksandr's debut was genius. You tell him this dress fits like a glove.' She ran her hands over the bodice and swished the tassels from side to side. 'You know,' she leaned in and whispered conspiratorially, 'I used to make my own costumes from the ones all the top actresses discarded backstage. I'd piece together bodices, combine rows of sequins, unpick tutus and refashion them under my skirts. I couldn't *bear* it when the seams dug into me, so I used to carry my own wax.' She patted Violet on the hand. 'What I'm saying, dear, is that it's the pure silk linings and their perfect seams that make this ol' lady part with her pennies.'

'Miss Carthage, Mrs James, lovely to see you both here,' said Lord Ashworth as he wandered over to greet them and join his wife. He pecked Lady Ashworth quickly on the edge of her cheek, slightly awkward yet endearing.

Waiters offered silver platters of Bulgarian caviar, limed shrimp and aioli. As the guests drank gimlets and old-fashioneds, a lone cellist started to play from the mezzanine, between the towering marble sculptures of Artemis and Apollo. Violet and Charlie stood apart from the others, taking in the spectacular art and sculptures around them.

On the other side of the room stood Conrad Mackenzie, his camera around his neck. Lady Ashworth had insisted he be the exclusive photographer for the gala, working with both *Harper's* and *The Times*—she hadn't wanted the evening polluted with flashes. Charlie had negotiated half a page.

'We should have Aleksandr's next show here,' said Violet confidently.

'What, among the Greek gods and goddesses?'

'Why not? That's why we came to Paris, isn't it? An audacious dream?'

'*Oui.*' Charlie stared at the twisted torsos, carved thighs, and translucent cheeks and stomachs. The ceiling shimmered with thousands of crystals threaded onto chandeliers. *La Ville Lumière.*

The eighty guests were soon seated at the long table, washing down platters of scampi and grilled leeks with white burgundy and bottomless glasses of Krug. Lady Ashworth patted her green chignon as she laughed, and Mercedes looked impeccable in an eggshell-blue fitted bodice and tulle skirt designed by Aleksandr. Lord Ashworth and the commander looked in good cheer, chuckling and laughing with the rhythm of the conversation.

After the mains were served and devoured—duck on a bed of polenta with grapes, lamb falling off the bone, a lentil and herb salad—Charlie told Violet that she needed a moment alone to collect her thoughts.

She stood in front of Vermeer's *Girl with a Pearl Earring*, examining the painting up close, her head tilted to one side. The young maid peered from the canvas, cautious and curious. Here was a girl on the cusp of adulthood. What would she choose— or whom?

Footfalls sounded near her, in the shadows at the corner of the room. Angry muttering. Out of the corner of her eye, she spotted

Lord Ashworth run up the stairs to the mezzanine, followed by Conrad.

She set her glass on a ledge then tiptoed up the stairs, holding her dress so she wouldn't trip. She followed the sparring voices as she edged past Apollo and pressed her cheek to Artemis, taking comfort in the chill of the marble but wishing she could hear what the men were saying in their low furious voices.

There was the sound of a scuffle. Tentatively stepping around Artemis's flank, Charlie saw Lord Ashworth on the ground, wheezing and panicking as he gulped for air. One eye was swollen shut.

Conrad had limped away and was standing at the edge of the mezzanine that overlooked the foyer gallery. He seemed to be composing himself. A sea of marble tiles stretched below him.

Lord Ashworth scrambled to his feet and approached Conrad, who lunged towards him.

'Stop!' Charlie rushed over to try to pull them apart.

'Be careful,' warned Conrad. 'He's dangerous.' He gently nudged her out of the way.

'That's rich,' Lord Ashworth shouted, 'coming from a murderer!'

Conrad struck out with a fist, but Lord Ashworth stepped back, raising his hands to protect himself. Darting forward, Conrad wrapped an arm around the older man's neck and dragged him towards the edge of the mezzanine.

'Please, stop!' yelled Charlie. Her words echoed across the floor, and she hoped the guests downstairs would hear her. 'Help!' she yelled, louder now, but the cellist had started to play again over the chatter.

The men were in a frenzy of punches when they reached the edge. Lord Ashworth scrambled out of Conrad's grip, the young man tilting backwards. He lost his balance . . .

'No!'

Charlie's cry was echoed by a guttural scream from below.

She and Lord Ashworth looked at each other, then peered over the edge of the mezzanine. Charlie gagged and covered her mouth.

Below them, Milly Goldsmith was leaning over Conrad's crumpled body and screaming.

Chapter 28

Inspecteur Bernard arrived ten minutes later with half a dozen officers, who attended to the doors of the Louvre. He looked as though he'd been called away from dinner, as he was wearing a smart blue linen shirt under his trench coat and a yellow silk scarf tossed around his neck with a flourish. Charlie imagined him at a tiny bistro, sipping pinot noir and enjoying slivers of duck terrine, slices of pear and roulade. He was man who was particular about his food.

The air in the Salon Carré was sticky with relief and mortification: relief that the sorry saga of Marchand's murder had been resolved; mortification at another dead body connected to *le tout-Paris*. Everyone, including the police officers, seemed to accept Lord Ashworth's statement that Conrad had confessed to killing

Marchand. All the guests were gathered around the dining table in pairs and small groups, hugging and consoling each other as they spoke in hushed tones, waiting to be told what to do. Men removed their tuxedo jackets and loosened their bow ties, while women pressed damp damask serviettes to their foreheads.

Glasses and crockery had been knocked over around the table, leaving stains in the gold damask cloth that looked like blood, and broken glass and porcelain that glittered around spills. Charlie realised that the guests had stood up in a rush to run to Conrad's assistance, although their swift action hadn't made any difference. The sharp twist of his neck, and the rivulets of blood from his mouth and nose, left no doubt that he was dead. All of Milly's pleading was never going to revive him.

Charlie looked across to where the young woman still lay with her head on Conrad's chest, quietly sobbing. She had insisted on staying right beside her lover, kissing him on his clammy forehead, his hands, his blue lips. Charlie doubted that she knew what had taken place on the mezzanine.

Lord Ashworth had explained the circumstances of Conrad's accidental fall to the other guests, and they had closed ranks around him and his wife, enveloping them with sympathetic hugs and consoling pats while someone raised the police.

Mon dieu! Mauvais. Evil.

Violet had draped a cashmere shawl around Charlie's shoulders and was waving away people who wandered over, demanding to know her version of events. She sat quietly, not knowing what to make of it. Conrad Mackenzie had been many things, but evil? She wasn't convinced.

Lady Ashworth sat weeping and trembling, comforted by friends. She looked bereft. Others fussed over her husband's injuries and pressed a silk scarf full of ice to his rapidly swelling face. Lord Ashworth was graciously accepting the attention while repeating his story to shocked faces. 'He just came at me. I was trying to hold him off, but he wouldn't stop.'

Self-defence or an accident? Or was there another explanation? Charlie thought of the two men arguing in an alley. The small white envelope. She was having trouble wrapping her head around the facts.

The gold picture frames and glittering chandeliers made Charlie feel nauseous. Violet was rubbing her back, but she barely felt it. She was numb.

Flanked by officers, Inspecteur Bernard marched to the centre of the Salon Carré and surveyed the room, his face inscrutable. He ignored the guests for the moment, walking straight across to Milly and Conrad. All the time he was barking instructions to his men. Two officers gently prised Milly from the corpse of her lover, wrapping her in an overcoat and placing her on a chair beside a burly officer. A second officer took another seat beside her, introduced himself and brought out a notepad for an interview.

Charlie tried to look up at the mezzanine from where she was sitting, but she realised that Lord Ashworth and Conrad would have been impossible to see from the dining area. The space had been designed to hide strange angles, to reflect light, so Milly could not have seen what unfolded above.

It was common in the newsroom to mock police and heckle when they didn't give up sensitive information. A reporter was always racing to break a story, and Charlie was no exception, but she couldn't help admiring the work of Inspecteur Bernard and his team. They worked quietly and efficiently, treating the corpse and witnesses with respect.

Charlie watched the inspecteur move among his team in his neat three-piece suit, taking notes and making small suggestions. His face was strained, sweat beading at his brow. He examined the body from every possible angle and took extensive notes. He spoke with one of the junior officers before pointing to Conrad's neck; the young man nervously chewed his moustache then squatted to gently remove the Leica camera and its strap. The camera was bagged by another gloved officer and whisked away.

Charlie looked across at Milly and remembered the beautiful American on the night of Marchand's murder, sitting in a police car. That night there had been a stillness about her—shock, Charlie supposed. But tonight Milly wasn't holding back, her body convulsing as she wept.

Charlie thought of the stolen looks she'd witnessed between Conrad and Milly, two young people besotted with each other and trying to make a new life together in Paris.

Why would Conrad have attacked Lord Ashworth at the gala? He must have had many other opportunities, including their meeting in the alley. She again thought of the white envelope changing hands—what had it been for?

As Inspecteur Bernard stood to stretch his legs, his gaze alighted on Charlie. She was still huddled beside Violet, and his brow furrowed with concern as he quickly strode over. 'Madame James, are you hurt?'

'I saw it happen,' she told him, just managing to keep her voice steady.

'You witnessed, *oui*?' His voice was gentle but firm. 'Are you willing to make a brief statement now?'

Charlie nodded.

The inspecteur turned to a clean page in his notebook, and took a seat beside her, leaning towards her so she would not have to strain her voice over the cries and tears of upset guests behind them. 'I understand this is difficult. But if you could give me a clear idea of what took place up there . . .' He pointed to the mezzanine. 'We can go into further detail tomorrow morning at the station in a formal interview after you have had a good sleep.'

'Okay. When I arrived upstairs Conrad and Lord Ashworth were already arguing. Lord Ashworth was nursing a bruise on his face—clearly caused by Conrad.'

'What were they arguing about?'

'Unclear,' she replied thoughtfully. 'Lord Ashworth called Conrad a murderer, and Conrad just . . . snapped.' She thought of her father's comments about reasonable people losing control when they were trapped. Or helpless. What had Lord Ashworth said to Conrad?

'And you think he was referring to Marchand?' queried Inspecteur Bernard as he took everything down in his notebook.

'Possibly. But also Conrad has—had'—she swallowed sadly as she corrected herself—'that manslaughter conviction. Perhaps he meant that.'

'*Homicide involontaire* is not the same as murder.'

'I know that. But Lord Ashworth . . . he has a touch of the school bully about him, doesn't he?' She imagined him in his posh English boarding school tormenting younger students.

'So you think Lord Ashworth was provoking Conrad Mackenzie. Can you think why?'

Charlie remembered the envelope of money exchanged outside Ashworth's Paris apartment. The money sent to Mary Mackenzie. 'Maybe Conrad was bribing Lord Ashworth.' She briefly described what she'd seen in the avenue, and her conversation with Mary and the money trail, deliberately omitting her visit to Western Union posing as Mackenzie's wife. Inspecteur Bernard would most certainly not approve of this investigation method.

'Blackmail! How interesting.' He scratched his chin. 'Now, I want you to think carefully: did Conrad Mackenzie fall—or was he pushed?' He watched Charlie closely.

'Conrad fell . . . I think. They were tussling. Fighting . . . I was calling for help.' She rubbed her eyes and tried to suppress a yawn.

'Very well. I appreciate this. Let's continue in a formal interview tomorrow. I have a piece of news for you.' He wrote something on a fresh page of his notebook and tore it out, handing it to Charlie. On it was neatly written just one word: *digoxin*.

'What's that?' asked Charlie, tired and confused.

'This drug came back in Marchand's blood tests. He was taking medication for his heart.'

'But you said Madame Marchand had told you he was fit and did not take medicine, didn't you?'

'Either she lied. Or Marchand lied to his wife. It would not have been the first time Marchand had deceived his wife.'

Charlie looked at the word in front of her, and a strange electricity flooded her fingers and toes. She had a theory but it was too early to share with the inspecteur—he would only shut it down. Instead, she said, 'I'll be at your office at 10 a.m., Inspecteur Bernard. Now, if you don't mind, before I go home I'd like to talk to Milly . . . to console her. Such an awful shock.'

They both glanced over to where Milly sat on a dining chair like a limp rag. Violet and Aleksandr were beside her, each holding one hand.

'Go!' he ushered Charlie in Milly's direction and walked over to where some uniformed officers were preparing to lift the corpse onto a gurney.

Charlie tried to block the unpleasant scene unfolding behind her by kneeling in front of Milly. Violet shot Charlie a consoling glance before indicating with her eyes to Aleksandr that they should give the women some privacy.

Violet let go of Milly's hand, and Charlie took it as she sat on the warm spot Violet had just vacated.

Charlie squeezed Milly's hand. 'I know Conrad cared for you. Deeply. Whenever I spoke with him, his first concern was for your reputation. Your privacy.'

Milly nodded and wiped her eyes with the back of her hand. 'Thank you. Whenever we had dinner together at my place—or he stayed—he always spoke highly of you too.'

'He was a good person. And very talented.'

Milly sobbed and placed both hands on her belly, hunched over.

Charlie clocked it and realised the truth. She said gently, 'Did Conrad know you were pregnant?'

'Not yet. I was going to tell him when we got home tonight.'

Charlie took a deep breath, trying to proceed delicately. 'Is that why you met Marchand in the garden?'

Milly nodded. 'I started seeing Conrad right after Marchand . . .'

'And you weren't sure of dates?' whispered Charlie softly. The clandestine meeting in the garden with Marchand at Villa Trianon now made sense. It also gave Conrad another motive for murder.

Charlie shivered, following her instinct.

'Conrad—I wanted him to be the father. Is that terrible of me?' She looked at Charlie with pleading eyes. 'He would have been a great father. Marchand . . .' She shivered with repulsion. 'But Conrad was always insecure about being with me. Said he didn't have enough to support me—he's Southern. Traditional. All good manners and the idea that he couldn't support his . . . well . . .' She started to cry again and her face crumpled. 'He couldn't accept that I had plenty for the three of us.'

'So Conrad stayed at your place often?'

'Always.' Some police officers started to talk loudly nearby and indicated that Milly should join them for questioning. 'I have to go,' said Milly as she stood up. 'Not that anything I tell them is of any use now.'

Charlie had to act quickly. 'Milly, I want to check Conrad's stuff. See if there was anything in his work that would help . . .'

Milly shook her head. 'No.'

'Milly!' Charlie pleaded. 'They are accusing Conrad of Marchand's murder. Saying he attacked Lord Ashworth too. They'll close this case tonight if you don't help me. Please, give me your keys and I'll retrieve his things. Spare his dignity before the police get to them.'

Milly bit her lip, 'I don't know. There're just some clothes . . .'

Charlie was willing to take her chances. 'Please!'

Milly turned towards the officers, but she slipped her keys into Charlie's hand. 'For Conrad. For our child,' Milly said as she walked towards the police.

Chapter 29

Charlie jumped out of her taxi as it pulled up at the Cité Metro Police Station. A bored-looking officer doing night duty on the reception desk greeted her with sleepy hooded eyes and a grunted, '*Oui?*'

'I'd like to see Inspecteur Bernard.'

The officer raised his eyebrows. 'Do you have an appointment?'

She sighed. It was four in the morning. Who made pre-dawn appointments? She knew the inspecteur would still be here— he was diligent and hardworking, and he would not sleep after tonight's tragedy. He now had two deaths to investigate, and he would be trying to join the dots. Except he didn't have all the information—not yet.

'*C'est urgent.* Please tell him Charlie James from *The Times* is here and needs to see him.'

The officer took in her unbrushed hair and skew-whiff hat. 'Take a seat. I'll call the inspecteur.' He held up a finger like a schoolteacher before he picked up the receiver and dialled a number.

Moments later, Inspecteur Bernard came downstairs and did a double take when he saw she was still in her gown. 'You haven't been home?' He looked concerned.

'Conrad hid this in Milly's apartment.' Charlie tapped the front of the envelope, then pulled out some photos and handed them over.

He studied them for some time, turning them at different angles and holding them up to the light. He whistled slowly. '*Merci.* I assume no one else has seen these?'

Charlie shook her head.

'This evidence is still circumstantial,' he said. 'We need a confession.'

'I know,' she said. 'I have a plan. Will you work with me?'

Chapter 30

Later that morning, Charlie took a deep breath before she pressed the brass doorbell at Villa Trianon. She had dashed home to change into slacks and ballet flats, and to get some copy to George, then hopped in a taxi. It was hard to believe that less than a fortnight had passed since she'd stood at this grand entrance, nervous about her interview with Lady Eleanor Ashworth.

As Charlie waited for someone to answer the door, she peered into the huge windows. There was no sign of green tresses or any movement. Over her shoulder, the magnificent garden was bathed in morning light. This splendour and magic had been stained by Marchand's murder. It was time to put things right.

She tried the doorbell again, then thumped the wood with her fist. As a few more minutes passed, she stepped off the grand terrace and onto the gravel driveway. Tiny white stones glistened like jewels in the sunlight.

Eyeing the stone façade, she thought how the villa carried the past proudly, but was stronger and prouder with every renovation. She thought about Lady Ashworth, the actress turned New York society darling turned grande dame of Versailles. Love, power, betrayal, war: Lady Ashworth had seen them all, and survived with wit and aplomb. Her husband always beside her, soothing cajoling . . . making the right connections.

Finally, the front door was thrown open and Lord Ashworth stared at Charlie James with considerable confusion. His face looked pale and dark rings sat deep under his eyes. He was clearly unwell and exhausted.

'*Bonjour . . .*' he said, clearly flummoxed.

'*Bonjour.* We have an appointment. I made it last week with your secretary, remember?'

His expression left no doubt that he had forgotten all about it. And who could blame him after the last fortnight's turn of events. The recent deaths were clearly taking a physical toll on the older man. It was likely he was still in shock after Conrad's accidental death, but this was all the more reason to get a doorstop interview as soon as possible. No other press would be getting into Villa Trianon today.

'Very well, you've come all this way. We did have an appointment,' he said grudgingly. 'I can answer a few questions for you if you make it brief.'

'Of course,' replied Charlie graciously as she was ushered down the hallway into the bright sitting room, where a tea set was laid out.

Lord Ashworth indicated she should take a seat, and he sat opposite her.

'I'm so sorry for your loss,' she began. 'Such a terrible accident.'

'Yes. Look, I understand you've been doing this little piece on my wife. And I'm happy to help where I can. But she's very distressed.' He took a sip of his tea and coughed, thumping his chest before he continued. 'Too much tea this morning . . . my good lady arranged for me to wake with a pot.'

'The English salve.'

'Exactly.' Another sip; more coughs. 'Sorry, I didn't sleep well. I know you're with *The Times*, and I agreed with London to give the exclusive. . . but I really think—'

'Understood.' Charlie spoke in a soothing voice and broke eye contact as she pretended to study a gold lamp base studded with sapphires and a matching silk cover. 'Lady Ashworth told me that when the two of you bought Villa Trianon, it was decrepit. No one had lived here for a century, so you had to replace every window, every architrave, all the parquetry. You had marble shipped from northern India for the bathrooms.'

'Yes. Lady Ashworth draws a bath every day and spends an hour in there with Bach on the gramophone.'

'Sounds wonderful.'

'You know my wife!' he said with a weak smile.

She turned and looked out into the garden where the avenue of ancient oaks disappeared into a black void. She knew that beyond it lay the perimeter wall and the dark lake. That far corner where Marchand's body had been discovered was so close to where she had sat trying to escape the crowds. Alone with the commander.

She shivered. At least she had *thought* they were alone. But Conrad had captured the moment . . . just as he had so many others.

He captures the truth.

'Lord Ashworth, I wonder if you'd care to look at these photographs?' She pulled the envelope from her satchel, took out the photos and sat them on her lap.

Lord Ashworth swallowed. 'Doesn't sound much like a question to me!' His pompous, school bully voice had crept in as his temper shortened.

Charlie held up an image of Lord Ashworth pinching powder into a champagne coupe. In the next photo he was passing the glass to Marchand.

'Circumstantial evidence. You've got nothing.' Lord Ashworth jutted his chin out, arrogant to the end.

'Would you mind stating for the record what was in your snuff box? You are not a smoker?'

'No. I will not be drawn into ludicrous accusations. Or speculation. Enough damage has been done.'

Charlie remembered the tender way Lord Ashworth had consoled his wife the night of Marchand's death, their connection caught in sharp focus in Mackenzie's photos.

Perhaps she was wrong. Perhaps there was another explanation.

She needed to engage Lord Ashworth. To use every reporter's trick to get him to talk . . . and keep talking.

'Why kill Marchand? And Mackenzie?' she asked. Charlie waited, biting her bottom lip as she counted to ten. When there was no response, she started to count over. When she got to six, her subject started to speak.

'You must be confused. I understand how this looks.' He was trying to be conciliatory.

'What about this?' Charlie pulled out a photograph of Lord Ashworth helping Marchand to the far corner of the garden.

'So? He'd had a little too much champagne. I was helping him regroup. It happens at large parties such as ours.' His tone was patronising. He looked up and down at Charlie's neat grey suit with obvious scorn.

Charlie was unperturbed. Instead she revealed the next photo, of Lord Ashworth placing Marchand on the ground. The last one with a hand over his mouth, checking for his last breath.

'Get out! You insult me. You insult my wife. This interview is terminated. You can tell George if he so much as thinks about printing any of this faff I'll tie him up in legal proceedings so expensive his future grandchildren can kiss goodbye to Westminster.'

Charlie started to protest, but Lord Ashworth was having none of it. He tossed his cup down on the silver tray and marched out the front door into the garden, slamming it behind him.

After a few minutes, not wanting to wait for the butler to appear and evict her, Charlie tiptoed down the hallway and let herself out the front door. Lord Ashworth was striding to the far corner of the garden, swinging his arms with fury. A warm breeze lifted her hair and anxiety gnawed at her stomach.

Inspecteur Bernard appeared from the side of the house, trench coat neatly knotted at his waist. The agreement had been that he would arrive once the interview had begun. Well, it had begun—and ended—in a precious few minutes.

'I lost him,' apologised Charlie.

She eyed Lord Ashworth's disappearing back. He had no idea the police were here. He had to be stopped before he destroyed any evidence.

She checked. 'Have you got your warrant?'

'But of course,' replied the inspecteur.

'And I have permission to observe?'

'*Oui.* Observe only. Granted by the commissioner, in exchange for the photos. But not once we take them into the station for formal statements.'

'I have permission to quote you as a source?'

'My name, *non!* Metro police source only.'

Charlie thought about the photos she had found in an envelope tucked under Conrad's dirty sports sweater in a cupboard at Milly's apartment. About the details she'd missed. She wanted to see it for herself, to make it right. So she marched into the garden beside the police.

There was no sign of Lord Ashworth in the far corner of the garden. Charlie and the inspecteur took a moment to gather their breath.

'You shouldn't be here,' boomed the deep voice, startling them. 'Not now. Lady Ashworth is inside sleeping. She's crushed about Mackenzie. We all are. It was a terrible misunderstanding. I'm devastated he fell.'

Lord Ashworth eyed Inspecteur Bernard warily. If he was surprised to see the police beside Charlie, he did not let on. 'I already told you everything last night at the Louvre. Can't whatever you need wait?'

'*Non!* Some photos have come to my attention.'

Lord Ashworth rolled his eyes. 'How ridiculous. Does *she* have something to do with this? He pointed scornfully at Charlie, and it occurred to her that the British aristocrat might not remember her name, even though they'd now met a handful of times.

Lord Ashworth stood in his burgundy smoking jacket in the garden. His eye had closed over now, the skin darkened and bruised. He was clearly upset about the metro policeman and Charlie walking about his garden first thing in the morning. 'There's nothing for either of you here. Call my secretary and make an appointment, Inspecteur. I'll be sure to fit you in. Not you, though.' He glared at Charlie.

Charlie returned Lord Ashworth's look, heart pounding. They were in the far corner of the garden at Villa Trianon, the dark lip of the lake just visible through an arbour. Maxime Marchand had been murdered just a few steps from here.

She pictured Conrad's crumpled body lying on the marble floor of the Louvre. Milly hunched over him, weeping and wheezing. Pumping at his chest and shaking his shoulders in a furious effort to revive her lover.

Charlie was sorry Conrad was dead. Paris had taught her to believe in second chances, and he had deserved better.

Three black swans huddled together, necks craned low under their wings to shelter from rising wind. As the breeze whipped against her cheeks the leaves shimmered like ghostly bats.

Lord Ashworth patted his jacket and cocked his head to one side, then the other as though he were trying to get a crick out of his neck. His face was composed. Thoughtful. 'The gardeners will be here tomorrow. Perhaps if there's something you want to see you can come back then, Inspecteur. It's been a night! It will take Lady Ashworth some time to get over this. First Marchand, now Mackenzie's accident.'

'Explain these to me, please,' the inspecteur said as he held out Mackenzie's photos.

'Conrad Mackenzie was a criminal. You know that—you've investigated him. He was blackmailing me.'

'Blackmail?' That explained the white envelope of cash exchanged in the street. The money sent to keep Mary Mackenzie in a fancy home. Honourable acts by nefarious means.

'Yes. Mackenzie was a hustler. Milly is better off without him, trust me. He was extorting money from me. Outrageous amounts.'

'To marry Milly, to make a home for their baby,' Charlie retorted. Her heart ached for Conrad, for Milly.

The inspecteur made eye contact with Charlie, indicating she should keep Lord Ashworth talking.

Charlie spoke: 'You borrowed huge sums from Marchand. Amounts you could never repay. You were running out of money and wanted more but Marchand refused you.

'However, Marchand did not want anyone to know that you were defaulting on your loan either—so he destroyed the evidence; that way his precious reputation was not destroyed. He was in the business of making money—taking advantage of impoverished factory workers. He would not have taken kindly to one of his own defaulting on a loan.' She thought of Jacob Marchand telling her about documents burned in a bin. She was making leaps—but hoping the pieces fell together.

She and the inspecteur had gone over and over this theory last night, testing for holes until he had finally applied for—and received—a warrant. Villa Trianon was registered in Lady Ashworth's name, and though she was by no means implicated, neither was she protected by diplomatic immunity. She was the decoy they needed.

Charlie continued to speak. 'Your diplomatic immunity meant that you could never be prosecuted for defaulting on a loan. Conrad somehow got wind of it and blackmailed you—threatened to tell Lady Ashworth the truth.'

Lord Ashworth's face was puce.

'Conrad wanted to use the money for good. To support his grandmother. To support his lover—and soon-to-be-wife,' she continued.

Charlie didn't judge Conrad. He'd had a rocky start to adulthood. Who could blame him for twisting the rules to find a way to get ahead, make a clean start. Had he known Milly was pregnant? Is that what he'd overheard when he'd followed Milly and Marchand into the far corner of the garden? Is that why he'd been chasing extra money freelancing, blackmailing . . . putting a nest egg together? Charlie felt a wave of sorrow for Conrad's misplaced good intentions. For the unborn child who would now grow up fatherless. For the woman who'd lost the man she'd loved. A good man.

'Tell us,' Charlie demanded. Her patience was wearing thin.

'Why did you borrow money from Marchand?' asked the inspecteur.

Lord Ashworth sighed. 'We would have lost all this . . .' He raised his arm and gestured to where the fairy lights flickered on the terrace. Just beyond, the stone columns of Villa Trianon soared out of the darkness, bold and proud like its mistress.

A swan lifted its head and hissed.

'Marchand . . . he wouldn't extend my credit. Nor would he release a pool of investments funds—my money—to me that were due to be realised in three months. Said he was keeping it to cover my loan. What difference would some extra francs make?' The Englishman shrugged, hapless. 'It was . . . different rules once Marchand died. We had a little money paid out last week. A gentleman's agreement with Jacob. Ask him!'

'We have,' replied the inspecteur.

Charlie looked at Lord Ashworth's drooping shoulders, his wide eyes. For a moment she felt sorry for the aristocrat. His privilege had made him blind. He'd been raised to believe he was exceptional. That it was no big deal to break a financial contract with a bank, or banker.

He had made poor decisions. Channelled money and energy into poor investments. Kept up the punting habits he'd developed in the Eton dormitories. First, silly schoolboy wagers. Next, horses. Then, the stock market. British inheritance taxes and death duties had brought Lord Ashworth to his knees. Cleaned out almost all the remaining capital his fastidious father bequeathed him.

To top it all off, the king had abdicated—Lord Ashworth had backed the wrong horse. But he'd had to grin and bear it—with the added ignominy of still treating the Duke and Duchess as special guests. He was a laughing stock in the House of Lords. Forced to leave his country with his tail between his legs, and given a token position in the British Embassy to keep him out of the way.

In Paris, Lord Ashworth had the façade of respect. He'd lost his standing with the British court, but with money and the right social partner, had gained membership to *le tout-Paris*. But this membership was expensive to maintain. Lord Ashworth had been constantly trying to keep up the masquerade of bottomless inherited wealth, despite the fact that most of his remaining capital had been squandered, or seemingly lost by Marchand. His mask had slipped.

Lord Ashworth took a step towards the inspecteur. He pulled a small pistol from his robe pocket. The pearl handle glinted in the sun.

Charlie's heart froze. Her lungs. Her liver.

The inspecteur had prepared her for danger and instructed Charlie to keep calm. Police were just steps away.

'Lord Ashworth, put the gun away. Come with me quietly to the station . . . we have uniformed police steps from here.'

'The money in Marchand's fund was mine.' Lord Ashworth lowered the gun, which hung loosely from his hand.

The inspecteur shot Charlie a warning look to keep quiet and shook his head.

The rules don't apply.

Just one more punt.

The sun was nudging its way higher into the sky, and the stonework of the villa reflected a faint golden glow. She studied the huge sash windows of Villa Trianon, and imagined the bunches of heavy silk curtains sashed inside, the thick woollen carpet, silk wallpaper, Clodion sculptures.

Less than a fortnight ago, these lawns had been dotted with circus tents, cocktail bars and acrobats juggling their way through the crowds. With knives.

All this would cease if Lord Ashworth had no money. She imagined Lady Ashworth would have invested every cent she'd earned over the years in Villa Trianon.

'Why did you pay Conrad extra cash?' asked Charlie.

'Pardon?' Lord Ashworth looked confused.

'I saw you with him in the alley behind the Luxembourg Gardens. You gave him an envelope. Presumably francs. Surely you could have slipped it to him at work?'

Lord Ashworth threw his head back and laughed. 'You obviously don't know my wife well enough yet.'

Charlie studied the drooping figure of Lord Ashworth, his shadow looming large against the wall. His face was pale and jowly—soured by rejection and worse: irrelevance.

'I didn't intend to kill him.'

'Who? Mackenzie or Marchand?' Charlie glanced at the menacing shadow and tried to get him talking again.

'Marchand, of course.' Lord Ashworth looked indignant.

Chapter 31

'Inspecteur Bernard?' The anxious shout from a policeman was close.

Lord Ashworth tightened his grip on the gun and lifted the weapon to his own neck. The muzzle sank into his jowls.

'Put the gun down, please,' urged the inspecteur. 'We just need to explain—'

Lord Ashworth's face fell and he looked like a hollow ghost in the moonlight. 'Explain what? Everyone will know I lost the Ashworth fortune. Everyone.' He gave a hopeless shrug. 'I misjudged and lost everything . . . Marchand, I . . . lost my temper. He wouldn't listen. Wouldn't agree to give me my money back.'

Footsteps. A twig cracked. Someone was close.

Lord Ashworth tilted his head, like a dog sniffing the wind. 'Stay back,' he warned as he pressed the gun deeper into his neck.

A policeman appeared behind Lord Ashworth, creeping towards them. He pressed his index finger to his lips as he crept along the shadows to the lake's edge.

Charlie made every effort not to break eye contact with Lord Ashworth as the uniformed man crept closer. She needed to connect.

'Please, put the gun down, Lord Ashworth.'

'It's over,' the inspecteur said firmly, but sadly.

Lord Ashworth gave a wry chuckle and nodded. He looked contrite. 'Ellie . . . she doesn't know. It has nothing to do with her.' He looked forlorn, as though the magnitude of his deeds was just starting to sink in. 'She's a remarkable woman.' He gulped down tears, and Charlie thought of all the tender exchanges she'd witnessed between these two. Theirs was an unorthodox pairing, but it was true enough.

Love showed itself in infinite ways. So did evil. Opposite sides of the same coin.

'It was all my fault. Ellie had no idea . . . The investment fund. The gambling. Conrad . . .' At the mention of that name, his voice quivered and broke. 'I need your word, Inspecteur. Mrs James. That Ellie will be left out of this.'

'You have it,' said the inspecteur. 'Now, put down the pistol.' His voice boomed across the trees.

The two men stared at each other, before Lord Ashworth closed his eyes and said softly, 'For what it's worth . . . I'm sorry.'

The inspecteur tried coaxing. 'Why don't you come with us now? Tell Lady Ashworth yourself. She'll be here any minute.'

Shaking, Charlie's eyes pleaded with the inspecteur, and he answered with the faintest nod.

'Now!' screamed Charlie as she ripped her brooch from her blazer and stabbed a shocked Lord Ashworth in the arm with the pin. The inspecteur lunged forward to grab the gun.

Lord Ashworth resisted and the inspecteur's tackle threw both men to the ground. A second uniformed policeman nudged Charlie out of the way and ran to help the inspecteur.

All three bodies thrashed about in the weeds and mud.

She caught a glint of light: the pistol. A hand reached for it.

Charlie dived onto Lord Ashworth's free arm to stop him from picking up the gun and hurting himself, or one of the officers. She received a swift punch to her head.

Darkness . . .

More hands, this time around her throbbing shoulder. She was being wrenched from the mud. Fingers pressed firmly into her temple to stem the bleeding from a cut on her forehead.

As they reached the edge of the lake she heard instructions: 'Careful. Take him straight to *l'ambulance*.'

Charlie looked up and through her blurry vision saw uniforms spanning the edge of the lake. Police were everywhere she looked.

The sun sat above the treetops, throwing a soft golden light across the garden.

Then he came into focus.

'*Merci*,' said a strained and tired Inspecteur Bernard as he squeezed her shoulder. He wiped a slick of wet hair from her mouth and started to speak. 'You—' He paused, then said nothing. Instead he indicated with a flick of his wrist that the doctor should attend to her at once.

Charlie was surrounded by policemen and ushered away from the corner. 'But—' She squirmed and tried to see what was going on, but the uniforms had a firm grip and she was placed on a stretcher and lifted into an ambulance.

Where was Lord Ashworth? She could see him at the edge of the lake on his back, motionless and surrounded by uniforms. Couldn't hear him.

More hands pressed at her temple. Her breathing was checked, as was her heartbeat. Light was shined into her eyes with a tiny torch by a medic. Charlie tugged her head sideways, craning her neck.

Lord Ashworth's motionless body still lay on the grass beside the lake.

But she'd stopped Lord Ashworth from shooting himself. Held his arm and knocked away the gun.

Charlie threw off her blanket and tried to sit up, but strong hands held her by the shoulders.

'What's happening?' she shouted at the policeman who restrained her. Her head was dizzy . . . it was hard to keep her eyes open. She needed to get back to the edge of the lake. Charlie tried to climb off her stretcher but the uniform stopped her.

Charlie's question was ignored. 'Let's get you to the hospital. Here, drink this . . .' Someone lifted a glass to her lips. Parched, she took a sip and felt her throat burn: vodka.

A black swan opened its wings and hissed at the trespassers.

Nobody took any notice as police gathered around Lord Ashworth's body. Fingers were pressed to a neck. A deep voice said, 'He's gone.'

The swan flapped its wings then screeched into the brightening air.

'What's happening? Why isn't he moving?' Charlie tried to shrug off the blanket around her shoulders.

'Hush.' A clammy hand wiped her forehead. Tried to reassure her as her eyes filled with swimming whitebait. Her head buzzed. As the vodka hit her system and she could no longer hold her eyes open, the last thing she heard was, 'Inspecteur Bernard, there's no pulse.'

Chapter 32

Light concussion and some stitches to the temple, the doctors confirmed when Charlie awoke in a private hospital room wearing a scratchy gown.

As she turned her head, the boulevards of Paris spun in the open window, dotted with plane trees, dog-walking pedestrians, and ice-cream vendors with striped umbrellas. The vibrant colours made her a little dizzy. Her forehead started to throb.

The summer sun tracked high in the sky, making the grey-tiled rooftops shimmer. Paris stretched out as far as she could see. The amber Seine looped through the middle of the city, its changing currents pouring energy into the city and emptying it of its garbage and secrets.

Violet pranced through the doorway in heels, flicking her high ponytail. She was dressed in a cream suit and pillbox hat, and a camel handbag hung from her wrist. In her hands was a box of red roses that matched her red lipstick. 'Bravo, Charlie James. George sends his best wishes, but we aren't allowed to visit. I'm just the delivery girl.' She kissed the top of Charlie's head, then winked as she put the roses on a side table.

Charlie James, Paris Correspondent xxx, said the note atop the flowers.

Bless Violet. There was no way George had added the kisses. But Charlie took this as a sign she was staying with *The Times*.

Violet's face crumpled as she took in Charlie on the bed. 'You did a brave thing. I'm not sure George would let you go home now, even if you wanted to!'

'Lord Ashworth—what?' Charlie mumbled.

'Shh.' Violet brushed a strand of hair from Charlie's face. '*Crise cardiaque*. He didn't make it. I'm sorry.'

'*Mademoiselle!*' A frowning nurse in a white uniform put her head around the door. '*Laissez!*'

'I'm going, I'm going.' Violet held up her hands in surrender. 'Just delivering the flowers . . .' She turned to Charlie. 'I'll pick you up tomorrow. This lovely nurse said I could take you home in the afternoon.'

'Thanks, Violet, the roses are beautiful,' croaked Charlie, grateful for the sweetness filling her hospital room.

'You'll be back at work soon enough. The pushy men in the office are trying to land your desk, but George won't hear of it. That Paris news desk is now well and truly yours. George is covering the news for you.'

'What about his wife?'

'Recovered and back cooking. George and Daphne are having us for dinner as soon as you are up to it. Beef Wellington, I believe.' She shrugged apologetically. 'Best of British food, I'm afraid.'

'And you?' asked Charlie. 'Will you be back in the office or are you leaving to run a couture empire with Aleksandr?'

Violet blushed. 'I'll be in *The Times* office with you. But we are working on another show . . . something spectacular!'

'I've no doubt,' said Charlie, who was relieved she and Violet were going to continue working together.

Violet beamed at the nurse, who rolled her eyes and said, '*Out!*'

'Going! *Au revoir.*' Violet blew a kiss towards Charlie and followed the nurse out the door.

Her head sinking back into the pillow, Charlie ruminated on the news that Lord Rupert Ashworth was dead. Cardiac arrest: a humdrum death for a murderer. Charlie's own heart ached for Lady Ashworth.

What a strange start to Charlie's life in Paris.

Paris. She sighed as she took the summer pollen deep into her lungs. *La Ville Lumière.* An enchanting city of light but also shadows. What had started as a girlish crush on the city had spiralled into something more dangerous. Paris welcomed suitors and encouraged them to dive into the couture houses, the bistros, the parties. The city dazzled like a woman who knew she was beautiful and did as she pleased. Charlie was grateful for this energy—each sip of champagne had washed away the hurt and guilt of home. But Paris stood still for no one. She was a spectacular seductress.

Charlie closed her eyes to stop the spinning.

Later that day, Inspecteur Benoît Bernard paid a visit to Charlie's hospital room. She supposed a senior policeman could not be shooed out by a nurse. He was dressed in his usual navy three-piece suit with a green cravat. His trench coat was folded neatly over one arm, and he set a newspaper and his felt hat on the side table beside the roses. '*Bonjour*. The nurse says you are leaving tomorrow.'

'A relief! I'm fine,' Charlie said lightly as she waved her hand. She must look a fright—pale and messy in a hospital gown.

'Your quick thinking saved my life. Also, the other officer's.'

'My mother's brooch saved the day.' They both looked at the small diamond brooch placed thoughtfully on her bedside table when the nurses removed her clothes.

He shot Charlie a grateful look then glanced at his shiny shoes; if she wasn't mistaken, his cheeks were slightly pink. He looked back up, studying her face with solemn eyes. 'Lord Ashworth's body is being repatriated back to England. There is some question about whether it will go into the Ashworth family crypt. But Lady Ashworth insisted he should not stay in Paris.'

'Lady Ashworth—how is she?' Charlie asked in a croaky voice.

'Indomitable! But underneath, who knows?' He lifted his felt hat from the side table, leaving the newspaper. 'When you get a moment, you might want to read that. It is fresh from London. Monsieur Roberts asked that I give it to you—along with his best regards.'

Ooh La La! Times Reporter Tracks Paris Society Killer

Charlie cringed. *Bloody subeditors.* 'I wasn't supposed to be the story.'

'And yet here you are, front page, Madame James.'

'It's Mademoiselle,' she said softly.

'Sorry?'

'Mademoiselle. I'm officially divorced.'

'Ah.' He coughed and studied his shoes again. 'Monsieur Roberts will be along to visit you later this week when the doctors give their approval.' As the inspecteur opened the door, he turned to meet Charlie's eyes. '*Bonne nuit.* Get some rest, Mademoiselle James. I'll be back tomorrow.'

The door closed. She stared out the window at the pink sky and Eiffel Tower in the distance, and thought, *I'm looking forward to it.* She was surprised by how much she meant it.

Epilogue

Charlie sat tucked into the same chintzy sofa opposite Lady Ashworth as she had sat on the day they met. The doors of the salon were thrown open, and Charlie could see room after room filled with dark timber French furniture, sideboards and bookshelves stacked with French memoirs, hardbacks stamped with gilt writing and covers in lilac, faded burgundy and tobacco. Their reflections floated from one gilded mirror to the next, the air heavy with perfume from vases full of white lilies and blush full-headed roses. A blue Persian carpet stretched across the parquetry and sunshine streamed in the window.

Her diminutive host was dressed in a Chanel black bouclé suit with gold buttons, and her green hair was pulled tight into a neat bun. The older woman had been in mourning since burying her husband a month ago, choosing to retreat within the grounds of her beloved Villa Trianon as the headlines raged.

Lady Ashworth was as elegant as ever, but her cheeks looked hollow and dark rings sat deep under her eyes. The two women stared at each other as the butler placed a tray with a Limoges tea set and raspberry macarons on a cream ottoman in front of them.

'*Bonjour*. Tea, Just Charlie? Or would you prefer champagne? I must admit I've not had any since . . .' Her shoulders sagged.

'I'm so sorry for your loss.'

Lady Ashworth's powdered face crumpled for a moment, then she nodded. 'So am I. My husband was a rascal . . . but a murderer! I never imagined . . .' She tugged a linen hanky from her shirt-sleeve and dabbed at her eyes. 'These deaths will haunt me till the day I die. And poor Conrad. He was a troubled soul to be sure, but he did not deserve to be killed.' She pursed her lips and shook her head.

'Thank you for seeing me. I understand you've not permitted visitors, especially from the press.'

'Ah, but you are not *just press*, are you, Just Charlie. You were there when my husband died.'

'Again, I'm sorry for your loss.'

'I received your letters. I apologise for not replying.'

'I understand. It's been a challenging time. How have you been getting on?' Charlie asked gently.

'Getting on? Yes, I suppose that's what one does. We keep moving. Paper over the cracks like those in this villa and put on a bright new face. I see your latest headlines have moved on to the prospect of war with the Boches. Have we learned nothing?' she said mournfully.

It was true. Somewhere beyond the northern French borders, conflict was brewing. George Roberts spoke of it daily and had demanded Charlie spend these past weeks meeting army majors, speaking with ammunition factories, making contacts. She'd visited hospitals, preparing for all eventualities. In the coming conflict women like Lady Ashworth, who fundraised and led the charge in hospitals and shelters, would be key to survival. No one needed strong women more than a country on its knees.

Lady Ashworth tipped her head sideways and said, 'You know, Charlie James, I've made a life by making magic. Dancing, acting, designing—all of these involve mastery and trickery. Performance. But do you know how I connect? On stage or with a living room— I never mistake the kernel of a person.'

Charlie sat quietly and forced herself not to interrupt.

'Conrad was a sweet boy who deserved a chance. I gave him one and he took it—gratefully, mind—with both hands. He and Milly, well, they were from different worlds to be sure, but they had love. Real love.'

'Milly's returned to the States to have her child.'

'Yes. It's important to be near family.'

'What about Marchand?' She thought of Mercedes's parents and brothers, their livelihood and pride stripped away. Aleksandr growing up in a freezing apartment block with his aunt. Milly assaulted and insulted.

'Maxime Marchand.' She laughed bitterly and shook her head. 'He took people and companies and squeezed every delicious and delightful drop out of them until they were shells. Stringy husks to be discarded. He hurt people. Killed people. Crushed companies.'

'Still, there are legal procedures . . .'

'You've been a reporter for some time, so you've seen how justice works in your own country. Do you think it's any different here? Or in Russia, for that matter? Poor Aleksandr . . . his whole family killed.' Lady Ashworth dabbed at the corner of her eye with a blue linen handkerchief she pulled from her sleeve.

Charlie continued to prod. Something had been niggling at her. 'Lord Ashworth loved you . . . I saw him lead you away the night of the party. His first concern was for you.'

'Silly man . . .' Lady Ashworth spoke softly now. 'I loved him. But then I discovered how callous he could be. So I focused on mitigating the harm—concentrating on causes that needed me. That bought joy—or essentials—to others. He was a fool. A greedy man with no head for money. Happy to invest in evil.'

Charlie's stomach roiled with sympathy for Lady Ashworth. Like Charlie, she had married a man who was initially charming and kind, but his kernel was soured with greed, pride and reckless privilege.

Lady Ashworth was upset. 'Poor Conrad.' She dipped her head. 'He was always holding his breath, thinking Milly would wake up and abandon him, but she loved him. We *all* did.'

Charlie nodded, but still said nothing.

'Marchand wanted more munitions factories, more deaths. That's why he wouldn't return our money. There would be other mothers and children dead. Like Aleksandr's family. More blood on our hands.' Lady Ashworth hung her head in her hands, her green bun bobbing to one side.

'You wanted to make life beautiful.'

Lady Ashworth's avoided eye contact as she picked up her cup and brought it to her lips.

Charlie sat back in the sofa, recalling their first interview, the Ambrine treatments, Lady Ashworth carrying eighty women downstairs herself to save them from German attack, the parties where her aim was to connect people. Managing an inept husband, nurturing a young, struggling artist and giving him a new life. The life he deserved.

Lady Ashworth took a sharp sip of her tea and nestled the cup and saucer on her lap. Her shoulders were square and she held her neck tall. 'Well, you have it all figured out.'

'*You* planned it all?'

'My husband was desperate . . . he could be persuaded to do anything. It was my idea to lace Marchand's drink and then to lure him to the woods.' Her face crumpled with distaste. 'While everyone was distracted, Rupert grabbed the knife from the acrobat and finished him off, just to be certain. That was his own idea—most certainly not mine.' She looked aghast. 'Unnecessary cruelty. Marchand was probably dead already.' Lady Ashworth eyed Charlie with respect. 'How did you . . .'

'In hospital,' the inspecteur brought me *The Times* newspaper with the headlines of Lord Ashworth's death. In it was an advertisement for heart medication. Digoxin. The same as was found in Marchand's toxicology report. He wasn't a young man, but his physician confirmed to the police that he'd never prescribed this drug. I only thought of it again today at the Louvre, looking at van Gogh's picture. Van Gogh was famously treated for a heart condition using foxglove. *Digitalis lanata*. Turned into digoxin.'

'I'm not sure I'm following . . .'

'The morning I visited you in your rooms, Lord Ashworth brought you a lovely breakfast tray. With two bottles of your heart medication.'

Lady Ashworth sucked in her breath. 'Lord Ashworth could have taken them, crushed them up and fed them into someone's strong cocktail.'

'He could have,' agreed Charlie, meeting Lady Ashworth's stare. 'In fact, that's the way it looks, now he's dead, doesn't it?'

Lady Ashworth sat completely still.

'It was a perfect plan. Civilised—almost. But you weren't planning on Conrad and Milly being nearby, were you.'

'No,' she said sadly. 'They were unfortunate bystanders. Conrad blackmailed my husband—as you witnessed. He didn't know, of course, that I was involved.' She hung her head and dabbed at more tears. 'Conrad was never meant to die, he was a beautiful soul. The son I never had,' she said with a breaking voice. 'My husband, he's in the same camp as Marchand. May they rot together. When you report this, Just Charlie, make sure people know it was me. Fate catches all of us.'

Charlie again considered the illustrated advertisement she'd seen for digoxin when the inspecteur had left her *The Times*. 'You spiked your own husband's tea, knowing he'd have a heart attack.'

'I gave him some sedatives. We were all upset.' Lady Ashworth stared at her, wide-eyed. A true performer.

Charlie studied the light dancing across the parquetry and the avenue of manicured plane trees dotted along the driveway. Behind Lady Ashworth, translucent Clodion nymphs swirled and teased. Magic.

Charlie put down her teacup, picked up her satchel and stood to leave. 'What you say is true, Lady Ashworth. Fate does come for us all. Marchand and Lord Ashworth killed innocent people in cold blood.' She looked the older women in the eye. 'But you have a villa to fill with good people. More hospitals to help—more souls to save. You have more stories to tell.'

With that Charlie slung the satchel over her shoulder and headed out the door. She had work to do.

Acknowledgements

The idea for Charlie James and *The Paris Mystery* series started percolating in lockdown when I felt an urge to write something a little lighter, sexier and more mysterious. I couldn't go to Paris, so I decided to make my own version. I wanted to feel joy and delight—to write something with loaded with panache and a feel-good factor paired with heavenly food, masses of couture, elegant houses and Champagne. I'm guessing my readers were looking for similar fun distractions.

I didn't want a traditional detective—I thought a writer might be a nice twist. Obviously, I needed the main character to be a smart, accomplished woman and fortunately I have many, many such women in my life to draw inspiration from. An honourable mention to my dear friend, Emmy-awardwinning journalist and foreign correspondent (and my favourite American) Sara James, for whom my heroine is named.

Charlie James is based on the early female correspondents who were not given formal accreditation nor the support of their male colleagues. The bones of Charlie's character is drawn from Australian reporter Louise 'Louie' Mack, borrowing elements (and plotlines) from other notable reporters like Janet Flanner, Clare Hollingworth (who World War Two in Poland), Dorothy Lawrence (who dressed as a male sapper and served in the trenches in France), and the indomitable American Martha Gellhorn. Charlie is without question a feminist, with views that sometimes surprise the French—and her family and friends.

Rather than provide a full reading list I thought I'd provide a few titles that stood over the past year as I was reading this book. For a masterclass in setting . . . and an analysis of crime you can look no further than John Berendt's classic *Midnight in the Garden of Good and Evil*. I also read two annotated compendiums of reportage and columns by the great Janet Flanner—the American writer who reported on European affairs for *The New Yorker*, including her famous '*Letters from Paris*': *Janet Flanner's World, Uncollected Writings 1932—1975* and *Paris Was Yesterday*, both edited by Irving Drutman. If you get a chance to stroll back through old magazines, Janet Flanner's razor wit and intelligence will spiral off the page. I read archive editions of the *The New Yorker* from the 1930s and 1940s, but any edition you can get your hands on will always be some of the best writing you've encountered. It is the only magazine I still insist on having the print edition delivered. The cover of this novel pays homage to the reportage of the great women of *The New Yorker*, and the timeless cover artwork.

For a real-life peek into the decadence of Pre-War Paris, the real-life Circus Ball of 1939 and the great Villa Trianon you must read *Elsie De Wolfe's Paris: Frivolity before the Storm* by historian Charlie Scheips.

Lady Ashworth is inspired by the indomitable Elsie De Wolfe and for those wanting to know more see Jane Smith's *Elsie de Wolfe: A Life in the High Style*, Mark Hampton's *On Decorating* and Nina Campbell and Caroline Seebohm's *Elise De Wolfe: A Decorative Life*. My version, Lady Ashworth, is a complete fabrication.

Furthermore, my versions of Villa Trianon and the Circus Ball are a departure from the actual places and events, so please do not conflate the two. I also feature fashion houses, particularly Mainbocher—but these are imagined versions (but please do look up the real-life dresses—they are so pretty!). My version of London's *The Times* is also fictionalised, timelines for telegrams condensed so the novel can crack along at pace.

To my Australian publishing team at Allen & Unwin: Annette Barlow, Christa Munns, Kate Goldsworthy and Ali Hampton—thanks for your endless belief, patience and care. Also to Clare Foster at Curtis Brown, who walks every step with me. And Sue

Peacock for reading early drafts when she had a million other things to do, and a new state to move to.

Lastly, I need to put on record that though the character shares a name with my youngest child (the only one of my characters thus far), I have no favourite child . . . even though Charlie has spent the last year telling everyone that he must be.

Oceans of love to my family: Henry, Jemima, Charlie and Alex who totally get that I need to spend days and months diving into different worlds for research, and then spend yet more months with people who don't exist. You are my anchors.